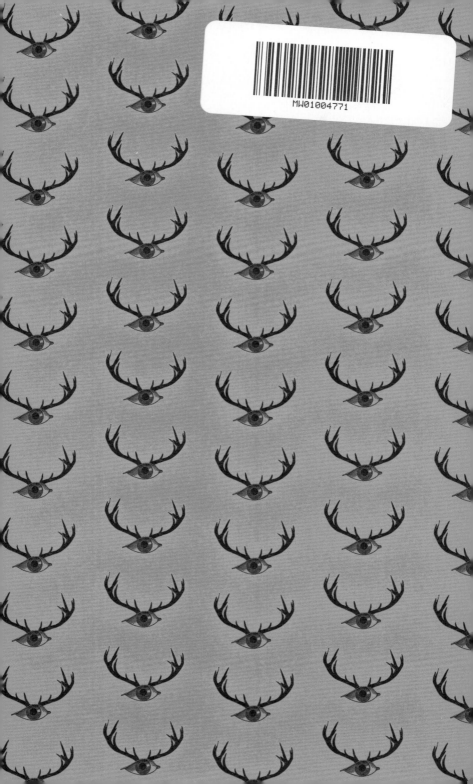

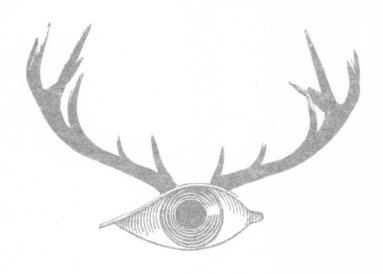

The
DARK
BETWEEN
the
TREES

The
DARK
BETWEEN
the
TREES

Fiona Barnett

SOLARIS

First published 2022 by Solaris
an imprint of Rebellion Publishing Ltd,
Riverside House, Osney Mead,
Oxford, OX2 0ES, UK

www.solarisbooks.com

ISBN: 978-1-78618-713-0

A CIP catalogue record for this book is available from the
British Library.

Designed & typeset by Rebellion Publishing

Printed in the UK

For Helena,
with love and a handful of trail mix

"When we returned to the hillside, I saw by the moonlight that there were but the two of us left. Pray God have mercy for the ones we left behind."

– The True Account and Testimony of Thomas Edgeworth, as Told by Him to the Reverend J. Garner, in Tapford Gaol

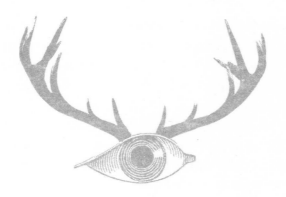

CHAPTER ONE

Nomansland

FIVE WOMEN IN a Land Rover, heading out towards the distant treetops. Kim was driving, since the car was hers, and Dr Christopher got the front passenger seat by default because this whole expedition was on her funding. They'd had BBC Radio 4 on up the motorway, but after the last stop at a petrol station it had gone off and no one had bothered to put it back on. Nuria, the graduate student whose rotten luck had meant she was perched right in the back among the bags, had her earphones in. The rest of them looked out of the windows, to the woods in the middle distance, and at the greying clouds overhead. The roads were much narrower by now, the car bouncing over pothole-riddled asphalt, which in turn crumbled into gravel tracks, and the signs of habitation got progressively sparser.

They parked the car about two hundred yards out from the treeline, in a patch of scrubby grass that would have served for a car park if there had been any need for one. From here the high wire fence around the forest was visible, the small, red, stay-away-by-official-order signs noticeable at intervals even if their details couldn't be made out yet.

"Is that us, then?" said Sue. She unfolded herself from a pile of waterproofs and opened the Land Rover door.

"Do we want to stop for lunch first?" said Helly, who had been sat next to her. "It's nearly twelve o'clock."

Dr Christopher—Alice—would far rather get going; she had been radiating nervous energy in waves since before they'd stopped at the service station, but she swallowed it and agreed to the passing around of the peanut butter sandwiches. She kept looking off towards the horizon—not just at the woods, but in every direction, getting a feel for the lay of the land, remembering the first time she had been here, almost exactly two decades ago. Thinking of the question she always told her students to ask, which was, *what must it have been like?*

In the distance, beyond the fence: Moresby Forest. It stretched out to the north-west, rising to a ridge and then falling away and further off rising again. To the south, and behind which the road had come, was a hill criss-crossed with falling-down dry stone walling. Here and there, dandelions poked up startlingly bright amidst scrubby grass, and patches of thistles grew wild and unchecked among the little cascades of rubble that crumbled from the intentional stone boundaries. There were no sheep.

"There ought to be a cairn up there," said Alice Christopher, gesturing at the top of the hill, "or something, at least."

"You'd better go and put it there yourself while we're eating," said Sue, "since you're about the only person who's ever wanted a marker at all."

"If there was a monument, maybe more people would be interested. What do you think, Nuria?"

Nuria had just taken a bite out of a banana, so took a moment to respond, but when she did she said, "I think they should put a blue plaque down the road in Tapford instead. That's where most of the actual legends came from. Far more interesting than an old battlefield."

"Does Tapford still exist?" said Helly.

"All three streets of it," said Sue. "It's about four miles that way." She indicated south-east. "There's still nothing closer. No one will build any nearer to Moresby Forest."

"Old superstitions die hard," said Alice.

Sue gave a little supercilious smile. "Oh, I don't think that's the problem, do you?"

"They last a surprisingly long time, although that's more Nuria's area than mine." Alice got to her feet. "Maybe there'd be more chance of a cairn if we could pin down the parties on both sides of the Battle of Sibbert Hill."

"Can't we?" said Helly.

"It's not in any of the reports. We know who the Parliamentarian group are, obviously—that's who we're looking for this week, we know plenty about them. Names. A few hometowns. Where they were going. And they definitely fought up on this side of Sibbert Hill, just over there—we dug it up about twenty years ago, found a few remains. A buckle, some bits of leather that might have been armour, the business ends of a couple of pikes. But nothing to tell us who the ambushers were."

"Royalists, surely?" said Sue.

"Probably. But they could be other Parliamentarians, if they weren't paying too much attention to their colours. Or very lost Scots. Or if you believe Nuria's sources, demonic agents of paganism."

"Oh!" said Helly. "They sound like fun, Nuria; tell me about them."

But before Nuria could reply, Alice said, "Later," and reached for a clipboard from the footwell of the front seat. "I want to get going as soon as we can." And she marched off in the direction of the foot of the hill.

Sue chucked away the core of the apple she'd just finished, and stumped off after her.

Nuria Martins sat in the open back door of the car, and watched them go. There were five women on this expedition, which was sort of a coincidence and sort of not. Alice Christopher had chosen three of them. Nuria herself was not very well going to say no to something she might later be able to get a whole conference paper out of, and which at any rate was being run by one of her PhD supervisors. Her other supervisor, as it happened, had advised her not to go, but nevertheless here she still was. She had met Kim and Helly in person for the first time only a week or two ago. They were from the National Parks authority—Helly newly seconded to the area six months ago; Kim having grown up thirty miles south and, by her own admission in the car about an hour and a half ago, knowing the rural parts of this county as well as anyone really could know them. Although that was an optimistic way of looking at it. Nobody went near Moresby Forest, not just because it was a bit out of the way, nor because these days the majority of it was fenced off, but because it was actively dangerous—a marshy microclimate all of its own. Rumour was, the army secretly used it occasionally, but if that was true it wasn't often. If she was honest, Kim Macleod had said, she was mostly on this expedition because she'd never been inside the forest before. The National Parks people called it the Black Hole. They didn't even go in to chop trees down.

The fifth member of the group was Sue Aitken, whose presence here was a condition of the whole thing taking place, and who seemed to have estimated her importance accordingly. She was from the Ordnance Survey, which did not in fact offer for sale a map of Moresby Forest— what would have been the point, since the general public could not enter it?—but nevertheless she was along for surveying-related reasons best known to herself and Dr Christopher. For the rest, the point was that this place was out of bounds, the chance to duck behind a gigantic sign labelled "PRIVATE" and keep walking, and take a shovel to a few of its secrets.

Alice and Sue walked a little way off, towards the bottom of Sibbert Hill. They were an odd combination, Alice gesticulating with the clipboard as her hair whipped about her in the wind, Sue with her hands shoved deep in her pockets. The other three watched them go, wading through knee-high grass untouched by person or livestock, almost as far as the first bit of tumbled-down dry stone walling.

Kim said to Nuria, "What are they looking for?"

"Comparing it against the map. The eighteenth-century one. Have you seen it?"

"Didn't know there was one." Kim had finished her sandwiches. She went around to the back of the Land Rover and started pulling bags out of the back. "What about it?"

"There are a few maps. Alice says the one from 1731 is more accurate than the one from 1966."

"That's the most recent one?"

"It's the one that gets used these days."

Helly said, "Apparently the standard map is rubbish, so she might be right." She went round to help move equipment.

Kim said, "Not possible. It might not be completely accurate but the '60s couldn't be worse than the eighteenth century."

Nuria shrugged. "That's what I'd have thought, but apparently... Anyway, they're getting their bearings. Since the compasses are a bit wonky in the forest. Why is that?"

"Something technical involving magnets," said Kim. "I don't know what it is exactly. Iron deposits underground, I suppose—but it's hard to tell for sure, we've not managed to get in far enough to pin it down. Like the Bolton Strid, I think. We're taking two tents?"

"Yes," said Helly. "I thought two would be easier to distribute among us than one big one." And she and Kim started discussing the sort of practical camping matters that generally made Nuria zone out.

There was a chilly wind coming from the west, over the treetops. Nuria looked up at the hill, where her supervisor was scrambling up a small cascade of rocks. Men had died here. There were, she thought, few places in this country where men hadn't died at some point or another. In the late library nights where she didn't move from her desk for hours on end and her brain felt like it had been tied in knots, it seemed stupid sometimes to fixate on so few people, in a remote corner of somewhere unremarkable. The disappearance of the Roundhead company led by Captain Alexander Davies in 1643, at the height of the English civil wars, had no direct consequences in the rest of the world. They weren't special on their own account or on account of any friends or near relatives, weren't pioneers or game-changers in any discernible way. If it were for their own sake Nuria would hardly have been interested in them, although she wouldn't care to guess at why Dr Christopher had been obsessed with them for so many years. But they had come this way, these perfectly ordinary men. They had ignored all the local warnings—or, quite possibly, had not even known about them, if they were just passing through—and then they had disappeared, leaving behind one, single, remarkable source.

And *that* was where Nuria's interest lay. The account of the deserter Thomas Edgeworth held her interest because her research was in folk tales and the supernatural, and the tale of the Devil of Moresby Wood might not have been the earliest of its kind but it was unusually long-lived. There was evidence that the story had existed as far back as the fourteenth century, and it had made it all the way through to the seventeenth century, mythology practically intact. It was not Captain Davies and his missing company that caught her imagination, although the words of Thomas Edgeworth still ranked among her favourite discoveries and she had a soft spot for his company on that account.

But what she really cared about, and why, in the end, she was here, was the creature called the Corrigal.

The woods looked wild. There was none of that expected uniformity of British woodland that comes from the trees having been deliberately planted. Which came first, the dismal wildness of an inaccessible place or the ghost stories? Surely, in this place, they were now too intertwined to tell.

Alice and Sue were heading back down the hill towards the car, and as they got closer Nuria could hear that Alice was on one of her favourite subjects. "—Third trench further up near the top of the hill back there, but there wasn't anything to find. No more bones, at least."

"I've seen the plans," said Sue. "You used the '66 map, though. I don't see that there was any problem with it. What year was this, '89?"

"I was starting my PhD, so yes, twenty years ago this summer. Doesn't time fly? We were just looking at Sibbert Hill on the '89 dig, didn't go into the woods. It had already been fenced off, anyway. Ah, fantastic," she said, seeing the pile of unloaded bags. "Are we nearly ready to go?"

They were, and this seemed to increase Alice's energy even further. She couldn't stand still. Clipboard back in the car. Map checked—both variations of it. Sunglasses out. Sunglasses away. Checking her watch.

"Okay folks. I've chosen this gate into Moresby Forest because it's the closest one we could get to the original Davies route. We're going to need to skirt around to the west on the other side of the fence, and then we'll try and follow the eyewitness account as far as we're able to. And go from there. The first thing we're looking for is a huge oak tree in a clearing, probably an hour or two's walk from the boundary. That's where they spent their first night, so it shouldn't be too hard to find.

"Just to orient everyone: in the middle of June 1643, twenty-six men led by Alexander Davies came up from the south, on their way to join the war closer to the Scottish border. They were ambushed on the side of Sibbert Hill, just up there,"—she gestured—"by our mystery Cavaliers. About two thirds of Davies's men, apparently, made it out alive—which is brutal, by the way, especially for what was essentially just a skirmish—and those survivors fled into Moresby Forest. On the first night, Thomas Edgeworth and Josiah Moody saw something in the woods on the edge of their camp. Edgeworth connected it with the big oak tree—the one we're looking for—but... well. Whatever it was, it scared them enough that an hour before dawn they chose to desert. They made it to Tapford mid-morning, still injured from the fight the day before, and Edgeworth told his story to the village priest, who was horrified enough that he wrote it down. There was still a heavy penalty for deserting, and in fact they were imprisoned—"

"Moody died," said Nuria, as much to head off the lecture as anything else.

"Yes," said Alice, and took the hint.

"And no other man from Davies's company ever emerged from the forest," Nuria finished.

"So what are we expecting to find?" said Helly.

"Bones, I assume," said Sue flatly.

"We'll find what we'll find. But I want to follow their route as closely as we can. No one has ever done this before."

"That's because it's awful terrain," said Kim. "It's marshy, there's a huge part towards the north-west that's riddled with underground caves, there's something in there that makes compasses inaccurate."

"No fear," said Sue, and she held up a handheld GPS unit. "New batteries this morning. The map isn't the *most* accurate, but it'll do. We're not going to get lost."

Kim gave her the smile of long experience. "Let's just see about that. Knowing where you are is only the start, anyway—you also have to make sure you're not up to your knees in water."

"Oh, well, yes, of course..."

"We'll probably be okay but we will need to watch out for each other. Any concerns, you talk to me, you talk to Helly. We've done stuff like this before, and much harder than it, hundreds of times. There's no reason to suffer in silence and we don't want anyone to get hurt if we can possibly help it."

There was a moment of silence. Helly kicked a bit of grass with her boot.

Alice said, "Are we ready to go?"

"I think we are," said Kim. They put their waterproof coats on, helped each other on with their rucksacks. Stood around awkwardly while Kim locked the car. Then walked with tentative purpose down the last of the hillside, in the direction of Moresby Forest.

There were two large padlocks on the gates, and they were stiff with rust and lack of use. On the other side of the chain-link fence a ladder lay a little way off, propped against a boulder and half covered in ferns. It was easier to get out of this place than to get in. When Helly opened the gate, the whole fence shuddered along its length, so that the nearest "KEEP OUT" signs clattered too loudly against metal rings.

Nuria had a sudden thought: *we've announced ourselves. They know we're here now*. But there was no one else around; "they" were no one.

Alice went first over the threshold. Then Kim. Then Nuria, Sue. Helly shut the gate behind them and fiddled the padlocks back into place. "Right," she said, brushing her hands off on her trousers, stashing the keys back in her pocket. "Round to the west, you said, then? Lead on, the person with the map."

And off they went, following the boundary, with one shoulder to the fence as if it would keep them grounded wherever they were going.

CHAPTER TWO

After The Onslaught

THERE WAS A little copse at the top of Sibbert Hill, which was where the attackers must have been hiding when Captain Davies and his men rounded the side of the ridge. By the time the captain had spotted the copse, though, it was already far too late: the shout of *fire* had come from over the hill and the man to his right had been shot in the head.

He thought later that it was a miraculous kind of shot that had felled Lucas Blashford in an instant—Blashford must have been nearly a hundred yards from the nearest place the shooter could have been hiding, and moving away from it. By rights that ought to have been impossible—whoever was on the crest of the hill must have seen them coming, must have been lying in wait for them, muskets at the ready. For nights afterwards he would dream of that crackle of musket fire, echoing around the valley as if it came from nowhere at all, from above, was an act of God Himself showing His displeasure, as if Davies and this motley assortment of men he had with him didn't know about that already.

Back on the hillside, the first thing Davies saw was Blashford flung forward down the slope, landing face first as a ribbon of red sprayed in an arc as high as a moment before the man had stood. Only when he hit the grass did Davies realise what was happening, that the popping to his right and a little behind him was not his mind playing tricks on him, but more muskets. He turned, and saw smoke rising from the copse, and that was when the shot hit him in the shoulder.

For a moment or two he couldn't place what had happened to him, and his thoughts felt like the last wisp of a snuffed-out candle, and in that time there was a flash of gold from the copse—which, was it sparkling? Gleaming somehow like the surface of a river?—and then a small mass of pikemen emerged from their cover at a run. This he understood, at least. He tried to lift his right arm to point at them, but it was suddenly, blindingly painful as his thoughts caught up with the agony and he was slammed back into the present. And then he was stumbling, using his still-sheathed sword to keep himself upright or close to it, and without the power to think fast he would have to rely on his men's training to save them. If you see the enemy, rush them. If they ambush you, move together, without waiting. The enemy mustn't have time to press the advantage.

A shout from behind—the unmistakable voice of Sergeant Thatcher from the back of the line, telling everyone to *move*.

But it seemed that the advantage was already being pressed: already other soldiers than Blashford were falling, cut down where they stood without mercy or fanfare. Davies tried to focus, but the pain in his shoulder and the flashes of silver in the sunlight were too distracting. Around him, the crashing of swords and the grunting of men fighting for their lives. One moment there had been nothing, and now this.

He had control of his arm again now, or some of it. He drew his sword. Out of the thicket, the pikemen continued to pour. He could hear their shouts, the rustle of knee-high grass as they came closer. There must be more than thirty of them, more than Davies's own entire company, such as it was, and still coming. And that wasn't even counting their musketmen, who must even now be reloading.

He spat on the ground and made a decision. There was a forest at the bottom of the slope—their best chance to escape. It could only be two hundred yards away. "To the trees!" he called, hoarsely, and looked around for Willis, the bearer of the colours.

But Willis was on the ground, maybe five yards from where Davies stood, and there was blood down his front, and a stranger in a dark red coat was standing over him, and still Davies could hear that crackling inside his head, and the shouts of men around him. He wanted to run to Willis's aid, to cut the enemy down where he stood, but his right arm was cold, the numbness beginning to set in. "To the trees! Save yourselves!" he bellowed again, and this time they all heard him, and Moody and Ames were overtaking him, already breaking rank and running down the slope as fast as they could go.

"Captain, help me," called the other sergeant, Harper, now on his knees in the thin grass with Willis leaning fully against him, still clutching the banner. The man in the dark red coat was gone, disappeared into the fray. All around Davies, men fought as best they could, and the snarls of the strange soldiers seemed somehow more urgent and unsettling than he had come across before, as if the Devil himself possessed them, which may yet have been true. To pay too much attention to them would have frozen him to the spot. So Willis was still alive, then. Thank God. Davies knelt down next to Harper and presented his left side—the one that wasn't next to useless. "Here, Willis, lean on me." Supporting Willis between them, they got to their feet and down they staggered, the three of them together on the steep, rubble-covered descent down to the cover of the forest. He couldn't see very well, which might have been tears of pain or sweat dripping into his eyes, but it didn't matter, the only thing that mattered was that if he stopped moving he would die, and Willis would die, and none of the rest would have any chance at all.

It was not so much the pain in his shoulder that preoccupied him, spreading out as it did in all directions, hot and cold at the same time; more it was the noticing of his own desperate, animal impulse to escape, to be somewhere, anywhere, else. But he fought that back down, both the impulse and the rising urge to vomit. He had been on a battlefield enough times to know that the only way to truly get out was to make it to the end, and he must throw all the strength he had into getting there. Into getting all of them there. The trees loomed ahead of him, and at the pace he, Willis and Harper were able to go, reaching them seemed less like a sprint and more like a long, shambling walk, drawn out over hours. His sword was still in his right hand, his grip on it next to useless, and at any moment he expected that someone might cut him down from behind. But the blow never came. He tried to turn around to look behind him, as much to see the state of his fleeing company as to see if the ambushers were following them down the slope, but even turning his head caused Willis to scream in pain from his shoulder. Harper said, "What are you doing?" in a tone that clearly appended, "you dolt," and he was right, as usual. So onward Davies staggered.

At the edge of the trees, which were now a matter of twenty yards away, Sergeant Thatcher was having a shouting match with Alwood, the sergeant's bulk making the other man's frame look even smaller and skinnier than it was. Davies couldn't hear what it was about, because they noticed his approach and Thatcher grabbed Alwood by the scruff of the neck and bodily dragged him into the shadow of the wood. Alwood struggled, calling out to Davies—"Sir, sir—"

"Further in, Alwood! That's an order!" And he shook himself free of Willis, and tried to straighten himself up without the nausea overwhelming him. He dimly registered through blurred vision that there weren't as many men around him as he'd expected. They had been on the lookout for the King's men for the last forty miles. Surely it was impossible for anyone to have got so close without them noticing. To have ambushed them so suddenly, so effectively. Surely... But he couldn't think, couldn't get any further right now than the thought that this shouldn't have happened. He staggered forwards.

"You're bleeding, captain," said Harper, who was red in the face from exertion.

Davies gazed at him steadily. He wasn't sure he could trust his own voice.

The sergeant continued. "We should stop. They're not coming down the hill. They won't follow us."

"We're not stopping. Further in." It came out hoarser than he intended it; his throat was dry. And where *was* everyone?

Harper started to say something in protest, at the same time as Cadwell said, "Shepherd is still out on the hill, sir. I'm sorry."

"If you want to go back and get him, Mr Cadwell, take your chances. We won't wait for you." Cadwell didn't move. Davies saw, superimposed on his vision, that image of Lucas Blashford pitching forward, the blood already soaking into his hair. "We march. We rest when I say so." And he turned to face forward again, feeling the light-headedness as he did so. Somehow he was at the front of the group. For a moment he had an urge to turn back, to at least try to rescue the men he'd abandoned on the hillside, but he knew in his gut that he could be no more use to them in his current state than he could be to the bleeding-out Willis. He was leading the way, and this was where he was leading. And he would respond no further to any arguments about it. He couldn't look at those who were left, did not want to know what state they were in. He felt nothing in his body that was not the pain of his right shoulder, and that was everything.

He did not know how long they fled, limping through the dense and dark trees, which seemed to Davies to muffle all sound but his own too-loud breathing. At any rate, it soon became clear that Harper was not going to be able to continue supporting Willis, whose head drooped lower and lower and who seemed increasingly unable to carry his own weight. It would have been slow going to pick their way across the debris-strewn woodland, even without their selection of injuries. They hadn't got far, but there was no going any further.

"Here," Davies said. "We'll stop here."

They were on the edge of a clearing, maybe twenty yards across, and off to one side of it was a gigantic oak tree, vast enough that it would take four men with outstretched arms to surround the circumference of its trunk. The long shadows of the trees at the edge of the clearing brushed the great roots at the foot of the oak, as if reaching out for it— it must now be getting into early evening. And above, the sky was a dim grey-blue, the light now the warm yellow of June evenings, turning the leaves and the ground a colour that was faintly uncanny.

They entered the clearing in twos and threes, helping each other along. Some were sorely injured, and there were desperately few of them—Davies could no longer stave off the inevitable, and counted his men. They had an undersized fraction of a company this morning, on their way up to meet the rest further north, but even so there had been significantly more than now settled at the foot of the vast oak; now, not including himself, there were sixteen. It hadn't just been an ambush. It had been a massacre. His chest suddenly felt very tight, his mouth dry. He'd not known some of these men very long, had been picking up stragglers on his way up north, and yet he felt responsibility for them. Who was missing? Hodges and Shepherd and Timms and Neville. Kilburton was here, and Edgeworth, and Moody—although it looked like he had been hurt quite badly—but Mance and Tomkins were gone. He felt an intense stab of guilt, which mixed quickly with something he couldn't quite explain, and came out somewhere near pity. Whatever it was, it squeezed at his heart, and he found he was blinking rapidly. None of the rest should see him like this. None of them should *have* to. He turned his body awkwardly and walked away from the group.

He had done everything he could, taken every possible precaution in this part of the world. And yet where twenty-six had stood, sixteen remained. The unfairness of it stung.

"Captain," said a voice behind Davies. Footsteps jogging his way. It was Sergeant Thatcher, tall and broad-set and apparently uninjured.

"What is it?" he said, irritably.

"They're saying that we should get out of this wood as soon as possible. That we can't stay in here."

"Who's saying?"

"Stiles and Alwood, sir. The ones we picked up the day before yesterday. They know this area better than I do. They're saying we should go east."

"Maybe Mr Stiles would like to come and tell me himself, then."

"Have you seen him, sir? He's wounded something terrible."

Davies didn't say anything.

"Not as bad as Willis, sir, but bad enough that we thought he should sit down for a while."

"And yet he wants to move on? Has he lost his senses?"

Thatcher said, "He says there's something wrong with the wood." But even as he said it he seemed to realise how it sounded, and frowned to himself, and didn't elaborate further.

Davies didn't ask. He straightened his back painfully, ran a hand through hair greasy with sweat and mud and God alone knew what else. "We'll stay here until everyone can move, if we can. As long as we can afford to. If they were going to follow us we'd know by now. In the meantime, post a watch. Two men. Tell them it's at my command."

"Harper wants to start a fire, sir." Thatcher sounded disapproving, like he wanted an excuse to squash the idea. Davies decided to give him this one.

"Tell him I say on no account. I don't care if we're staying here all night, no fire for a few more hours. And if he'd care to come and help me with this,"—he indicated his own shoulder, which was soaked through with his blood and which now ached like it was immersed in quicklime—"I'm sure I should be able to spare a minute to indulge him."

Thatcher nodded and retreated. Davies thought: *that'll hold his tongue for a bit. Give him something to do, stop him trying to make up his own orders when he thinks I'm not looking. Else his fancies will run away with him, and I don't have the patience tonight. It's the best way.*

Later, when Davies returned to the group, it struck him afresh how small it was. How many now lay dead barely a couple of miles away. This wasn't the first time he had seen a third of a unit wiped out so smartly, although it was the first time since he'd been a captain, and he knew that he'd never get used to it. Remembering his first bout of soldiering in the Low Countries felt dully painful now, as if it had more in common with loneliness than grief, which it probably did. At any rate, his duty was, as always, to the living.

Harper had got Willis settled by now, and had moved on to Richard Jessop. He wiped his arm along his forehead and nodded at Davies, who was still feeling the dizziness in the front of his skull, throbbing in time with the pain in his shoulder.

"There must be water somewhere near here," said Davies, weakly. "Ames, you look fighting fit. Go. Take someone with you."

Ames went, not enthusiastically, but he went.

"What is it, Mr Alwood?" For the young man had approached Davies again, and was wringing his hands. A stained rag was tied around his waist—he seemed to have caught a piece of shot of his own. In the lengthening shadows, he looked ghostly pale, and his hairline was flecked with blood and muck.

"We can't stay here, sir."

"Well, we're going to. You can't expect us to go further in, soldier. Not everyone came out of that as lightly as you."

Alwood winced. He could only have been nineteen or twenty, with a face still full of spots. "This wood, sir—Bill and I have heard talk of this place, and they say that you should never... We can't stay in the forest after dark."

"Or what?"

But Alwood did not seem inclined to say.

"Well then. We'll set a watch tonight and woe to anyone who tries to sneak up on us again. I don't want to stay here any longer than we have to, but it would be an idiot who would move on so soon." And he gestured at his own shoulder, from which a thick, dark ooze still spread down his arm. He flexed the fingers of his right hand experimentally. "We set up camp here, and move on in the morning. That's my final word."

Davies lay back exhausted, although it was still early. By and by Sergeant Harper came around to see to his shoulder, and he swore heartily and gritted his teeth but did not black out or cry in front of his men. It was the best outcome that could be hoped for. He could still use his arm, to an extent. The piece of shot, when it came out of his shoulder, was tiny, as small as a fingernail. He held it in the palm of his left hand when Harper moved on to the next man, then slipped it into the coin purse that hung around his neck. He was not willing to let go of it just yet.

Sergeant Thatcher organised the watches—of three men at a time, just in case, not that any of them were expecting whoever had ambushed them before to creep up and massacre the rest, but you never knew. Alwood sat away to one side, with little Bill Stiles, who came from the same village two days' march away, and they put their heads together and steepled their hands compulsively in prayer every so often. Captain Davies considered asking what they were talking about, or else telling them to knock it off, but his shoulder hurt like the very Devil and therefore he was preoccupied. He didn't want to hear the local ghost stories, anyway. There were more things to fear than ghosts. Blashford had been the handiest at foraging for food, which meant that the chances of a good meal were now vanishingly small, and Timms and Shepherd were gone too, who might at least have put the company in mildly better humour. It was a terrible way to die, for that it went so quickly, as well as that it went unmarked. There was not time for so much as a short prayer over their bodies, never mind burial. But Davies had been a soldier long enough that he took his life in his hands far more deliberately than many of the others.

Later into the evening, Harper found him again. "How's the shoulder?"

"Feels like it's ascended to the next life without me. You did good work today, Sam."

The sergeant sat down next to him on the ground. A fire had been lit a little way away, eventually, and it was light enough still that in general the firelight drew the eye more than it cast shadows. Both of them stared at it.

Harper said, "I suppose so. It's bad business."

"Never gets easier."

"You did the right thing, pushing on ahead. I think they were all more willing to follow you than if you'd brought up the rear."

Davies took this for what it was intended as, which was absolution. "Mmm. We'll take our time heading north, I think."

"Some of them can't travel." Harper shifted uncomfortably. "One or two I wouldn't wager at making it through the night. Willis. Jessop. Onslow. They'll go if you tell them to, but I'd counsel to rest a few days if such can be spared."

"If we'd just been able to go back and bury them," said Davies. "It doesn't seem right to leave them out there to be picked over." He felt the bitterness of one who had seen it before, and who at times had been responsible for the picking over.

"We did what we had to."

"Did you see who they were? Any markings?"

Harper shook his head, retrieved his pipe from a pocket, started fiddling with it. "Just that they were Cavaliers, King's men. A whole company, full-sized, judging by the speed they were upon us. Though how they all managed to stay hid I'll never know." He spat on the ground. "Whoever they were, there's nothing we can do about it now. It makes no difference."

Davies looked at him. "Except to Blashford. Shepherd. The others."

"All with higher matters to deal with now. Shepherd's almost certainly giving the Devil a piece of his mind, and welcome he is to it. Got a drink?" Harper accepted a swig from Davies's flask without looking at it, still staring towards the little bonfire in the middle of the clearing. It was definitely growing dark now, which at this time of year would make it late in the evening indeed. He got up not long afterwards to go and check on the injured men; the scent of his pipe smoke remained in the air.

Captain Davies surveyed the pitiful remainder of his men, scattered in the darkening shadow of the gigantic oak tree, and felt a stab of unease. He could hear the vague murmurs of their low conversations, but it was only reasonable that they were thinking the day through as well.

The air was close, and the sky cloudy. They could do with some rain, but perhaps it was coming. He dreamed of musket fire, but couldn't tell where it was coming from.

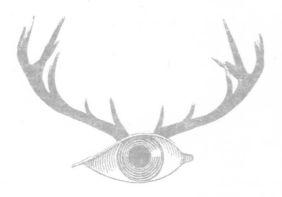

CHAPTER THREE

Follow My Lead

THEY HAD WALKED along the chain link fence marking the boundary of the woods for less than half an hour when Alice said, "I think we should turn inwards now, don't you?"

"What makes you say that?" asked Sue.

"The soldiers were injured, they couldn't have gone too far. And I don't want us to overshoot."

Helly said, "It looks like there's a ridge on ahead, is there any mention of that in your eyewitness account?"

"None," said Nuria, who knew it by heart.

"Then I think here is as good a point as any."

There was much fidgeting about with maps and marking of routes—for all that it was probably better than the alternative, the modern map of Moresby Forest was still not very detailed—and then they began to cut a path away from the boundary, almost due north into the depths of the forest itself. Only Nuria took a deliberate last glance at the outside, so as to carry it with her on the way in. She couldn't be quite sure why she did it, except perhaps that part of her wished she were indoors, with the thesis which she really ought to be concentrating on instead.

Up ahead of her, Alice was clearly spellbound by the prospect of walking the same path as the Davies group, now that that might be actually what they were doing. "The deserters say once they got to the edge of the woodland, they fairly ran for cover, carrying the ones who couldn't walk themselves, leaving trails of blood behind them as they went." And she cast about the ground, as though expecting to see the very spatters, now hundreds of years old. Nuria caught Sue and Kim exchanging looks.

It was by now early afternoon, and they carried on walking in the same direction, picking their way around particularly thick areas of bracken rather than attempting to bisect them directly; their walk therefore took on the feel of a ramble or a gentle exploration. Here and there the ground sank a little underfoot, less as if they were steering into a swamp than if they were walking over a layer of soft peat. Kim tested the ground with her foot, frowning, before deciding that it was safe to walk on, even with all that they carried, and waved the rest of them across.

If there were no human-made paths in this wild and untouched area, then after an hour or so they found themselves moving north-east along what might almost, if you squinted, constitute a corridor through the trees and brush. Surely the work of animals—deer and such—but, Nuria thought, if you were the sort of person who believed in such a thing, then you'd be forgiven for thinking that there was some kind of design here. No woods were completely random, but there was a spectrum, between the deliberately cultivated and the purely natural. Moresby Forest was manifestly not the former, but there was something about it that precluded the latter. It was hard to tell how, exactly. Nevertheless, the path they were travelling looked like a corridor, and it seemed to be going in the direction they wanted, so they followed it.

"Go on, then," said Helly, in the tone of someone resuming a conversation after having been temporarily forced to pause it. "Tell me all this about the Corrigal, then."

Four faces turned expectantly to Nuria.

"Would your soldiers have known about him?" Helly continued, as if for all the world she hadn't noticed that they'd been silent since not long after they'd left the boundary. "Or is he too old for that?"

"It's not a 'him'," said Nuria, as the same time as Alice said, "The deserter's account mentions the Corrigal." She paused. "But Nuria has a whole chapter of her thesis about this."

Nuria said, "The deserter's account doesn't mention it by name. It just calls it, 'the beast in the trees'."

"But you think that's the same thing, yes?" said Alice, with the tone of an academic encouraging her undergraduate to summarise the reading.

"Probably. Edgeworth couldn't write. He dictated it to the local priest, James Garner. Edgeworth probably hadn't heard of the Corrigal, but Garner would have done. Some of the details match the Corrigal stories, but that could just be Garner's influence."

"What details?" said Helly, her eyes shining.

"That it was tall, that it seemed to move silently. Edgeworth describes its black eyes even though he admits he only saw it at night. And he connected it with the weather, which is interesting—a bit of a departure from the older stories, but not too far off. Anyway, the Corrigal is older than all that. It might even predate the Norman invasion."

"It probably does. There's pretty good evidence for it."

"Alastair says he's still not sure about the dates," said Nuria.

"Alastair is a wet fish. If only he was half as anally retentive about his own research. The fourteenth-century reference was already old, and—"

Helly interjected, "But how local is it to Moresby Forest in particular?"

Alice seemed surprised to be asked this question, or at least to have the direction of conversation shifted for her. "Very. The Corrigal is tied to this wood, long before it was ever called Moresby's Wood—all the sources say this is where it lived. But the Corrigal is *old*."

"Moresby Wood isn't in the Domesday Book," said Nuria.

"But it wouldn't be, would it?" said Alice. "The Moresby name wasn't attached to it until the 1350s."

"Is it not a forest, rather than a wood?" said Sue. "Technically speaking?"

Alice said, "If you're a geographer, sure. But I'm afraid in this case the name came before the geographers. And as far as I've been able to tell, the Corrigal came long before both of them."

The way ahead of them started to slope more sharply downhill, and they paused their discussions to negotiate it. A wall of thick bracken snaked along a little below them, stretching out in both directions, as if—and it was a stupid thought really, although Nuria found herself thinking it— as if the wood itself wanted them to change direction. To left or right? It was hard to tell, which was why the idea was so silly. Either way, the academics and Sue hung back, and Kim and Helly strode forwards wielding short knives as if they were machetes, clearing the way at least a little so that the others could file in behind them. It was slow going, especially with backpacks on, and the slope of the descent was deceptively steep under the thick ferns which came up to their waists.

At the bottom of the decline they paused, and Sue got out her Thermos flask, and they all took off their backpacks and sat down on them to recover. And the subject of the Corrigal, like scum on a pond, floated back up to the surface again.

"So it's always been in this bit of woods?" Helly asked, as if the conversation had never been interrupted in the first place.

Nuria took the Thermos lid of tea being offered to her. It was strong and stewed; Sue must have left the teabag in. Nuria briefly registered that she wasn't surprised. Sue was that kind of person. "It's hard to tell, too far back," she said. "Certainly by the time the wood was called Moresby, it was supposed to be where the Corrigal lived. Before that, there's hardly any sources." She looked across to Alice for confirmation, but Alice was looking into the middle distance, apparently thinking about something else.

"What? Oh, yes. I've not come across anything that might place the Corrigal too far from Moresby. It could be wider than just this forest, but this is where the Black Hole is."

"What's that?" interrupted Sue, who had stood up again and was tying the arms of her waterproof jacket round her waist. "Is it a landmark?"

"Folk term for it," said Alice. "This is one of the things I want to find. There's allegedly a cave of some kind, on the 1731 map, called the Black Hole or Corrigal's Nest."

"It's not on the OS map from the '60s." Sue frowned. "Not names, at least. But this place is riddled with caves. It could be any one of them."

Kim said, "There are some old cave networks in Catterley to the north-west. I suppose you've ruled out any chance of it being one of those?"

"Definitely not Catterley. Although I know the ones you mean."

"Corrigal's Nest, or the Black Hole," said Helly, approvingly. "Fodder for generations' worth of ghost stories, no doubt."

"Oh, hundreds of them."

The tea had been passed around to all of them and completely drunk by now. Sue turned the flask upside down to get the last drops out—the teabag fell out with an unceremonious *plop*—then screwed the lid back on and tucked it back into her rucksack. They relifted the bags onto their backs. They felt heavier this time. Nuria thought, *it's because I don't do this often. I'm not used to it, that's all.* She straightened up.

Sue was holding the GPS unit. She raised it to her eyes and shook it experimentally. "It's not getting a signal."

"None at all?" said Helly. "Give it here."

For a moment it looked as if Sue wasn't going to, but then she passed the little unit across. Helly waved it about over her head. "Huh. How about that."

Kim said, robustly, "Maybe it's the tree cover, means it can't find the satellite. It's very thick, after all. Never mind, we know where we're going now, don't we?" And she made to start walking.

"But we came from that way," said Helly, pointing to their left. "Down that slope. See, up there? That blasted bracken?"

Kim was silent for a moment. Then, "So we did. I should have checked my compass. So we should be going..." And she turned to her right, and stuck her hands in her pockets, and started out again with purpose, now in the correct direction.

She did not get her compass out.

Nuria caught sight of Sue's pursed lips as they set off, and decided that was a problem for someone else to deal with.

They walked on, into the afternoon, changing direction here and there as the way ahead was blocked (although never nearly so much as on that first downhill slope), but keeping roughly to the same course overall. There was no rush, no need to pick up the pace—after all, the company that had come before had consisted of sixteen men who were injured. There was no chance of the historians being slower than that. The route before them rose into a gentle sort of hill, dense with silver birch and holly, and then they followed along the side of a ridge thickly covered in trees. It was overgrown, and seemed to show no signs of the squelchy marshiness they had been promised. In fact, although the uniform grey overhead still suggested that rain was approaching, the ground itself was quite dry. After an hour the way levelled out, and although the tree cover was still fairly thick, the first few drops of rain made it through the treetops.

*   *   *

THERE IS SOMETHING about a longish afternoon's walk with people who don't insist on conversation. You find yourself not having to pay too much attention to navigating or negotiating terrain, and even with a hefty pack on your back your mind is able to wander far enough that after a while it is almost like having an out-of-body experience. So it was in Moresby Forest for Dr Alice Christopher, who felt, now that the first wave of excitement had subsided, as if she were walking against a backdrop, a kind of stage setting. It was the oddest sensation, and as they made their way in a snaking line along the ridge, it only grew stronger: a hunch that this ground where she was putting her feet was not *the* forest floor, that the landscape she saw to left and right was not *the* landscape. It wasn't based on anything in particular—except perhaps that she had built this place up in her head to be something vast and mythical, and instead here she was tramping through rainy woodland. And yet the feeling remained, that what they were walking through was not all there was to walk through, and what they were seeing was not all there was to see.

Her mind wandered. She put that thought to one side of it.

What would this place have looked like three and a half centuries ago, more or less, when Captain Davies came to it with his half a company of injured men? Would he have had to cut his way through foliage, or clamber and lift his men over fallen trees? If the deserter's account hadn't specified that they had travelled almost due north, she might have been more content to veer off intuitively, the way the woods seemed to want them to go. That way it might have opened up to her a bit more, have given her the chance to see the woods *behind* the woods, or *under* them, or however it turned out to be.

Thinking about how the Davies company might have gone this very way—a way that few other people had gone in the intervening time—made her enthusiasm flare up again so that she had to keep a careful hold on herself, to stop herself speeding up to the front of the group ahead of the rangers. There was no rush, no reason to get ahead of herself. This was a long time coming, an interminably long time preparing, and she could afford now to take her time and just enjoy the surroundings. She could relax.

Relaxation did not come naturally to Alice Christopher.

At the very back of the group, Nuria Martins trudged along in everyone else's wake. It was not, Alice thought fairly, that Nuria was not excited to be here. If she wasn't, surely she would have said something. But Nuria was not one of life's natural wild campers, and Dr Bell had not been thrilled about her going on this trip this late in the writing of her dissertation. He'd cornered Alice in the department kitchen more than a month ago, to ask if she'd mind putting the expedition off for a few months, or taking someone else.

"It's a camping trip, Alastair," she'd said as airily as she could manage, because inside she'd felt the sting of offence. "No one wants to do it in January. And I've got the funding now, I can spare Nuria an extra six weeks to catch up afterwards."

"I'm her first supervisor," he'd reminded her, "and I don't like it." But Nuria had seemed pleased to join in, and in the end she'd come, hadn't she, so there couldn't have been too much of a problem after all.

Then she thought about her own PhD supervisor, Deirdre, and decided that it was more than permissible to push for what she wanted. If Alice couldn't stand up for her own interests, then nobody else these days was going to do it for her. Deirdre had been the biggest advocate for Alice's academic interests, and as Deirdre herself had said, if a thing was worth doing, it was worth fighting tooth-and-nail for. Whatever strange looks it might get you from people who didn't understand. And that was that.

Round about four o'clock, they came across a clearing, and a remarkably clear one at that, for such a wild place. It was dotted with patches of long grass, and in the middle— oh, joy—in the middle of the clearing was a huge oak tree.

"Oh my god." Alice ran ahead of them, almost at a sprint. "This is it. I can't believe it!"

Sue said, with some satisfaction, "You're sure this is the one? This is your oak tree?" She slung her bag down at the clearing's edge and followed Alice, who was standing turning slowly about, as if she were in some great cathedral. The tree really was phenomenally tall, and its branches spread wide; presumably its roots were responsible for the wide berth given it by the silver birch around it.

The others were smiling, sharing Dr Christopher's delight at their discovery. The rain had even lightened up. The eyewitness account from the past had turned out to be an effective map to where they now stood, three and a half centuries later— a connection to the past suddenly made tangible. Thomas Edgeworth himself had seen this tree, had perhaps stood beneath it staring up through its branches at a sky a similar silver-grey. A "towering oak," he had called it, "more grand and unlike any other near by." His words now echoed around Alice's head. "In our ill state we sought to shelter beneath it." A reminder that they were real people in a real place, and that place was here.

"There are bodies buried nearby, if it's the right place," she said. "Edgeworth doesn't mention them, but there have to be."

"Let's not go digging everything up right away," said Sue, as if she thought Alice was about to go off the deep end.

"Of course not." But she looked at her watch anyway. "Have you got the camera though? Let's document the lay of the land before it starts to get dark."

"We've got a few hours yet," said Kim. "I take it we're camping here tonight?" A look at Alice's face told her the answer was yes, and truth be told it seemed like an ideal place to stop. "Take your pictures, then. Then Helly and I can put the tents up while you do your paperwork with the maps."

The maps, it turned out by the time they had taken a load of pictures of the clearing from every angle, and finally sat down to compare them on laminated sheets, diverged.

According to the later one, they had probably gone just over six miles, which (said both of the park rangers) seemed about right. By the reckoning of the 1731 map, they had only gone about four.

"Miles weren't really standardised yet," said Alice, while Sue's explanation was, "Bad scale."

"This is why I'm less inclined to trust the older one," she continued. "It's not uncommon, you know. As I say, the technology has just got so much better." That being said, technology was not on Sue's side today. She held the GPS unit up again. "I can't understand why it's still not finding the satellite. And the battery's three-quarters gone already! I've barely had it on!"

"Maybe it switched itself on in your bag?" said Alice.

"Maybe," said Sue, doubtfully. "But no, at the moment, I can't tell you definitively how far we've gone. Sorry."

"Here's a thought," said Kim, and she pulled her phone from the front pocket of her rucksack. "There's a pedometer on here somewhere."

"Oh!" said Helly. "Good idea. I've been keeping mine switched off, just in case."

Sue said, "Mine's saying nine thousand steps. But it's not very accurate."

"Thirteen thousand, apparently," said Kim. "That's 6.1 miles. Sounds about right to me. Any more for any more?" She peered at Alice and Nuria.

Nuria shook her head. "I don't have a pedometer. I should have thought of it."

Alice smiled apologetically. "Too technologically advanced for this old lady. Besides, I left mine in the Land Rover. I thought you told me there wouldn't be signal in here, Kim?"

"Probably not," said Kim, "but just in case—"

"It must have crashed when we stopped for tea," said Sue, who hadn't been listening. She was holding her phone in one hand and the uncooperative GPS unit in the other. "It's a few years old now." She had gone quite red.

"Never mind," said Helly, bracingly. "Maybe it's better like this, in a way."

"Run that one past me," said Kim.

"Well," said Helly, without a hint of self-consciousness, "the soldiers didn't have a GPS, did they? They had to rely on their instincts—you know, on understanding the woods intuitively. In which case, logically, maybe our best chance of following them is just to trust the woods. To trust ourselves to understand the woods. Don't you think?"

"Logically," said Alice.

"That's what's so great about old maps. Because they're more focused on landmarks than measured distances, you have to interpret them a lot more by *feel* than by specific A-to-B measurability."

Silence greeted this remark; the sat-nav emitted a hopeful beep and its screen went blank.

But Helly was not to be dissuaded. "Anyway, that's why I think old maps are actually more practical than modern ones, because they're focused more on the experience of travel than a set of arbitrary numbers."

Sue stood up very suddenly, walked off about five yards with her eyes fixed on the GPS, and walked back again. Alice clicked the cap of her biro a few times, almost without noticing she was doing it. Then she cleared her throat, and returned her attention to her notebook.

BY THE TIME they had done all the particularly pressing note-taking, and put both of the tents up, there was less than an hour left before sunset, so the fun job of digging out the metal detector and hunting for bodies was put off until the following day. But that was okay—it was what they were here for, after all, and they had plenty of time. It would be no good at all to rush something so important and—said Alice—so groundbreaking.

They sat around the little stove eating sausages and baked beans, and drinking tea, talking about not terribly much as the air grew colder and the shadows got longer. The smells of the woods rose up around them, and there was the occasional crack of twigs in the semi-distance, as if the trees were settling in for the evening. Then Helly said, "Tell me about these demons. You mentioned them by the car."

Nuria ducked her head and stared at the bottom of her empty tin mug, but she wasn't about to escape that easily. Alice said, "Nuria wrote a whole chapter on this last year, didn't you? The different stories of the Moresby family?"

"Yes," said Nuria, dubiously. "And I still have nightmares about drafting it."

Alice laughed too loudly. "Nonsense. We all thought it was some of your best work. And this isn't a conference, I'm not going to mark you on spookiness."

"It's a ghost story?" said Helly.

"Oh yes," said Alice. "Go on, Nuria."

They were all turned towards her, so there was nothing for it. Nuria accepted a fresh mug of tea from Sue and shifted her weight, tucking her feet up underneath her. "Do you want the history or the ghost story?"

"The history," said Sue, as Helly said, "Definitely the ghost story."

"I'll try and do a bit of both. Well then. It takes place many years ago, in the fourteenth century, when England was much younger but its forests were already old. And this one in particular was old, and no one lived in it, and Robert Moresby decided he wanted to get out of Tapford and move with his wife Margaret and their three children to the wilds. In the fourteenth century there was a lot more woodland in this area than there is today, and I think the forest stretched out a lot closer towards Tapford itself, although the story is still that nobody went out there alone if they could help it. Except the Moresbys. Robert, and Margaret, and their three children, Geoffrey, Essie, and baby Mary. They thought to hunt in land that nobody else would hunt in, and to burn charcoal, and make a home for themselves. So they went out in the springtime, although the villagers warned them against it—"

"Why did they warn them against it?" asked Helly.

"Good question. By this time there was already a rumour that something lurked in the old forest. That's the ghost story version. In real life it was probably the climate— remember, the Little Ice Age had just kicked in and winters were long and cold—as well as the superstitions."

"But climate change is not as fun," said Helly. "Carry on."

It was definitely beginning to get dark. Kim had a hurricane lamp, which she switched on and which lit their faces in eerie, yellowish light.

Nuria pushed her knitted hat a little further up her forehead. "After a few weeks, people began to get worried that they'd not heard from the Moresby family. They hadn't come back to church. They hadn't come to trade. Geoffrey Moresby had a sweetheart in Tapford and he hadn't sent word to her at all since he'd left. And as weeks turned into months, the villagers began to worry. So eventually as the summer became autumn, a few of the men from Tapford went out into the woods to look for them."

"How old is this version of the story?" said Sue.

"I'm picking the best bits. Some were written down in the 1970s, some are Victorian. The oldest ones are much, *much* older than that, but it's hard to say how old."

"What's the actual version, then?"

"There isn't one, not really. It's folk tales all the way down." She expected Alice to object—that was the sort of statement that usually baited her into joining in—but Alice wasn't paying attention. At any rate, there were no further questions from the jury. Nuria took another sip of tea and continued.

"They went out into the woods. Rather like we did today, actually. And they looked everywhere and found no sign of the Moresby family. Finally, in the deepest part of the wood, where the trees lay thickest, they found a little cottage, and in front of it sat Essie Moresby, only thirteen years old, holding her baby sister in her arms and rocking her gently. And she wouldn't say a word, and after a while someone realised—the baby was dead. And not a mark on her."

Kim sucked in her breath. Helly's eyes were wide in the lamplight, but she didn't interrupt. She leaned forward.

"Inside the cottage, Margaret the mother, was dead too.

And just like the baby, there wasn't a mark on her. The father and brother were nowhere to be seen. After a few hours when Essie still wouldn't speak they took her back to Tapford with them, but by the morning she was gone again.

"After that there was uproar in the village. No one knew what was going on, only that it couldn't be natural. In the end, they found out that Robert Moresby had made a pact with whatever it was that lived in the forest. In exchange for his family's lives he gave his soul to it. And in the depths of the forest that now bears his name, on Midsummer's Eve, he paid it homage. Margaret objected, had tried to get him to change his mind, but he wouldn't, and so the Corrigal had put the pestilence on her and her baby, and taken her son away, and all that were left were Robert and his daughter.

"It was around this time that the Black Death hit England, so it's possible that that's what truly happened to the Moresby family: the Black Death could kill overnight, and if you didn't know to look for the buboes, it could seem to kill without leaving a mark. Or that's why they left Tapford in the first place—lots of people did go out into the wilds, to try and outrun the plague."

"But," said Sue, "you said the mother and baby had no mark on them. And surely they'd know to look for evidence of the plague?"

"That's the legend."

"And the son?" said Helly. Her face was still rapt. "What happened to him?"

"Dragged into the Corrigal's Nest and devoured, or so the story goes. But none of them were ever seen outside the woods again. They say Robert and Essie walk the woods to this day, restless and regretful."

Kim said, thoughtfully, "That's not the version I heard."

"Did yours have the witch in it?"

"Yes."

"That's another good one. Maybe one for another night, though."

Helly stretched her legs out in front of her. "Good story." She wiggled her toes experimentally in the lamplight. "Do any of you feel like you're being watched? I've felt it for a while."

"Very funny," said Sue. She shivered and pulled the ends of her sleeves down over her hands. "I might turn in early."

Alice was staring into space. Kim prised the tin mug from her hands and she shook her head, the train of thought visibly dissipating.

They split into their tents not long afterwards: Kim, Helly and Sue to the larger one, Alice and Nuria to the smaller. Just before she turned the torch off, in her sleeping bag, Alice said very quietly, "Did you see it?"

"See what?"

"The other wood."

"What do you mean?"

But Alice shook her head and turned the light out. "Goodnight Nuria. Sleep well."

Outside, the leaves of the gigantic oak tree that linked them to the past rustled in the ghost of a breeze.

CHAPTER FOUR
Omens And Escapees

THE OAK TREE had gone. It was impossible to see how it could have happened, and yet there was no arguing with it. The clearing remained, and apparently every single one of the skinny trees marking its boundary; the massive oak that had seemed so solid, so permanent the night before, was no longer there.

To begin with, there was stunned silence, as the realisation spread among those who were awake and nearest. Captain Davies was woken by the sound of someone telling someone else what he'd do if the other one wouldn't shut up, and then he recognised the high-pitched muttering of Francis Alwood.

"What's going on?"

Then he saw. And scrambled to his feet, sword in hand. "Where did it go?"

None of the terrified men seemed to want to get any closer.

Alwood and Stiles, the two from one of the nearby villages, were praying aloud in tones of pure fear, signing the cross in front of themselves over and over with trembling hands. The others were giving them a wide berth, eyes wide and untrusting. Stiles and Alwood were not the only ones with faces the colour of milk.

Davies took a couple of tentative steps into the middle of the clearing. As he approached where the oak had been, he could see all the eyes on him, the flinches as he stepped forward. But the ground was smooth, as strewn with leaves as the rest of the clearing. There was nothing to suggest that a tree had been there—of any size, never mind one so gargantuan. He stepped forward again, and at an awkward sort of half-run launched himself across the middle of the clearing.

Nothing happened.

The oak tree had gone.

Alexander Davies had only just woken up; he could still feel the thickness of sleep tempering his fear and making it difficult to think. The ache in his shoulder was duller now, and mixed in with the stiffness of his back after another night sleeping on hard earth. "Who was on last watch? Which of you?"

They stared from one to another. Then, "Moody," said Thatcher.

"Where is he?"

And that was how they discovered that Willis had died in the night, and that Roberts, Edgeworth and Moody were nowhere to be found.

The body of Willis lay where he had slumped the night before, when they had first entered the clearing. If it hadn't been for the grimace of pain on his muck-streaked face, he could have been asleep, but a dark stain of blood discoloured the earth where his head rested. It was perfectly still. He had ceased to bleed some time ago.

Edgeworth and Moody, it quickly transpired, had made up the last watch, and although nobody was terribly surprised that they'd all deserted at the first opportunity they'd got, there had been several such opportunities in the preceding weeks.

"Why now?" said Harper. "First chance where nobody's likely to chase after them?"

"I think it's clear why now," said Thatcher. His eyes kept darting across to Alwood and Stiles, as if he held them personally responsible for this.

Byrne said, "Roberts sat up with Willis last night. He didn't want to leave him to... to be alone. Roberts has more honour than to leave his post."

Thatcher rounded on him. "Well, what do you say happened then? Clearly he's not here any more."

But there was no answer to that, or at least none that didn't involve wild speculation. Byrne said only, "I know him better than that."

Seeing Thatcher rise an inch taller in protest, Davies turned his attention to Francis Alwood. "What do you know about this?"

But Alwood seemed unable to get any words out. He was deathly pale, still signing the cross over his chest again and again. Davies felt a moment of pity at how young he looked. But it was immediately drowned out by his own fear. "Stop that," he barked, and Alwood's hand immediately fell to his side.

"It's the Devil," said Thatcher. And he stalked across to where the tree had once stood, and inspected the ground, more slowly and carefully than Davies had just done. Then he rounded on Alwood and Stiles. "That's what you think, isn't it? What happened to them?"

Bill Stiles was shaking violently. He seemed to be trying to say something, but couldn't get his voice to work.

"Enough!" said Davies. "We'll move on this morning, as soon as we can. Next town we get to, I'm putting a warrant out for the deserters. Any more insubordination and you'll feel the point of my sword." For some reason he was feeling defensive. He made eye contact with Sam Harper. "Look to Willis. Do what you need to do before we move on." And he stumped off into the forest for a piss.

A few minutes to himself in the cold morning air, and he was able to think more clearly. They needed to get out of this God-forsaken wood, get back on the road north and try to meet up with someone else who could make the decisions.

A low mist hung about the trees, and in this early light— it could not, he saw now, be long after dawn—it looked almost beautiful. Or it would have done if Davies had been in any mood to appreciate it. Had he imagined the oak tree after all? It might have made sense: the day before he had been delirious, in no fit state to keep a close eye on the world around him. But the tree had been the most obvious thing to notice, an anchor point in a world that had been spinning, sometimes fast, sometimes slow. And besides, they couldn't all have imagined it. Whatever was going on, it wasn't right. And it hadn't been right since yesterday afternoon.

He had, he realised, a splitting headache. He needed to drink something. He needed *a* drink, which wasn't quite the same thing, but he'd take what he could get at the moment.

The hair was standing up on the back of his neck, and he didn't know why. Aside from the obvious, of course— this wood was different in some way, something hard to put his finger on. He concentrated on it, frowning out into the trees stretching away from the clearing where they had made camp: mostly ash and birch and, yes, one or two other oak trees. Even so, it was as if… as if there was something insubstantial to it, like if you leaned too hard in the wrong direction you might fall right through something you had thought was solid. Davies wanted to say he had been surprised by the oak tree's disappearance, but now in the morning didn't the wood look perfectly right without it? Hadn't it not really made sense after all, for there to be such an enormous tree, in such a densely wooded area? Maybe they were in the real wood now, and the oak tree… But it was a stupid thought, and it made even less sense than everything else going on. Less sense than the Devil walking among them, even. He wiped his forehead with his sleeve.

After that he took his time, because if everything was buggered then it was buggered, and there was nothing he could do about it. Then he took a deep breath, because if Rod Thatcher was going to start rattling on about demonic forces beyond the ken of man, then someone needed to behave like an adult around here. And then he went back to the rest of them.

His absence seemed to have given some of the men a bit of perspective, because at least the immediate sense of panic had subsided. Of course Moody and Edgeworth and

Roberts hadn't been stolen away in the night by the Devil incarnate. They had deserted, like men often did, every day of the week. Soldiering was hard enough to stomach when you had signed up for it, when there was peace across England, when it wasn't your home in particular that was under threat of being burned to the ground. For men who were desperate to go home, now was as good a time as any to slip away, and probably better than most. It was cowardly, but England was not short of cowards at the moment.

Someone handed Davies a fist-sized hunk of stale bread, and a few of them moved along a fallen tree lying near the edge of the clearing to make room for him. He eyed it warily before sitting down.

"Was this here last night?"

"We think so," said Cadwell.

Davies took a bite of the bread. He could barely force it down, barely swallow. "Anyone got a drink?" A quarter-full water skin was passed along the fallen tree trunk. It tasted worse than the bread. "Did someone piss in this?"

"It's all that's left," said Ames, sourly. "We couldn't find the river yesterday."

They were all watching him, Davies realised. He cast about for the sergeant he liked better. "Where's Harper?"

Half a dozen men turned away to where the body of Willis still lay, and Harper bent over him. Harper was whispering something, that was evidently not for the rest to hear. When he straightened up there was a moment before he noticed all the rest of them looking at him, in which loss was writ large across his face.

They didn't have a priest. Davies had felt bad about it yesterday, when they'd had to leave so many comrades on the battlefield unburied. But this was worse—now they had time to spare, and no way to give Willis the absolution he deserved. A few more days and they could have met up with the rest of the companies heading north, and one of them, surely, would have a chaplain. Too late for Willis now, though. No chaplain, no quartermaster, barely so much as a drummer with Jessop in the state he was. Thank God for Sam Harper, otherwise Davies would almost be inclined to desert himself.

He called Thatcher and Harper over to one side. "We need to move on, quickly. Get out of this hellhole. No, don't look at me like that, Thatcher. How long 'til we can get everyone moving?"

"An hour or so," said Harper. "Taylor is weak, so's Onslow. We need to go slowly." He glanced back across at the clearing. "Speaking professionally, I think we should wait a few more hours." Thatcher started to try to cut across him, but Harper continued as if he hadn't noticed. "Personally, of course, let's go on as soon as we can."

"Right," said Davies, doubtfully. "You'd better patch up Taylor, then, before we go."

Harper nodded.

"We need to get out of this place," said Thatcher. "Alwood—"

"I didn't want to hear Mr Alwood's opinions last night, and I don't want them now." Davies looked across at the rest of them. There were pitifully few of them. Alwood and Stiles still sat apart from the group, looking down at the ground, still praying quietly. "Are you sure no one saw what happened? Someone must have."

"The entire last watch has gone missing," said Thatcher.

He appeared to be gritting his teeth. Davies ignored him. Where the oak had been, there was nothing at all.

They buried Willis in a shallow grave. Byrne and Kilburton dug it; Byrne had known Willis the longest. They set up a makeshift cross made of sticks to mark it. The rest sat around, either still too injured for such exertion, or just lost in their own thoughts. Davies sat near Jessop the drummer, who had been bleeding heavily the night before. Today he was subdued, and sweating under the muck of travel and battle, but seemed in reasonable spirits given the circumstances. Harper and Taylor lashed a few makeshift crutches together and handed them around to those who needed them, and they all gathered around the hole where Willis's body now lay. Most of them had known him for a year or more, a few for most of his lifetime. They were all from the same part of the world, after all. It was more than the fallen man's banner that kept them together.

They were a sorry-looking lot, quite apart from the crutches. Coats which had been patched several times already were soiled and bloodstained, and would likely remain so until they made it to an actual garrison. Beards grew patchy and rat-tailed, whether their owners intended to have them or not—they hadn't had much choice about that lately. And, thought Davies, under all that they were thin, sickly, underfed. This war was no good for anyone.

Taylor led the prayers for Willis's spirit, and for the men they had lost the previous day, in a voice whose flatness seemed to be belied by how tightly he shut his eyes while he was doing it. They stood around the open grave, and for a short while after he had finished the only sounds were low wheezing, and the leaves shaking in the trees around them, and Bill Stiles's muffled sniffling.

A respectful amount of time; not enough that it would tip over into something other than thinking about the dead. After that they dispersed, and prepared to leave. Willis's banner lay on the ground next to the spot where he had spent his last moments. They all eyed it nervously—it must be bad luck to take up a man's banner so soon after he was in the ground. Davies thought he saw Charley Ames smirking, and it was enough: "Ames, you take the colours. They're your responsibility now. Stop whining, man, your missus would be proud." No one laughed, and he wasn't sure he'd expected them to.

He avoided everyone's eye, and barked orders at them until they had assembled in a way that wasn't completely desultory. Then he picked a direction to what he recalled had been approximately the north-east, and started to walk in it.

"Sir!" Davies wheeled around. It was Cadwell, halfway down the line. Of course it was; no one else would have dared interrupt. "I thought we were going north-east?"

"We are," he snapped, and turned back around.

"Beg pardon sir, but north-east is that way." Cadwell was pointing to a direction almost at right angles from where Davies had been intending to take them.

Davies didn't move. "Are you suggesting that I'm going the wrong way?"

"No, sir, only—I'm sure it's that way."

Ten others—only ten!—all staring at the two of them, from one to the other. On any other day Davies might have had Cadwell flogged for insubordination. But something wasn't right in this place, and now he was doubting himself. He squinted up at where the sun would be, if it hadn't been obscured by thick grey clouds. Now he looked, the weak shadows fell in the way Cadwell was suggesting. That couldn't be right; they'd come from the south-east, which was... nearer to what he thought was north than it was to south. His head hurt. "Harper, Thatcher, to me."

They shuffled off to one side.

"Which way did we come from last night?"

They pointed in two different directions.

Davies swore. "It couldn't be bloody simple, could it?"

Thatcher's eyes were bulging. "It's the Devil's doing. It must be. We should get away from this place."

"The river can't be far off. We can't go wrong when we get to it." He called out to the rest of the group. "Alwood! Pull yourself together. Which way is the river from here?"

Alwood said, "It runs north to south, east of here. But they say in these parts that you should never—"

"Alright, shut up. I don't want to hear what your mam told you not to do. We'd better go Mr Cadwell's way, then." He was being petty, and in the back of his mind he knew it. But he was the captain here, not Cadwell, and the rest of them could put up with it if they knew what was good for them. At the back of the line, Bill Stiles was now staring wildly into the trees in all directions. He was visibly shaking. Davies ignored him. They set off, slowly so that the injured ones could keep up, in a direction that was probably to the north-east.

* * *

SOLDIERING, WHEN IT comes down to it, involves hardly any fighting—not on the regular, at least. If you're unlucky there's a little of it, and if you're very unlucky there's months of drilling that immediately disperses to the wind the moment you go near a real battlefield with real enemy soldiers in it. But no matter how lucky you are, the fighting and the drilling bits of being a soldier pale into insignificance next to its two chief components: trying to sleep in terrible places, and marching. Sometimes—and again this is about how lucky you are—you might find yourself in a bit of garrison that isn't soaking wet and doesn't smell too much like something rotting. But the marching, that's non-negotiable. Even at the best of times.

It is not fun. It hurts—acutely, if your boots are too big or too small, which is likely, and otherwise it's a long, dull ache in your legs and your heels and your back and your shoulders.

The ones who could afford the coin to boost their luck often ended up as cavalry. To do that, you needed to be able to buy and keep a horse. These were not those men. This was a company of foot, and when it came to marching, the clue was in the name.

And yet, thought Davies, somehow, when all about was uncertain or just plain dangerous, marching was better than the alternative. It was better than what you might be doing. He had been a soldier of sorts for more than half his life, had walked half the length of England more times than he could count, and plenty of France and the Low Countries besides. England was worse; there were more hills in it, and the food was scarcer. Even here, though, in a bitter kind of way he almost enjoyed the walking. It was better at any rate than standing still and waiting. At least nobody had ever succeeded in co-opting him into the navy.

Behind him, he could hear the murmur of whispered discussion from some other part of the line. It was one of the things Davies usually found most comforting about the march—occasional conversation lapsing sometimes into companionable silence, or sometimes in high spirits into singing. There was no chance of singing now, besides which it was still threatening to rain, but there was something in the character of the conversation that seemed different from usual. It was something about the whispering, which spoke of intending not to be heard.

That probably meant one thing. "Should my ears be burning?" He turned and saw that the few at the back of the group were walking in a clump, like young girls. Ames with his banner held at an alarming angle like a pike, Cadwell, Alwood, Thatcher. Frowning and serious. In front of them Bill Stiles looked like he was about to burst into tears again.

Sergeant Thatcher looked like he'd been caught doing something illicit. He flushed red, and stomped forward with his head down. Turning back around, Davies heard Ames say, "I want to hear what lives here, even if *he* doesn't."

Davies said, "You're a bunch of superstitious old wives, the lot of you."

"How do you explain the tree?" said Cadwell, slightly too loudly. They all looked at him.

"I don't care to, soldier. I only care to get far away from it, and I can't do that if you're busy gossiping, can I now?"

Francis Alwood whispered something inaudible, and
Stiles took a step closer to him. They were both so young,
Davies noticed now—under Alwood's patchy attempt at a
beard he could only have been seventeen or eighteen, and
Stiles even younger. A bad influence on each other, surely.

"What did you say?"

And now the group had definitely stopped walking, and
were all goggling, and a sense of unease seemed to leap
from man to man, growing and becoming stronger as it
went.

Alwood tried again to speak, but the words seemed to
stick in his throat. Stiles said, "You can't say it here! It'll
hear you!" His voice was uncannily high pitched, almost
a squeak.

"What will hear you?" said Davies, helplessly.

"For pity's sake," said Thatcher. "He said, it's the
Corrigal."

CHAPTER FIVE

Health And Safety

ALICE CHRISTOPHER WOKE with a sore back and a cold nose, and lay in her sleeping bag staring at the pale blue canvas above her and listening to the birdsong. Judging by the quality of the light, it was still overcast outside, and without dislodging whatever comfort she'd been able to eke out to look at her watch, she was unable to gauge even roughly what time it was. And so she lay there, feeling her nose go numb, sure that if she moved an inch from her cocoon of sleeping bag her feet would immediately freeze.

From outside came the sound of the other tent unzipping. Someone rummaged around her waterproofs, got to her feet and stumped a few steps into the clearing.

And then silence.

Kim's voice. "Helly? Can I borrow you for a second?"

The sound of shuffling. Another tent zip. Alice was

suddenly alert, eyes open, listening hard. Next to her, Nuria made no movement at all, but Alice had the distinct impression that she was also awake.

From outside, a sharp intake of breath, and a muffled "Ssh." Alice sat bolt upright, and started shovelling on a second fleece jumper. Nuria next to her started to say, "I'm sure it's—"

"Dr Christopher?" It was Helly, outside.

Kim's voice said, "Sue? Have you got the camera in there?" Alice pitched herself forward through the inner tent opening, grabbed her boots without putting them on, and lunged for the outer zip. A wave of freezing air hit her, damp and misty from the early morning.

She immediately saw what they were looking at. What they weren't looking at. Because it was gone: that enormous oak tree that had been the source of their triumph the previous evening, that specifically mentioned star that lit their way and proved they were on the right track, that Alice was on the right track, was not there. It had gone.

It was like she had run into a brick wall at full speed. She sat awkwardly in the door of the tent, boots in one hand, mind almost completely blank, staring agape at the middle of the clearing.

There was movement behind her, as Nuria said, "What's going on?" and looked past Alice's shoulder. Then she too saw what was out there and fell silent.

Sue had by now found the camera and switched it on; it gave a cheerful little bleep, and she took it across to where Kim and Helly stood while it booted up. Her expression was curiously thin-lipped, almost angry, and she averted her eyes from the middle of the empty clearing as if it offended her. Kim took the camera and flicked through the last few pictures.

"Look. There it is. Tree." The little screen was barely two inches across, but the image it showed was unmistakable. There was the oak, at 18:31:14 the previous day, trunk so thick that it could conceivably have been a thousand years old if you didn't know any better, branches mingling with the rest of the canopy so that it was unbroken in places. There again at 18:31:32, 18:31:48, from another angle at 18:32:19. Solid. Real.

Alice put her boots on slowly, tying the laces entirely by feel—she couldn't take her eyes off the space in the clearing where the oak had been. Surprisingly, after that first moment of shock, she felt far calmer than she had expected to. It was completely impossible, of course, and yet somehow... it slotted into place in her mind quite easily. Last night she had had the strongest impression, after all, that she had not been looking at the *real* Moresby Forest, that somehow there was a wood tucked in behind the wood that she was seeing, that something about this place was not only not true but—and she had not been able to put her finger on it then, although now it felt as natural as the absence of the oak tree—that it was actively deceitful.

If there were bodies here to be found, she might just have the best shot anyone had ever had at finding them. This was her chance to *know*.

The others were talking, and it occurred to her that she ought to be listening.

"...have to come back another time," Kim was saying.

"This'll take a much larger team," said Sue. "There's no other way to do it. I can't do anything under these conditions, and neither can you."

"What's this?" said Alice, and she went over towards them.

"I'm sorry, Dr Christopher," said Sue. "But you have to admit we're out of our depth here. Let's come back a different day with more people. I'm as disappointed as you." But she didn't sound like it. She was still looking at where the tree had been.

"Are you joking?" said Alice. "Nobody has ever had an opportunity like this before, and you want to just turn around and go away?"

"Yes. In case of a natural disaster, I'd want backup. But this isn't even... What is this? I've never heard of anything like this at all. We need to go home, right now." She addressed this last to Kim and Helly, as if their say-so would swing it.

Kim said, in the tone of a mother being placatory, "Surely the real waste of an opportunity is trying to rush it, and not do it justice? We should definitely come back, but..." She trailed off. She too was looking back at the place where the tree had been.

Alice wanted to say, "But what if it's changed by then and we never get it back?" but she bit that back. "There must be some kind of reasonable explanation. What do you think, Nuria?"

It was a cruel thing to ask, because she knew what Nuria was like and that Nuria would back her up no matter what her private opinion was.

"It is a unique opportunity," sad Nuria doubtfully.

Sue threw her hands up. "It's a stupid idea. With respect. I don't know what's going on, I can't explain it, but—"

"We need backup," said Kim, firmly. "The safety of this expedition is my job. I've never seen anything like this before, or even heard of it. It's my call to make, and I say we're going back."

Helly sighed. "I don't like it either, Alice. I see why you want to explore. But—*but*—with my professional hat on, which I have to have and so do you, I agree with Kim. So let's take a few more photos, just for comparison, and have some breakfast, and come back another day."

"You don't understand," said Alice. She could hear her own voice wobbling. Something was slipping out of her grasp.

"You've worked hard for this, I know," Helly said. "We've all seen the risk assessments. But this is beyond a risk. How do you even explain that?"

And Alice couldn't, not in a way that she wanted to say out loud to people using their best reasonable voices on her, so she stumped off angrily on her own, and the rest of them let her go.

She should have known that the excitement of yesterday couldn't last, that anything she tried to hold onto with both hands would immediately be yanked away. That was about the shape of it. This part of the forest was wild, and thick, and there was something about it that was not as it seemed, that was being deliberately hidden in plain sight. She kept thinking she could see flashes of it out of the corner of her vision, and she was loath to leave until she had a chance to understand it properly.

Which she would not now get to do.

She had a sudden urge to scream, and gritted her teeth.

The planning of this trip alone had taken months; the permissions and funding had been in the works for more than a year. The risk assessments alone had been a nightmare, for getting into this fenced-off bit of forest—completely outsized in fact, even for a place the military was supposed to sometimes use, not that she'd seen any evidence that they ever did. And that was before she could even think about making a case for the trip's academic importance, and for bringing any other participants along with her. She had had to fight for it so hard, against people who didn't think it was worth the money or the paperwork. Then there were people like Alastair Bell trying to poach her grad students, to make out that her research was more obsessive than important—as if he or every academic ever didn't think a little more highly of their own work than it strictly deserved. As if a mystery like this and the opportunity to answer it weren't both worth their weight in gold. Alastair would kill to have something like this.

And then there was Deirdre, Alice's own PhD supervisor, from the first time Alice had come to Sibbert Hill. The woods had already been fenced off by then, and they'd been there to excavate the hill, and perhaps to find out who the mystery attackers mentioned in the deserter's account were. In the event, they had been out of luck—there was not a shred of evidence one way or the other, which had done nothing to sate either Alice's curiosity, or Deirdre's. But two decades ago Alice had been where Nuria was now—or a few miles to the south at any rate—stringing along in Deirdre's wake, already casting jealous glances at those tantalising "KEEP OUT" signs while Deirdre did exactly the same. The wild theories had been Deirdre's to begin with, and Alice found herself inflicted with the same fascination, drawn by the same compulsion to make it inside this place and see it for herself. Deirdre hadn't managed it, in the end, and now Alice had gone where her mentor never could. They had said it was a lack of funding that was the problem, or else that it no longer "fit with the currents of contemporary research", whatever that was supposed to mean, but the upshot was that every time she had tried to apply for permission to come here, she had no support at all from her department, and the permissions had been flat-out refused more times than she could count. It had taken twenty years of stonewalling and jumping through bureaucratic hoops, but she'd got here.

There was nothing for it, though. The park rangers had spoken, and that was the whole point of their being here in the first place.

She did her best not to sulk while they were packing up the tents, and eating their cereal bars and drinking their tea. It was hard not to, and there wasn't a lot she wanted to say. She should have learned how to contain her disappointment, or at least not to show it so transparently, years ago. Maybe in other circumstances. Or anywhere else on the planet.

The mood amongst all the others was equally subdued, although for different reasons. Sue in particular seemed to have been shaken by the disappearance of the huge tree. Every so often as they were packing up, in the midst of everything else she would look like she was about to say something, and she seemed to be suddenly hyper alert, aware of any small sound or movement not only in the clearing but around to either side. Kim was all monosyllabic pragmatism in the way of someone used to dealing with extreme conditions. You could almost see the to-do list painted on her forehead, checked off item by item— focusing the attention, getting through this.

Helly was the opposite. She muttered to herself quietly and constantly, narrating what she was doing in a way that see-sawed between inaudible and one half of a conversation in which the others might be expected to engage. None of them took her bait. And honestly, thought Alice, that might just be how Helly naturally was, rather than her chattiness being any particular response to stress: of all of them, Helly seemed the most at ease with the... you know, the tree. Presumably it made some kind of intuitive sense to her, although whether that was anything like the sense it made to Alice was debatable. She would've asked Helly about it, whether Helly too had noticed something strange about the landscape around them—aside from the obvious, of course, but she was afraid Helly would say something embarrassing. And then the others would think both of them were strange, and it wouldn't help Alice's own chances of coming back.

It had been barely half past six in the morning when Kim had first got up out of her tent and seen that the tree had gone; by the time they had all argued over their decision, and eaten and cleared up their things to leave, it was shortly after half past eight. They should be out of the woods and back at the Land Rover round about eleven-ish, shortly after that they'd have reasonable phone signal back, and they should be able to let the department know they'd be home by the end of the day. It was a shame, of course, but for everyone who wasn't Alice, that was all it was. It was all she could do not to be bitter about it, not to snipe at them.

The GPS unit was still not working. The batteries—"Fresh yesterday morning! You all saw me put the new ones in!"—were completely flat, and even when Sue replaced them with a backup set, it wouldn't acknowledge any satellites.

"Did you charge the camera, too?" said Helly.

"Yes, before I left the house yesterday. Don't say it's—"

"Down to its last bar, yes. Must be those magnets," she said, carelessly. "My phone battery went in the night too. Not that it's much use in here. You did say you'd left yours in the car, didn't you, Alice?"

"Mm-hmm."

"And I know Kim has a charger in the glove box. We'll be fine, then. Not too long without. I'll take a last couple of pictures, anyway." And she did so, of the space where the tree used to be, and where now was nothing. It looked normal. It looked like there *ought* to be nothing there.

Kim said, "It's a bit dodgy in this place, but I do have a proper compass with me, just in case." She extracted it from a pocket of her bag and hung it around her neck from a string. "We'll be alright. We'll just do it the old-fashioned way."

So they set off, back the way they had come.

Where the previous day Alice had been at the front of the group she now hung back. She was being childish about it, and she knew it—but to have the brakes applied so cruelly and so quickly on the fulfilment of such a lifelong dream was more than a person should have to bear. The morning was overcast and gloomy, and the greenery was thick and seemed to intersect their path with a frequency that felt almost deliberate, just like it had done the previous day. Nevertheless, they had walked for barely more than twenty minutes, when she began to get a vague hunch that they were not in fact retracing their steps. Really she wanted to keep quiet about it and let them get further in, to spend as long as she was allowed in this forest, but she was not as childish as all that so she said, "Have we been this way already? I don't believe we have."

Sue was the one with the map—the 1960s map, that was, requisitioned since the GPS was out of commission— and she brandished it now. "I think we're about here. We should be coming up along a ridge to our right, in a few more minutes." And she traced their trajectory with the tip of a chewed-up biro, produced from the depths of a trouser pocket.

Alice nodded. This wasn't her expedition any more, after all.

Kim held a hand out for the map. "Let's have a look." But she seemed placated.

Ten minutes later, they still hadn't come across the ridge.

"Let me have a look at the compass," said Helly fairly, and when Kim handed it over to her she said, "We're going almost due east?"

Kim flushed. "That's not what it said when I looked at it. Are you sure?"

But that was what it said.

"I could have sworn..."

"Let's check it against the map." But there were no obvious landmarks to compare with the map.

"Maybe we went past the ridge and didn't spot it," said Alice. "Should we double back?"

It was not the right thing to say. Sue shot her a filthy look, then returned her attention to Kim. "We definitely set out in the right direction." It wasn't a question.

"I thought so too," said Kim. "And I've checked since then and it said south. But then, there is something wrong with the compasses round here. Magnetic." She squinted up at the sun. "It's so dark today, I can't even see which way the shadows are going."

In the end they changed direction, to what the compass insisted ought now to be due south. Sue clearly wanted to take control of the offending item herself, but since she was loath to give up the map she instead had to be content with handing the compass over to Helly, who kept it face up in her flat palm as she walked, as a show of good faith. It was a bad compromise, at least judging by Sue's increasingly sour expression, but there was no way the map was getting relinquished to the possession of Mrs I Prefer To Understand Grid References Intuitively. Which on the whole was probably fair enough.

They went on, and although the silence among the group was more strained, and they could not be entirely sure exactly where they were, Alice felt herself start to slip into her own mind again. There was a weight in her chest, dense and heavy and recently chipped with the pain of failure, but at the same time the rhythm of walking was comforting, calming almost, and this place might after all be her favourite in the whole world. She ought to enjoy it while she could.

If they were not making their way out of the woods, though, then they must be instead going deeper in. Deeper wasn't a bad word for it, not least because the tree cover here was so thick. She could see the sky only in intermittent patches. And there was something too about the smell of it, of fresh leaves and also of something earthy and damp. Now and again she thought she caught a whiff of wild garlic, but there was none to be seen.

Nuria had not said a word while they had been arguing over directions—nor in fact since they had left the clearing. That was just what Nuria was like, though, and another opinion in the mix would hardly have improved matters. Alice stole a glance at her now; she looked like she was trying not to cry, but it didn't do to judge people like that and maybe Alice was reading into things. What was she going to do, ask? She looked away again.

One thing that she kept coming back to was that there shouldn't be any paths in here, because nobody ever came through it, and yet there were—just now and again, criss-crossing the way they walked, and sometimes they followed one along for a bit before it dissipated into nothing again. Deer, she assumed, must be responsible for it, or some other animals, perhaps—but it felt like the paths were features of the wood itself, that somehow they were a way for the place to express itself. It *was* expressing itself, Alice thought, the longer she was inside it. The wood was a liar, but beneath that was buried something true, and fascinating, and the wood was telling her what it was, if only she could tune into it properly, or decipher it.

Whatever it was, it was something big. She thought of the oak tree again—the tiny, incontrovertible one on the two-inch screen of a digital camera, and the real one, or the maybe real one, which had so dwarfed everything else around it. How old did a tree have to be to grow that size? Well, let's see: it was hard to tell the diameter of the trunk, since it was so gnarled, but let's put it at five feet, or sixty inches. Multiply that by pi—and she was nearly getting somewhere, when Helly planted herself face first into the ground.

"Are you alright?" Kim was the first to react.

"Yeah," said Helly. But she didn't get up; she slid the rucksack off her back and sat down. "I think I've jarred my ankle."

Then they were all concern, piling their bags to one side and rummaging for first aid kits and bottles of water. Helly winced when she tried to get up, and was nearly in tears the first time she tried to put any weight on it. The ankle, it turned out, was not just jarred but in all likelihood broken.

Kim pulled her phone out. "No signal. Of course not." She waved it about. "Look, it only thinks we've gone about half a mile today. Definitely not right."

"Mine hasn't got signal either," said Sue. "I don't think it has since we left the boundary."

"Two people should go ahead, then," said Alice. "To get help."

Sue looked like she was going to object, and Kim said, "Not if we can possibly help it. We'd never find our way back here, and the air ambulance would be no help in these trees." She said to Helly, "If we bind it up, and you double up on paracetamol and ibuprofen, do you think you can walk for a while? Just back to the car."

Helly was very pale. "Just about, if that's how it has to be. I'm sorry, Kim, I don't think I can carry my bag like this."

"We'll split it between us," said Nuria. She held out a box of pills and a bottle of water. Helly took them, and popped two paracetamol into her palm.

"Will that be okay?"

Sue said, rather brusquely, "Of course. You can't carry a tent on your foot."

Assent now given, the majority of Helly's pack was divided among them. They drank some of the water, and opened a few of the tins between them, since it wasn't worth carrying them back to the Land Rover. Kim bandaged Helly's ankle up and gave her an arm to lean on until a stick or two of adequate size could be found. It was all very straightforward. They were professionals, making the best of a bad situation.

Nobody mentioned the oak. Not once.

And, slowly, on they walked.

CHAPTER SIX

The Devil's Dance

GOSSIP TRAVELS THE length of a military marching line at speeds that shouldn't be possible, even in double file. Part of the reason for that, of course, is that discipline often leaves a lot to be desired. In this case Sergeant Thatcher, who was supposed to be at the back and supervising the line ahead of him, was in fact one of the worst offenders. Sergeant Sam Harper, two rows from the front and resolutely staring at the back of Captain Davies's head, knew that Thatcher had not been Davies's first choice of right hand man—anyone with eyes could see that, not least Thatcher himself—but aside from Davies, Thatcher was the longest serving soldier here. He'd be damned if he wasn't going to hang onto the crumbs of power and scoop them up with both hands where he could.

Frankly, Harper thought the captain was too lenient on Thatcher—on most of them, really. Maybe it was because the gossip hadn't made it that far up the line. And here was Harper, the killjoy that was stopping it. It was better for everyone that way.

He himself, being a bit further along, could hear better what was being said at the back, and he didn't like it one bit. Rod Thatcher spent far too long loudly contemplating the state of his immortal soul at the best of times, but now he was really taking it too far. Usually everyone else would agree about that—they'd all been subjected to it enough times. Not today, though. Today they were joining in. The parts he could hear were getting more and more far-fetched—now Charley Ames was sure that the ambushers on the hill must have been a rogue company of Irish Catholics set on driving them into this forest to their certain doom; now the Devil himself was watching their progress through His own domain.

It was strange. Harper's own memory of the hill featured more of his own men than the others. He had been focused on Willis, for a lot of it. But he remembered next to nothing about the enemy: no colours, no uniforms, except maybe that they were red. No faces, or voices. All that was unusual. True, he had not fought anyone man to man this time—but Sam Harper remembered faces, often for longer afterwards than was comfortable. He could still bring to mind some of the men he had killed in France, although he didn't like to if he could help it these days. He could picture the opposite line outside Banbury weeks ago—that was easy. And yet... He must have been too focused on Willis. That must have been it. He held the thought in front of him, as if in his hands, and then set it somewhere safe. Sometimes it was like that, immediately afterwards. You found out the truth of the matter sooner or later, if the Lord intended you to. Or you didn't.

As for the rest of what Ames was bleating on about, now that there was a name to it, he could see there being some devil or creature lurking in these woods. It was unclear how it might be related to the disappearance of the oak tree, but there was more in this world than Samuel Harper understood, and demonic forces were as likely an explanation as any other he could think of.

When it came down to it, and now he was thinking about it in particular, Harper also believed the Devil could walk among them, if it chose to. You had to be on your guard. Whatever the others had to say about it.

To either side, taller trees had given way to thick, sprawling bracken. It reached its tendrils out, almost to waist height in places, whispering and snapping as the men in front brushed it out of the way when they passed. The tops of wide-canopied birch bent lower than they had done in the morning, their trunks gnarlier and more twisted. Older, maybe, or just different. There was an odd smell in the air, deep and verdant and cloying. Harper blinked.

Corrigal. The Corrigal. He had never heard of it. But now that the idea had been planted in his head... Yesterday it had felt like someone or something had been watching them. He had blamed the feeling on the fact that they'd just been ambushed.

He nearly tripped over a protruding tree root. Luckily none of the rest were paying attention. He could have sworn it hadn't been there a moment ago—but then he had been peering through the trees, rather than down at his own feet, so it could yet be that he was mistaken. A freckle of damp touched the end of his nose. It was going to rain soon. He cast around again: did he feel like anyone was watching them right now? It was hard to tell.

At any rate it did not seem likely that there were demons running around uprooting trees and leaving no trace of them. For a start, the Devil was cleverer than that. But the thing that had shaken him most this morning was the fact that his sense of direction had failed him, and the captain the same. In all the years they had travelled in the same company, Harper couldn't remember that ever happening before. Now north was not the way he had believed it to be, and the one whose gut feeling had been true was Cadwell, of all people.

And yet, Harper could only rely on his own senses. That was the only chance he had of knowing things as they were. Now that he considered the matter, it seemed to him that the place that they walked now was as natural as any other forest, whereas the day before he had barely noticed his surroundings, had hardly been aware of anything that wasn't the men whose lives he had tried to save. Richard Jessop limped beside him now, his frown of pain so intense that Harper was amazed that he still continued to walk. No, yesterday Samuel Harper had not been paying attention to anything around him.

Which led him to believe that if there were any demonic meddling going on, then it had happened the day before. Yes. And therefore, this must be the true wood—and it stood to reason that the one they had been in yesterday, the one with the giant oak tree in it, had not been truthful.

Had been, perhaps, some kind of false thing, some mirage.

If that were how it was, which made sense—it did!—then it must have been the other place where the Devil had been, the untruthful one with directions that didn't make sense and foes who seemed to appear and disappear from nowhere on the hillside; and if they had been in the false place yesterday, with the oak and all the rest, then they were there no longer. Now they were safe.

Clear though this seemed to him, it was a conclusion of his own: if anyone further down the line had come to it, that never reached as far as Harper. He could hear now that Alwood and Stiles were refusing to talk about the Corrigal any more, and indeed Alwood seemed to be regretting naming the fiend in the first place—he was three ranks behind Harper and still distinctly audible. "If you keep saying it, I'll—I'll *get* you."

"Oh, you will, will you?" came back the sing-song voice of Kilburton. "You're bigger than me, are you? Well, I'm scared. I'm scared of the Corrigal."

"Cut it out, Kilburton," said Thatcher, sharply, and then, "Oi! No you don't, you little oik, back you go..." and a shuffling as Alwood was sent to the back of the line. "What are you looking at?" he continued. "Eyes front." And Harper wasn't the only one to hurriedly turn back around again. He caught a glimpse of Alwood's face as he did so. Wide eyed. Desperate.

Still, at the front of the line, Captain Davies seemed to be lost in his own thoughts, or at least he did not turn around to look at the bickering going on behind him. Harper decided to follow his lead, and pretend it was beneath his own notice too.

The more he thought about the nature of the woods, the more he found himself thinking about the men who had disappeared in the night. The fact that men had deserted wasn't surprising; in the army you got used to that sometimes happening. There were cowards all over, especially these days. The company had had a few deserters already, further south. The further you got from home, the less men wanted to be there. Moody and Edgeworth, he believed, had been waiting for their moment to make a run for it for days, had been looking shifty and muttering among themselves as far back as Leicester. But if they had in fact been in a false wood, rather than the true one, when they had finally gone, then where could they have run to? And the further the line now walked, the more outlandish the idea of a true wood and a false one seemed to him, the thinner the comfort, and it itched at him like lice.

Two woods, though, and only one of them containing the enormous oak. Was a moving forest any more impossible than a single disappearing tree? Harper had never been this far north before, or not in England at least. Maybe such strange things were more common up here; maybe people took them in stride. Or, judging by Bill Stiles's continued snivelling, maybe not.

The whispers behind him were becoming more agitated. He resented them and tried not to hear them.

A little before midday, they heard a telltale sound off to their right, and upon veering that way they finally came across a fast-flowing stream, running almost parallel to the direction they'd been walking. It was a minor triumph—even if it wasn't the main river they'd been expecting to find, it was at least a sign that they were going in the right direction. Water skins were emptied and refilled, and it ought to have raised their spirits—and would have done, most likely, if they hadn't been comprehensively dampened by the last day, by the oak and the deaths of so many friends. The deserters' names were bandied about now that those who remained were out of marching order—wishing that they would be eaten up by demons, calling them cowards, so on, so forth.

Harper had no time to stew on it, however; while they were walking he had not been paying very much attention to the limping Jessop next to him, or the others who were injured, and now they had found running water there were bandages to be stoppered, broken bodies to be inspected. Jessop was deathly pale and sweating, and he wasn't the only one—Onslow on his makeshift crutches gritted his teeth, declining to sit down as if he feared he wouldn't stand up again; the anger he directed at the escapees from the night before could easily have been directed at his own leg, which was smeared with dark, oozing red-brown. Harper had thought this morning that Francis Alwood was being too dramatic, and frankly the boy was still laying it on pretty thick given the state of some of the others, but when he lifted his shirt the bruise on his ribcage was something special. It wasn't just deep purple, but black in places, and larger than a handspan across. Whatever had hit him had not been mucking around.

Now that the company had had something to drink, they began to remember how hungry they were, how little opportunity there had been to find food over the last week. They were in a forest; this ought to be a better place to find sustenance than the villages they had passed through which had already been looted to empty by other soldiers before them. Ought they eat in here, though? Or was that like accepting food from the fair folk, the striking of a bargain on who knew what terms? Who could tell? How hungry did you need to get before that stopped mattering?

In the meantime, Rod Thatcher had developed a swagger. Harper was reminded of a stray cat, puffing itself up to try and look as big as possible in the face of a threat. It would be pitiful if it wasn't irritating. And the captain was saying nothing, which was almost worse, because he couldn't possibly be unaware of it by now. He should be reining it back in, thought Harper, before it got out of hand and drove the rest of them to distraction.

Still Davies paced back and forth, a little further off, looking out into the thick trees beyond the stream. They looked normal, that was the thing—they looked like any other bit of English woodland that Harper had ever been in. It wasn't all the same trees you'd get in the New Forest, but it wasn't far off. Nevertheless he was restless. This place was getting to all of them.

The captain must have been listening to the group more carefully than they had realised, though, because almost without warning he spun around, and snapped at Charley Ames, "That's enough! I don't want to hear your dullard opinions!"

Ames, who had been holding forth on ghostly trees he had heard of near Newark and wondering aloud if this might be something of the same kind, looked abashed.

Next to him, Thatcher was stony-faced. "Pray with us, captain. Only divine guidance can get us out of here."

Davies rounded on him. "And you should know better,

sergeant. I'll have no more talk of anyone's immortal souls in relation to these fucking trees until we join the main camp. Not a word of it, do you hear?"

Thatcher said hotly, "Do you think you're above the laws of the Lord, captain?"

Davies looked as if he might be about to hit him. "I won't pay the Devil more mind than he takes for himself. I won't tell you again." For a moment it looked like Thatcher was about to square up to him. Then Davies turned away again. "Pick your things up," he said to the group at large. "We're moving on. Let's get out of this pisshole of a place." As the rest shambled their way back into the semblance of a line, he said quietly to Harper, "Did you see it?"

"See what?"

But the captain shook his head. "Keep an eye out to the back of the line, won't you?"

"Everything alright, sir?"

"I can trust you, can't I, Harper?" Without waiting for answer, he said, "Of course I can. Just… keep a lookout." And he resumed his place at the head of the march, and pretended not to hear any of the muttering behind him.

There was a scuffle along the line, apparently over the order of march: Ames was attempting to foist off the pole of the colours onto Byrne, who was enough of a goody-goody arse-licker that in any other circumstances he might have jumped at the chance to carry the colours. Now, though, even he was unwilling to take it. "Ames," said Harper, warningly, and the other man gave up his vain attempt and wove through the points of the others' pikes towards the front. Alwood took this opportunity to try to sneak further forward up the line, to his original spot about halfway up it, until the great bulk of Sergeant Thatcher towered over him, grabbed him by the scruff of the neck, and thrust him back to the end. He protested no further, but several of the others averted their eyes. It seemed somehow an indecency.

They crossed the stream—which really was no more than two feet wide in a lot of places—a little further along. For a period the bracken became heavier again, and then as the stream turned (according to Harper's best guess) towards the west they left it behind and ventured back into thickish woodland, wending their way between patches of holly that grew unchecked higher than almost all their heads. A mile or so further still, the way—such as it was, for it could not reasonably be called a path, they forged it themselves by walking it—turned steeply downhill, and presently they were walking through a deepish natural gorge, with thin marsh-like clumps of reeds underfoot, travelling roughly by Harper's reckoning to the north-north-east. On an ordinary journey, he might have imagined to himself an old story in which an ancient giant had cleaved the hillside in two with an axehead bigger than a man, splitting it as you might split a log. Today he couldn't bring himself to. The thought sank to the pit of his stomach as soon as it came to him and he made no effort to examine it any further.

It was overcast, and as the cut to either side of them levelled out the sky began to get ominously dark. It was by now maybe an hour or two after midday, certainly no more, and already they'd had the best of the weather for the day. The sky grew progressively darker grey, and then very quickly the mist rolled in. If he hadn't known better, Harper might have guessed that they were within a very few miles of the coast.

The mist grew darker and more impenetrable, and the line grouped closer together, the better to see and follow the people ahead of them. Davies at the front seemed to be watching where he was stepping as much as he was casting around the gloom ahead of him. He had drawn his sword, Harper now saw—there was nothing in particular to suggest that such a weapon might be necessary, but somehow it did seem like the natural thing to do. Harper himself loosened his grip on the pole of his own halberd. He had been holding it so tightly that his knuckles felt numb.

And with the mist came again that nagging feeling of being watched. It wasn't true, of course, but the feeling of it was inescapable in this world which was suddenly made of long dark shadows and looming shapes which were trees but which might also not be trees.

The most uncomfortable of somethings are those that might easily be nothing, and that's how it was here. There seemed to be a low hum in the air, or perhaps it was only inside Harper's head—either way it reminded him of wasps. After a little longer he started to think he was seeing dark spots blink in and out in the thick greyness— like the spots you see if you stare too long at the sun and then look away, in the corners of his vision.

He shivered like it was cold, but it wasn't, not really— only humid. His hair was sticking to his forehead; he was sweating. Still he held the halberd upright, feeling rather than seeing its point drag through thin branches overhead, and next to him Richard Jessop limped along, eyes wide, with an expression of greatest concentration.

And then from behind them came a shout—not of men arguing, or even of someone trying to get their attention. For the second time today he heard the shouts of pure panic.

The dark spots blinked out. Once again, Harper found he was gripping his halberd very hard. He swung around.

For a moment he thought there was no one there, that the front of the line had left the back of it behind, or been abandoned by them, but it was just the fog—there were their indistinct figures, further back. It was alright. It was alright. His heart was hammering in his chest.

Captain Davies strode past him. "What's going on?"

Taylor was crying. Harper didn't think he'd ever seen that before. He looked from one to the next. Bill Stiles was curled up on the ground, his pack still on his back. He was shaking violently.

"What's happened?" said the captain. "Where's Alwood?"

None of them said anything. They were all staring at him, wide eyed. On the ground, Stiles was still rocking back and forth. The air was thick; Harper could hardly breathe. Davies rounded on Sergeant Thatcher. "You were at the back. What happened to Mr Alwood? Where is he?"

Sergeant Thatcher's face was blank; his swagger from earlier now faltering. The hair on his forehead dripped with sweat or condensation or both. "He wouldn't shut up about the Devil, he was snivelling like an imbecile so I sent him to the back of the line." He lifted his chin, daring Davies to object.

"So he ran off," said Davies, but there was something in his voice that made it clear: he knew it wasn't true.

"He never—" Onslow started to say, but he stopped short. Stiles was pulling himself to his feet.

"Oh," said Davies dryly. "So he's good for something after all. Pull yourself together, Billy."

Stiles wiped his eyes with the heel of his hand. The gesture made him look very young. "It must have taken him off the end of the line. It must have been following us. All morning." His voice was uncannily flat.

"What are you—"

"We're dead men!" Stiles was screaming now. He was getting hysterical. "Francis tried to tell you. And now he's... he's..." But he couldn't say it.

Harper could hardly bear it. He tried to put a hand on Stiles's shoulder, but the boy flinched away and stared at him. "You think I'm going mad. You think I'm a madman. We should never have come here. I should never have let you take us in here."

Harper said, "We don't think you're mad, son."

But Sergeant Thatcher had had enough. "None of this pagan horseshit! We all know what that means, and if you don't you're deluding yourselves. Whatever it is, it's not of God, so it must be of the Devil."

"There is no *it*!" said Captain Davies, but he sounded afraid.

"This is a matter of the immortal souls of every man here," said Thatcher, and there was something very dangerous in his voice, a spark of something that Davies hadn't thought he was capable of.

Harper said, "Careful now, Thatcher."

"I am the commander here!" Davies spat. "I will get us out of here, and you will do as you're told, sergeant, or I'll have you flogged!" Davies and Thatcher were squaring up now, the younger, stockier man up to the older, steelier. Next to them Stiles was shrinking away, his hands over his head, as if to try and push himself into the ground itself, away from this, away from all of this.

The rest of them seemed transfixed, packs still on their backs and bedraggled from the rain into which the fog had broken, unheeded.

Harper said again, "Thatcher. Come with me, man. We have to—"

"Go with him," said Davies, apparently feeling like he had the advantage.

But Thatcher made a swift movement. There was a long-nosed pistol in his hand. He cocked it and pointed it at Davies's forehead. "That's enough. You're going to get all of us killed, just like Alwood, and Willis, and the others. Who's with me?"

CHAPTER SEVEN

The Deeper The Mist

HELLY'S ANKLE HAD slowed them right down, and tempers were beginning to fray. Sue strode on ahead, the 1966 map in both hands, turning around every so often with barely concealed impatience while she waited for the others to catch up.

Kim and Helly walked together, in silence. Kim had found a pair of large branches which Helly used as crutches, and both seemed to have decided that grim professionalism was the only thing that would get them through this. Alice walked alongside them, picking her way through the undergrowth and apparently in a world of her own. And behind them all, her eyes on her own feet, came Nuria Martins with dread in her heart. Nuria generally found that she preferred nature from a distance, and preferably from the inside of a nice warm library. She was happier to read about the countryside than walk through it at particular length, should never have agreed to come on an expedition like this so close to the end of her thesis. It would be slow going now; it would be agony. It was already both of those things.

She reminded herself: she was here to back Alice up. All she had to do was keep her head down, let other people make the decisions, and wait it out. There was nothing she could do to make any of this easier, so the only way to make this as painless as possible was to do as she was told and follow where they went. That was okay. Nuria was quite practised these days at letting other people choose a direction and then just falling in with them. In one sense, that was what having a supervisor was all about.

There was a different kind of atmosphere to the group now that they knew they were lost, and they were relying on instinct and Sue's map-reading skills. It seemed to come quite naturally to Kim, who at any rate must be used to keeping a wide-ranging eye on the landscape around her, although she was far more serious about it than she had been the day before. That much made sense, at least. There was the oak tree to think of, after all—and if Nuria did think of it in any detail, it threatened to root her to the spot.

Too much of that could drive a person mad.

Helly was being relatively stoical, and Nuria was behind her so couldn't see her face, but her limp was quite pronounced and she must be in some considerable pain. She wasn't complaining at the moment, or at least she was complaining very little, but to now be lost on top of a broken ankle must be miserable.

This whole trip was a mistake, and Nuria wanted out of it. It would be over soon, anyway. She'd be home tonight, and in the morning, she'd allow herself a lie in before getting back to work on her thesis.

Sue did not appear to be at ease, but then she hadn't been from the start—something about not being able to trace the route they had taken with the tip of her finger. That was the trouble with having two versions of the map, neither of which was strictly accurate. Not even satellite pictures were much use in here, not with all the tree cover. There were patches where the trees were so close together that hardly any light got through at all, even if much managed to make it through the thick clouds overhead. Add that to the inadequacy of the compass: the light was so diffused that finding distinct shadow to point south was barely feasible. No wonder Sue was on edge. It would be stranger if she wasn't. Nuria couldn't blame her. She couldn't blame any of them for the fact that everything was currently terrible.

She had to keep reminding herself: none of this was anybody's fault. Not really.

*   *   *

OUT TO ONE side of the group, Alice was not paying attention to any of the rest of them. She was forging her own path, present in body but mentally alone in a deep, dark wood. When she walked on the ground it was somehow not quite this ground that she walked on; when she traipsed through puddles (for there were several increasingly boggy patches, the further on they went), it was not quite these puddles she squelched through. The others at least tried to avoid them—a walk like this was bad enough without also having soaking wet socks inside your boots—but Alice Christopher barely seemed to notice they were there at all.

It wasn't even that she was imagining herself somewhere else, nor that she was seeing the place as in some way other than it was. She felt she was apart from them, in the moments that she was aware of their presence in some meaningful way at all. In her own mind she might as well have been alone.

Alice had spent so long in preparation for this that she was, she thought, probably the one out of all of them who was the most truly present. This place made sense to her, in a way she surely wouldn't be able to explain if anyone had asked her. She had known on some level that the oak wasn't precisely real—or rather she had understood it as inevitable after the fact. The truth was that the oak was somewhere else. In a different wood. The other one.

There had been one other person in the world who would have understood, and she felt another stab of regret. Professor Deirdre Ellison had been enough of an all-rounder that the university establishment had been forced to put up with her fringe views on Moresby Forest, or failing that, to pretend that they didn't exist. Deirdre would have listened, and her eyebrows would have twitched in a way which meant she was considering what Alice was saying, and she wouldn't have interrupted until the end, and then—and this was something Alice missed intensely about Deirdre, which she had never quite been able to replicate herself—she would have come out with the perfect question.

"How does that fit with your broader thesis?" Deirdre would have said. "I'll reserve judgment until you can bring me a few more facts, but if you're on to something, what then?" And then, airily, "I know what they say about *you can't always trust your gut*, but that's what they're all doing too, they're just being coy about it."

Deirdre had known there was more to this place than met the eye. She knew it as soon as she saw the deserter's account. Alice had come to all of it—Captain Davies, the wood, even the Corrigal—by following Deirdre. And now she had outrun her, and it was as strange as she could possibly have imagined.

That was about the extent of it, anyway.

Something moved out of the corner of Alice's eye—a flash of something bright in the dark trees. She paused to look, and Nuria and Kim both frowned at her curiously. But there was nothing there.

She had had a horrible thought: something was walking behind them, following them through the woods at a leisurely pace. It was an improbable thought, more a fantasy than anything else, but if she spun it out in her head she could make quite a convincing story out of it. Whatever it was, it was probably what they were talking about when things were attributed to the Corrigal, which for all purposes meant that whatever it was, *was* the Corrigal. In the other forest, that was a fanciful thought. Here, anything could happen.

Did she believe in demons? Not as a general rule, no, but the Corrigal in particular? Maybe. It was hard to tell. That was the trouble with ancient legends—the further back you went, the harder it was to distinguish between speculation about what actually happened, and falling deep into the stories. And then suddenly here you were, believing in dragons and monsters as if they were real, rather than the attempt of someone eight hundred years ago to understand their own fear.

Or that was one way of looking at it.

The mentions of the Corrigal in stories were unusually consistent, and localised, and long-lived—as if the Loch Ness monster had been spotted every few generations for eight hundred years. Always a large, loping creature, in these woods, with eyes the colour of night and sharp teeth. Those things the same, across the centuries. It was tenuous, sure—but those facts alone ought to be enough to give one pause. Perhaps.

There was some feeling in her chest right now, something tender and anxious, but if she'd genuinely thought there was some kind of mythical monster in here, she would have said something about it. She was not that irresponsible. And who would have believed her, anyway? She'd had a hard enough time getting the go-ahead to come here at all, without that muddying the waters as well.

The air was warm, and close. There was a smell of damp earth, slightly sweet in a way that wasn't completely pleasant. Underfoot, the ground was springy, layers of peat or humus which left deep indentations where your feet had been. Alice thought, *this will play havoc with my knees, but is it really what everyone meant by boggy?*

They had been walking for probably coming up to an hour, when Helly said through gritted teeth, "Wouldn't it have been easier if we did this about thirty yards to the right?"

It was almost a shock that someone was speaking aloud.

"I'm following Sue," said Kim, in the sort of voice that abdicated responsibility.

Sue was five or six yards ahead of them. She turned around. "I was just going straight."

Helly said, "We've been veering left. If we were going straight we'd have hit that stream by now."

"I've had an eye on it," said Sue, "but if you have a better idea which way we're going maybe you should be the one doing the steering."

"You keep wandering off," said Kim.

"Well why do you keep following me, then?"

"It's more than a stream, it's practically a proper river," said Alice. The rest of them stared at her.

"Fine!" said Sue. "Fine. Since I clearly can't walk in a straight line. I was trying to get out of here the fastest way, that's all. But let's follow the stream along, if you prefer."

"That's probably the most sensible thing, at this rate," said Kim. "Since we're not sure which way we're going," she added quickly, seeing Sue's face become suddenly stormy. "Which way does the compass say it is?"

Sue gave it a shake. "North-east. North-north-east. I don't believe it. We're supposed to be going south. We're going the same way as the river, for Pete's sake."

They took a break where they stood, in frosty silence, passing around Twix bars and handfuls of dried apricots. Helly took another paracetamol even though she technically wasn't supposed to yet. She kept her head down so as not to meet Sue's eye. Alice Christopher had the air of someone forced to wait in a queue for forty minutes to fill out a form she wished she didn't have to bother with.

Nuria spoke only when spoken to, which might as well have been not at all.

They sat there for perhaps twenty minutes before Kim evidently couldn't stand it any longer. "How's the foot, Helly? Painkillers kicking in?"

Helly said nothing, but she looked up, at least. Then she seemed to remember her professionalism. "As much as they're going to, I guess."

"Maybe," Kim went on, "we should get going. Can you manage?"

"I think so."

"Yes," said Sue. "Let's get out of this bloody place." But even though she was addressing Kim, it was Alice she was watching—and Alice who looked away first.

They picked the bags back up and made their tortuously slow way up to the stream. It was indeed sizeable, five or six feet across in places and fast-flowing over long-smoothed pebbles. The ground to either side of it was muddy and slick, so they couldn't get too close to it.

"Can we *perhaps*," said Helly, "walk on ground I can lean on with my leg?"

"You wanted to come up here!"

"Sue," said Kim, warningly. "We all want the same thing."

"Dr Christopher doesn't," Sue pointed out. "She's loving every minute we're still in here."

"Not if you're going to be sniping at everyone," said Alice, and meant it. "We can follow the river without being in it."

They walked on, towards the end of the morning, and the sky grew darker and the clouds lower and the air thicker.

It started to spit.

CHAPTER EIGHT

Down The Middle

CADWELL WAS ON Thatcher's side, it turned out. So were Ames, and Kilburton, and to a lesser extent Jack Onslow who was much the worse for wear by now. Apart from his physical injuries, which were causing him considerable pain, he was scared for his soul. So were the rest of them: they had seen that tree, and the ones who had disappeared must also have seen something or else why would they have run off? It must have been something big, too, and devils and demons fit the bill. That wasn't what Alwood had called them, nor Stiles either, but it made sense, and *something* had picked Alwood off the end of the line.

The trouble wasn't so much that Alwood had disappeared as that he had done it completely silently, and nobody had noticed. That was what was most disconcerting. That something could sneak up on them so completely;

that they had felt like they were on their guard and yet whatever it was had got right up to them, and plucked one of their number from under their very noses. If the Devil himself had been there, nobody had seen him, or sensed his presence. If it was something else… well. Maybe Edgeworth, Moody and Roberts hadn't just deserted after all.

Billy Stiles was in no state to take an ideological stand on the nature of the attacker right now. He was so young; it had been obvious from the start that he was very young, but now that was thrown into even sharper relief. He was a crying child, barely fifteen years old and terrified—not Stiles nor even William but decidedly Billy. It had taken the waving of Thatcher's pistol at him to get him to even stand up. He and Alwood had been outsiders here: guides picked up a handful of days back to navigate the local terrain, and then coaxed into joining Lord Fairfax's army in the north. The weight of that difference had hung in the air, not only because most of the others knew each other well, nor even that the accents and customs of the newcomers had marked them as different. Alwood, being the elder of the two, had navigated most of it. Now young Billy was alone and friendless, even more than the rest of them, thrown into something he could not hope to understand. If they weren't careful, his despair would rub off on them.

Byrne also seemed unwilling to throw his lot in with the mutiny, which undoubtedly was what it was, but then Byrne was an arse-licker and always had been. Taylor followed Byrne, and had done for years; Richard Jessop was the company's drummer, and had been doing so in one place or another for near on a decade, and it was his considered opinion that Sergeant Thatcher was being an idiot. Jessop also was badly injured, however, and slowing down by the hour; his remaining strength was much more focused on walking, on getting out of this God-forsaken place, than on who he followed in order to do it.

That left only Harper, whose eyes were full of fury but who didn't speak. "Where do you stand?" Thatcher asked him, although everyone knew already that Harper was the captain's man through and through—the question was only how much he'd bend in the face of a pistol. Enough, seemed to be the answer. Enough to keep his head down, to only stare down at his own feet and keep his counsel. *I can trust you, can't I, Harper? Of course I can.* What was he supposed to do?

Truth be told, he hadn't even remembered until today that Thatcher *had* a pistol. It was a rare acquisition for men who weren't officers—usually involving a sizeable amount of money, or the pulling in of a very large favour. Harper had one which he had acquired some years ago in France, although it was badly made, temperamental, liable to blow up in a man's face if he wasn't careful. It was uncommon enough that he didn't tend to wave it about, even at the best of times. If only loading it didn't take an achingly long time, and if only the rest weren't so very vigilant right now. Well. Come the night time, maybe they'd see. But the night was a long way off yet.

"We're going that way," said Thatcher. He pointed off to the left, as if he was expecting someone to object. No one said a word, but Cadwell nodded. It seemed to appease him.

The ones who were sure took the captain's weaponry, bound his hands behind him—he swore at the pressure on his injured shoulder, but resisted no further—and dragged him along like a prisoner. Cadwell, emboldened, kicked him and gladly took the end of the rope, but would make no eye contact either with his charge or with Sergeant Harper. The others who had seemed doubtful were pushed to the front of the group where an eye could be kept on them, a grumbling Ames took the opportunity to hand off the bedraggled banner to Byrne, and Davies was dragged along at the back, in case whatever had snatched Alwood came back again.

And then they prayed. As they walked. They prayed aloud.

"What are you doing?" said Billy Stiles.

They stared at him.

Thatcher said, "The Lord Almighty will save us. If He wills it that we survive this place, we'll survive it."

"But it'll hear you!"

"And He will strike it down," said Thatcher, as if he were explaining to a child. "We're safer if we pray. We walk in the path of the Lord. He—"

"But this is its place," said Stiles. "It lives here."

"As Daniel into the lion's den," said Kilburton—which if he'd said a few days ago, they would have assumed was the beginning of a joke, but now he wasn't smiling.

Stiles looked as if he wanted to say something else, but that was as far as his boldness could take him now. His lips were pressed together so tightly that under a film of grubbiness they were white.

They limped on, the semblance of any kind of line or marching order giving way to just trying to not leave anyone too far behind. Now into the afternoon, it became clear that there were few who had escaped the previous day without lasting injuries, and that even injuries that had seemed superficial the day before were turning out to cause their carriers unexpected grief. The shot wound near Jack Onslow's collar bone was still oozing thick, dark gore a day after it was inflicted. Several times Harper caught him worrying at it with his fingers and flinching, or else turning aside so that his face was hidden. He didn't join in with the prayers, not out loud, and it was that more than much else that made Harper think it was serious.

Taylor, noted whinebag and wet blanket, drifted further behind, dragging his right leg at a strange angle. The further they went, the stranger the angle got—if it had been anyone else he might have got more sympathy but Taylor was known for not having the highest tolerance for pain. Which is to say, they were used by now to ignoring him.

By and by, the weather began to turn again, and the mist which had previously been heavy now became a soft rain that plastered itself to breastplates and settled deep in your bones, turning daylight into something grey and shimmering. The decreased visibility did not improve the general mood. Ordinarily, they might have had Jessop play on his drum for a bit, to help them keep pace apart from anything else, but today it was more than he was able to do.

Then the line stopped. Byrne, now carrying the standard, saw it first—something on the ground a little way ahead of them. No higher than knee-height, barely visible maybe a dozen yards away in the translucent wet. Whatever it was, it wasn't moving. Byrne stopped, and the men behind him nearly walked into him, and at the same moment Thatcher spotted it as well, and drew his sword.

"Stay here," he whispered, "and if anyone makes a move, I'll kill him where he stands." And he crept forward, a few yards. Pause. A few more. For a heavily built man, he was deft on his feet, and quiet. The rain pitter-pattered gently around them: now that they were trying to be quiet themselves, it felt uncannily as if the wood itself was also holding its breath to listen. He looked around, apparently saw nothing suspicious, and beckoned with an arm to follow him.

The company—or its remains, all eleven of them—approached: it was the body of a dead deer, its head snapped to one side, a huge gash along its ribcage. It was waterlogged, covered in flies which crawled across its skin in spite of the rain, and could only have been dead a day or two. Otherwise, it was untouched. Uneaten.

"What did that?" said Charley Ames, and went closer. "Are there wolves up here? Boar?"

"A wolf wouldn't leave it like that," said Kilburton. "Not out in the open." He knelt down next to it, examining, sniffing. "It's nothing I've ever seen before. Look at the size of that claw-mark." He spread his own grubby hand out an inch from the deer's flank. Whatever had mauled it was clearly larger.

A few feet away, Harper knelt down. "Does anyone know what made this?" It was the muddy outline of a footprint—animal of some kind, with the pad of a paw clearly visible, but elongated. The whole thing was as long as a man's boot, and whatever had made it had been heavy, heavier than a man.

There were no more prints, not that he could see.

Bill Stiles made a sudden movement, and eleven men spun around, but he only buried his own face in his elbow—his whole arm was trembling, and Harper thought immediately that it was to hide the fact that he was crying. Then he lunged for a nearby clump of holly and vomited into it, hard, painfully, embarrassingly.

There was silence, except for the whispering of the trees, the tapping and shimmering of raindrops. Stiles began to dry heave.

"That's enough!" said Cadwell, as if he were able to give orders simply by virtue of having charge of the rope Captain Davies was tied to.

Thatcher looked daggers at him. "Shut up the lot of you. Shut up, shut up. Anyone says another word, anyone doesn't do exactly what I say, we'll tie you to a tree and leave you here." He had got out his pistol again, and was waving it about, loaded and cocked. Stiles, meanwhile, was a shivering heap.

Harper said, "Let me help him, and then we can get out of here." And he made momentary eye contact with Captain Davies. The captain's face was a mask.

Thatcher regarded him, for the briefest moment a man who was visibly unused to power, wielding his pistol like a too-heavy sceptre. "Aye. Go on then. Quickly."

Harper bent down to the boy on the ground. He fumbled for his water skin. "Here you go, lad. Drink some of this."

"Is it from the stream?" Stiles whispered.

"Yes, but we haven't much choice about that now, do we? Come on, son. It'll go the worse if you don't, now." He spoke as he would to his own son, who was ten years old now—or as he thought he would speak, since he hadn't actually seen the boy in nearly a year. Now he felt a stab of panic, of missing his family—it wasn't unusual when he was trying to help some of the younger recruits, but the more the danger, the worse it would generally get.

Stiles wiped his vomit-covered chin on his sleeve and hid his face again until the shuddering subsided. With eyes screwed tightly shut he put out his hand and fumbled for the skin that Harper was still holding out. He took an unwilling sip.

"That's right," said Harper.

"We're moving on," said Thatcher, suddenly. He wasn't looking at the two men on the ground, however, but further out into the mist, the way they had come from. "Get up, everyone. We're going, right now. That's an order."

"What do you see?" said Onslow.

But Thatcher wouldn't answer. He only shook his head, and lifted the pistol again. A few of them helped Stiles to his feet and on they went. Grouped more tightly together. Definitely tense.

* * *

HARPER PLANTED HIMSELF on the edge of the group. He was filled with unease. Why did Davies not do anything? Most other captains—any other he knew—would have resorted to violence by now, and either be back in charge of the platoon, or two miles back with their throat cut. Probably the first of those, looking at this sorry lot. And yet. Davies had been a captain for several years by now—Harper should know, having been alongside him for most of that time. He was a good captain, most of the time, which was more than could be said for some of the bastards out there. It was hard to imagine that he had no idea what he was doing.

But then, he wasn't a genius either. Sometimes there wasn't some kind of secret plan. It was just a bad situation.

There was something in the air, he thought, after they had got back into the swing of walking again, and the rain had once more started to ease off. Thatcher was being unusually reckless; Davies unusually reticent. Stiles was just unusual, although he'd not known the boy long enough to tell if that was just the nature of him. He was awfully young, after all, and the loss of a friend went hard on anyone.

Am I behaving unusually? Is this all in my head? Because there's something in my head, and it's not just because of the fog.

Or maybe not. There was an occasion a few years before, in France, when he'd been marching along a deep, narrow cut, with the hillside stretching high above on either side. Slate and stone were dotted with yellow moss. Above, the sky was the thick grey of wool. It had rained then too, and the marching of the men in front had churned the ground to a thin grey mud underfoot. It spread up over their boots, up their legs, a single line of grey, dejected men in that landscape almost without colour. Even now he could remember it exactly, although nothing dramatic had happened there. It had felt at the time like a world unto itself, the strangest and most uncanny place he had ever been, and in a small way it had changed him. He had felt it in his heart and in his bones, where it had remained ever since. If he saw that shade of grey again, the feeling would return, just the same as the first time.

Then the sun had come out and got into their eyes and made everything worse. But the point was, places could do things to you.

That didn't mean you were being hunted by demons.

It was a strange sort of mutiny anyway, the sort you might expect from men who had paid no mind to what they would do next, or how this would end. That was how Harper felt too—as if the whole world had melted away that morning when the oak tree had disappeared. Were they all behaving this way because secretly in their bones they didn't think they'd be leaving these woods? It couldn't be. He didn't dare ask. He'd only end up with a pistol pointed in his face.

Slow progress. The company walked on.

CHAPTER NINE

The Hole In The Woods

IT WAS A little after two o'clock, and on the basis that they'd not hit the border yet it was pretty much a given that they'd been going the wrong way. It had rained briefly, on and off, and the weather seemed to have settled on merely threatening; there was an occasional gust of unexpectedly chilly wind but that was about the worst of it.

They stopped once or twice more, every hour or so, to give Helly a bit of a breather. Helly's attention, quite understandably, was mostly focused on her own foot, but she seemed at least by two o'clock to have regained her grip on her own temper.

Sue was sulking, although it was the kind of sulk that she would have called "just being quiet".

Alice was still thinking about that feeling of the hairs prickling on the back of her neck, of being followed by something that already she had half-convinced herself must be a monster. If it was somehow able to track them and follow them without being seen—again, she thought she heard a noise, and turned around, but it was only Nuria, stepping on a stick—and if there were some continuity between that, and the disappearance of the Davies company... then what? At the time, a few of the contemporary accounts had ascribed the company's disappearance to the Corrigal. The local ones at least, which was to be expected. But they connected that, too, to the Moresby family, centuries earlier, and to a handful of other disappearances over the years. Lost woodsmen. The occasional runaway. Nothing that, by itself, would make this place out to be some kind of Bermuda Triangle.

And yet Deirdre had sensed that there was more to this place than met the eye, and as soon as Alice had got anywhere near it she had sensed it too. It was hard to pick out what it was, exactly. Harder still to explain it to anyone else. She had gone quite long enough without expecting anyone else to properly understand, but that didn't mean it wasn't real.

Part of her had known, in her gut, that she would put herself in harm's way to see what it felt like to be here. To see what it felt like to fit the folklore in with everything else. She hadn't expected or understood until now that it would feel like being lost, and watched by something unseen and half made up. Like prey.

She could feel herself slipping—now she wasn't even thinking of the stories as made up, only *half* made up. The others mustn't know about this—unless, and she couldn't even ask for fear of them calling her mad, they were thinking all of this too.

She surfaced from her thoughts to Kim saying, "What's that?" For a moment excitement gripped her, then preemptive disappointment, and then excitement again—when she saw through the trees what Kim was pointing at.

It was the burnt-out husk of a structure, off to the right hand side up ahead.

Kim said, "Is that on the map?"

Sue was already looking. "Not that I know of."

They approached. It appeared to be the remains of a small hut, about twice the size of a garden shed. That was what it had been, at some point, at any rate—now there were a few charcoal spikes where beams had once been, and a shallow, darkened dip inside where the roof must have collapsed in. The burnt remnants of wood were mossy—evidently neither the hut nor the damage to it was new, although it was hard to pin down how old it was or how long it had been since it had burnt down beyond a ballpark of a couple of years. The hut itself was on the near edge of a clearing maybe a dozen yards across, now overgrown in patches with yellow scraggly grass. In the middle of the clearing was a mound of earth, as high as a person and maybe eight feet across. The mound had been hollowed out from one side, and the exposed core of it was carbon-black.

"Someone's been burning charcoal," said Helly. "That's what it looks like."

"Not recently," said Sue.

"They shouldn't have been in here at all," said Kim. She was making a slow circuit of the little clearing. "This whole place has been off limits for decades."

Helly settled herself on the ground at the edge of the trees, watching the others explore. She squinted at the burnt-out hut. "How old do you reckon it is?"

"A year or two, maybe. The wood's quite rotted. And this pit hasn't been used in a long time." Kim kicked at the edge of the mound. Dry earth crumbled where she struck it.

Alice had dropped her rucksack. She stood inside the burnt rubble, and turned slowly on the spot. It was well and truly destroyed. The highest remaining spike of former beam came up barely to her shoulder. For a second she thought she smelt a whiff of smoke, but it was just in her imagination. "Funny," she said. "I don't see any metal at all. Looks like it was just wood."

"Not too funny," said Helly, from her perch a few yards away. "If they weren't supposed to be here, then they probably weren't going to be bringing sheets of scrap metal in. And any fabric is probably long since rotted away by now."

"No nails, either," said Alice, squatting down to sift through the ashes. "That's more strange."

"Not unheard of, for hobbyists," said Helly.

But Alice wasn't listening. "Maybe a bit of metal, after all." She held something up to the light. "This looks like a piece of shot."

"Has someone been shooting pigeons?" said Kim.

"Maybe. It's quite big, I'd not want to be the pigeon on the end of this." She rolled the little ball between her thumb and forefinger, and scanned the nearby ground for more.

Nuria said to Sue, "Can you take a few photos? You have the camera, don't you? Is it working?"

Sue blinked. "Yeah."

The camera battery was flat. Completely flat. And not only that, but when she opened the compartment to change it, one end was furred over—the acid was leaking out of it as if it had been left in the back of a drawer for too long. "Maybe it's the air pressure," said Helly, although that couldn't possibly have been it. "I guess we're going the Luddite way for a few hours."

Sue didn't reply.

Alice was still squatting down inside the little ruined shack. The floor of it was a good two inches of a silt made of dirt and the ash of the broken building itself. "Nuria, the metal detector is in the left hand pocket of my bag. And my trowel should be in there too. Do you mind?" Nuria brought them over. "Thanks." She hit the switch on the metal detector. Nothing happened. "Oh, blast it. Sue! Are you all out of spare batteries?"

"You're joking," said Sue. She was still holding the camera in both hands. But Alice's attention was already back to the floor of the hut.

Kim was poking around the remains of the charcoal pile. There was not a lot left of it, and what there was hadn't been touched in a long while. She was fidgeting, and unlike Alice she didn't seem to be interested in sifting through the muck too closely, only shifting it about with the toe of her boot. Even that she gave up quickly when Alice straightened up, trowel in one hand, and said, "Come and have a look at this."

Alice had found a coin—a thin, hammered coin, of scummed-up greenish metal, about the size of a fingernail. Whatever inscription was on it was faded and hard to make out. "This is *old*."

She held it in the palm of her hand like a talisman.

"How old?" said Helly. "There's more light over here, if you need it." She indicated a spot where the fog was thinner and a weak beam of light filtered through.

Alice brought it over, and stood in the patch of overcast light. She held out her hand with the coin in it to Nuria. "What does that look like to you?"

Nuria picked the little coin up between thumb and forefinger, slowly and deliberately, half expecting to feel something quite strong and visceral. It was lighter than she had imagined it would be. Insubstantial. Hard to make out the details on it. She squinted. "Wow. Seriously? It was just lying there?"

Helly said, "What does it say?"

Nuria turned the coin over in her hand a few times. There was nothing remarkable about it, except that it was here at all. "Edward III," she said.

"When's he?"

Alice said, "1327 to 1377."

"Is that really a seven-hundred-year-old hut?"

"Of course not. It's a recent hut with a much older coin next to it." Alice held out her hand for the little coin and Nuria gave it back to her. "How it got here, now, that's the question."

"The bit of shot's not that old, I suppose?"

"Ah, yes," said Sue, "from those well-known guns they definitely used in 1350."

"Someone must have dug it up first," said Nuria. Her voice was unexpectedly hoarse, all of a sudden, and she felt that her mouth had gone dry.

"Well I think we could all get that far," said Alice flatly—

but the flatness was covering for the fact that she had no idea how the coin got here, and Nuria had known her long enough that she could see right through it.

Across by the fire pit itself, Kim was kneeling down. She looked up. "Is this what I think it is?"

Nuria went across to her, regretfully leaving the coin to Alice. "What do you think it is?"

It was a piece of bone, a couple of inches from one end to the other, smooth and flat and slightly curved, and maybe a finger's width across, stained dark with ash and the mud that had covered it for who knows exactly how long. It was broken off quite cleanly at one end, and ragged at the other.

"That's a bit of rib," said Nuria.

Kim said, "Is it human?"

"I'd say so." She knelt down to sift through the mud with her fingertips, to search for any more fragments. The mud was thick after the rain; Nuria scraped her fingers off on her trowel.

Alice came across to help, the coin stowed in one of the pockets of her coat. There was no more by the fire pit, but inside the doorway of the burnt-out hut they found a few more fragments, a piece of skull, something that might have been a knuckle bone, a piece of pelvis. Recognisably human. It was hard to say more than that. Nuria fetched a groundsheet and they spread the pieces out on it, cleaned a few of the bones off with paper from a loo roll. Even Helly moved to sit closer to the pit, joining in with the conversation even as she wasn't able to help scrabble around in the dirt.

"Are they recent?" said Sue. "Is this animal damage?"

"Most likely animals," said Alice. She was more animated than she had been all day. "Especially out here. I'm not seeing anything that would suggest otherwise, but this is hardly a full skeleton. I wouldn't even like to say for definite that it's one person."

"No chance that it's your soldiers, either?" said Helly.

"I'd place them somewhere between the very old coin, and the very new fire," said Alice, contemplatively. "But as much as I'd like us to have found them so easily..." She tailed off.

"But then," said Kim, "why was the coin so near the surface? It doesn't make sense."

They took a break at around four o'clock. It remained unspoken that they probably wouldn't make it out of the woods tonight; first thing this morning that would have been bad news, and at midday several of them might have pitched a fit at it. Now it was easier, but only because it didn't feel like it was anyone's fault in particular. Doing something practical, something different from just plain walking, was reassuring in a way. It was better for the imagination than walking—reined it in, stopped it running amok. Let them think of things other than vanished trees and (in Helly's case) a white-hot ache in the ankle. They passed around apples, and hastily assembled cheese sandwiches on plasticky bread. Food for the soul, fitting with the glimmer of progress they'd just made. Paltry, but welcome.

There was a brief scuffle over how to mark their location on a map when they didn't know it. In the end, Helly broke the stalemate by drawing a new map on torn-out sheets from a reporter's notebook. "The old-fashioned way," she called it. Sue scowled. Nevertheless it was the best they could do to collectively attempt to plot their route as they had taken it that day. It did not line up with the 1960s map. The river, the formation of the ridges, none of them lined up with what they had seen in real life. The compass was no help at all, and it was still so cloudy that it was hard to be sure which direction they had come from. The GPS unit was lifeless.

Interestingly, the real landscape was not that dissimilar in the grand scheme of things to the 1730s map. They weren't identical, but the rivers seemed to roughly match. And there was something, marked as a cairn or tumulus or something similar, that might even have matched up if you squinted with where they could be now. Maybe.

It could still be coincidence. Alice put on her best giving-an-undergraduate-tutorial face, and participated in the compiling of the makeshift map only to the extent that the professional surveyor invited her to. It was probably more scientific that way.

She touched the little coin, wrapped in a piece of tissue in her pocket. It was not strictly speaking the way such an important artefact ought to be transported, but then that coin wasn't just an artefact, was it? It was a sign, aimed at Alice Christopher in particular, and although she didn't yet know exactly what it meant, she would do sooner or later. Moresby Forest was speaking to her, personally. More than that, it was teaching her its language.

She felt no wave of dread at the idea, but held the thought secretly in her head, like the inexplicable coin in her pocket.

After they had eaten, and now that the afternoon was drawing on and there was finally some distance between them and the disastrous events of the morning, they rallied a bit. Alice and Sue had each done something that made them feel important. Helly was much perkier for not having had to stand on her busted ankle for a few hours; her mood too seemed to have lightened considerably. Kim felt less like she was trying to stave off an all-out argument. At half past four on the second day, things weren't necessarily any good, or even just fine, but they were at least tolerable.

They decided, since it wouldn't get dark for a few more hours, to pack up the things they had found and move on a little further before they made camp for the night. They could always come back here with a bigger team—in fact it would be prudent to—and now that Helly had had a chance to rest her leg they might as well get as far as they could while she could still stand it.

So they put away their notebooks and trowels and groundsheets, and took out their waterproofs again because it looked like the rain might very well come back, and a little before five o'clock were ready to get going again. Helly took two more painkillers, and grimaced like a woman doing the rest of them an extremely big favour, and picked up the pair of sticks she'd been using as makeshift crutches. By unspoken agreement, they couldn't have spent the night in the clearing anyway. God knows what they would have been sleeping on top of.

Sue took the lead again. The makeshift map had been a good idea; it gave her a modicum of control, or at least it felt like it.

"How's your ankle, Helly?" said Kim.

"Not too bad. Distract me."

"Maybe Nuria should tell the story with the witch in it."

"Yes," said Helly. "I'd like that. Nuria?"

Nuria had been drifting along at the back of the group, but at the mention of her name she shook her head to clear it and picked up her pace. "What did you say?"

"The Witch of Moresby Wood," said Kim.

"Oh. Now?"

"Might as well."

Helly and Sue made encouraging noises. Alice's hands were in her pockets; she was still holding the little coin, and she kept silent.

They were walking at a slow pace. There was a soft breeze, which smelled faintly damp. Nuria began to talk.

"This is the story, or something like it, I think, that the Davies company deserters were told when they got to Tapford the day after they ran away. The very same time that the Davies company were here, Matthew Hopkins the Witchfinder General was starting to conduct his own witch trials in East Anglia. Witches were topical. The civil war was happening, and this part of the country was on the front lines of the fighting. Bands of soldiers roamed the country, royalist and parliamentarian, and they were scared of each other, and everyone else was scared of them. Any news that arrived in your local town was weeks late, and probably full of misinformation, rumours, propaganda. There were stories all over the country of ghosts, devils, portents of evil, and for people at the time they were about as believable as anything else that was going on. They didn't understand what was happening—and in a very religious society, well, you can see how stories like the Moresby Witch might have come about.

"You remember the Moresby family: Robert and

Margaret, and their children, Geoffrey, Essie, and baby Mary. Well, the story of the Witch doesn't appear until centuries later than them—the first written record is from 1604, and the Witch is supposed to be Essie Moresby. She's very different from the earlier Essie Moresby, though— there are more similarities with other witch stories of the early seventeenth century than with the original legend of the Moresby family. The tales about the Witch say she was an adult woman of unnatural height—maybe six foot two or three, at least as tall as the tallest men—and she sent a gigantic beast to do her dark bidding."

"That's the Corrigal?" said Helly.

"Yes."

Kim said, "That sounds more like it. I never heard of Essie Moresby as being a child. They used to say at school that she set the Corrigal on her whole family."

"That's the old version, yes. What's quite interesting, or I think so, isn't her—it's that there's some actual description of the Corrigal. It's supposed to be an enormous creature of mists and shadows, with razor-sharp claws and pitch-black eyes."

"Perfect for scaring people round a camp fire."

"Exactly. And the scariest bit of all is that it seems to fit with Thomas Edgeworth's testimony."

Sue said, "But Edgeworth didn't write it himself, did he? He told it to the local priest, who I assume would have known the legends already."

"That's my argument, in my chapter. The Reverend James Garner, he's the priest, did write the story down. And if Edgeworth had got most of his details from Garner, you'd expect to see certain things, like the Witch, and maybe something that looks like a familiar, perhaps some kind of obvious clue to connect them to the local legend. But it's more subtle than that—what the narrative actually says is that in the last hour before dawn, a fog came down, and there was a great rumbling of wind. The ground under them shifted, and Edgeworth was aware of a huge presence flitting from shadow to shadow."

"That's… Okay, that's creepy," said Kim.

Alice was still silent, but she had ceased to turn the incident of the burnt-out hut over in her mind, and now she was listening. A shifting of earth, and a rumbling of wind. She knew Thomas Edgeworth's words off by heart, of course. Did it seem familiar? Did it sound at all like what had happened under the oak last night, to Alice? Not really, no—but then she'd been asleep. If it had all happened again, just like in the story, she couldn't possibly have known. She felt a flicker of frustration.

Nuria was still explaining. "One of the men had died in the night, and his first thought was the Devil, come for the man's soul, but come too late and looking for a substitute. Edgeworth ran away quietly, and Josiah Moody, and another man called Roberts."

"A bit higher than their pay grade, I suppose," said Kim.

"It *sounds* like Edgeworth trying to explain why he ran, rather than Garner trying to authenticate a local legend."

"What happened to Roberts?" said Helly. She was gritting her teeth. Her ankle must be hurting more than she let on.

"Edgeworth doesn't say. He's only mentioned once. I suppose they got separated, and then Edgeworth and Moody ran into some marshland that they weren't expecting, and—"

At the front of the group, Sue stopped up sharp. "We've been this way before."

Kim said, "Are we doubling back on ourselves?"

"No, I think we were going in this direction last time, too. I think we were over there." She pointed off to the left, where a birch tree split into two smaller ones, a third of the way up its length. "I remember that specifically."

"So do I," said Kim. "I think you're right."

Sue threw her hands up. "Then I've no idea where we're going, or where we've been going. We'll probably never find that ruin again."

"Maybe it's the tree that's moved," said Nuria. Any other time, she might have been making a joke. Nobody laughed.

Helly said, "Do you remember where we went after we passed here the last time?"

Kim said, "I think so. That way, wasn't it?" She pointed.

"Then," said Helly, "let's keep going forward, and try not to go that way."

"Are you okay with that?" said Kim.

"I'll be fine. There's no alternative, is there?"

Sue shook the GPS unit, holding it over her head, but it remained resolutely inert. "It still won't even switch on. But the batteries were new out of the box! What's going on with this technology?" She put it back in the pocket of her coat. "Okay. Try again."

They carried on in anxious silence. And now it was approaching six o'clock, and there hadn't been anywhere particularly obvious to stop and set up camp. It felt later than it was, and for a little while Alice couldn't tell why, but then the first fat drops of rain fell onto the outside of her glasses, and she looked up to see that the sky between the treetops was almost charcoal. The air was thick with humidity. They had been very lucky so far, apparently—and also very distracted.

Now that luck failed, and the deluge began. They hadn't been following a path, so it had been slow going before this; now the ground underfoot was slick with half-composted leaves, and mud. The trees over their heads were no cover at all, not in rain this heavy. Alice put her hood up and pulled the sleeves of her anorak down over her hands; the world reduced to a small window of grey framed by bright red canvas. She saw the outline of Sue's rucksack ahead of her, and tried to follow it. She could hear only the rain and the sound of her own breathing, unnaturally heavy inside the hood. She was walking alone; she was walking with thousands of disembodied footfalls under the rain. In the whole of the world, there was only Alice and the back of Sue's backpack, bobbing indistinctly in front of her. And now there wasn't even that, there was no whole of the world, she was outside all of it and the only things that existed were dim grey framed with red, and the smell of rain after weeks of drought, and the freezing trickle of water into the top of her socks. Alice herself was receding, her body was an irrelevance, at the same time as it felt too big, it was weighing her down. There was cold water on her face and her nose was running. Her socks were definitely starting to soak through.

There was a heavy thump, and a scream. For a second she was suspended, still outside the world and herself, and then Sue turned around—slowly, why was everything moving at half speed?—and her face twisted into shock and Alice realised, something had happened.

She lumbered around, not quite in control of herself. This must be what it felt like to be in space, to be in a space suit.

Ten yards behind her, a haze of purple and pale blue on the ground. A person. Three people. She could just about make them out through the rain, and as she registered what she was seeing Sue came sprinting past her, heading for them.

Helly Wheeler was on the ground, and Kim and Nuria were kneeling over her. She'd fallen over again, was Alice's first thought, but no one was helping her get up. The roar of the downpour was so much that she couldn't hear what any of them were saying. Ahead, Sue reached the group and dropped to her knees.

Alice made her way over, tentatively, feeling her boots threaten to slip in the wet mud. As she approached, the three on their knees looked up at her, and she knew what had happened, even as she didn't know how it had happened. She had known, not when she had heard the scream—she had still been too far away, then—but the moment Sue had turned around.

Now she stopped and faced them. Helly lay on her back, makeshift crutches still digging into the earth at an angle that was unnatural, obscene. There was bright red down her front, the same colour as Alice's own anorak. She was soaked through with it, diluted and chilled. The edge of her fringe trembled where it poked out from under her hood, quivering as raindrops continued to hit it, and the water ran down her face into her eyes which were wide open. And again, involuntarily, Alice Christopher receded. She felt the little coin in her pocket, warm and solid. Everything else was elsewhere.

CHAPTER TEN

Keeping His Grip

RICHARD JESSOP HAD been looking bad all day. The bloody gash under his ribs was doubtless worse under his coat, but even outside the coat it was beginning to smell as bad as it looked. Privately, Harper was quite impressed that he'd made it through the night. So in the grand scheme of things it wasn't that much of a surprise when Jessop finally sank to the ground, eyes half closed and pain etched across his face, and declared that they should go on without him, for he could walk no further.

Thatcher was antsy, even when it became clear that Jessop was not going to be able go with them. "I say we're going on, so we're going on!" The rest of the party had lapsed into quiet; even Charley Ames had gone from loudly proclaiming his various wild conjectures about devilry to keeping his head down. Gregory Kilburton still muttered prayers under his breath and fidgeted, shooting glances back at Cadwell as if he expected him at any moment to slip and be overpowered by the captain.

But even Kilburton was taken aback that Thatcher did not want to stay still, not even for a minute.

It was all the more uncanny that Jessop seemed to agree with him. "Go," he said. His face was white with agony and he leaned against the base of a large ash tree. "I can't go further, and I don't want you to watch me."

Harper said, "I can give you some—"

"No. No more. Tell Lizzy I love her, when you get back to Canterbury." There was a silver-coloured ring on his left hand. "Can someone get this off me?" Taylor bent to do it. He wouldn't make eye contact with Jessop, and when he quickly went to straighten up again, he faltered, and caught his own breath.

If Jessop noticed, he didn't say so. "Give that to her, won't you? When you get home." His eyes were leaking a little bit, or maybe he was still wet from the rain. His gaze moved onto Captain Davies, whose hands were still tied behind him, and whose face was set.

"We're going now," said Thatcher. "Walk on. Move. That's an order." He shifted his weight from one leg to the other and back again, back again, his hand on his halberd.

Jessop only watched the captain. He didn't say anything, or even try to. He no longer had the strength for it. Then he lay back against the tree and closed his eyes, and, after a moment or two, relaxed his shoulders. When Harper looked at Davies, he saw only loss. Jessop's drum lay slack at his side; he had carried it for nearly a decade now. Nobody tried to take it from him.

They went on and left him there, and it felt like a betrayal. But staying still would have been worse, and somehow without saying so, they were all agreed on it. He had wanted to be alone. There was a chill in the air, and it was even more discomforting than the rain.

Harper had the terrible feeling once again that something was following them. Whatever it was, they had not managed to shake it off, not that they had really been trying. And it had not stopped for Jessop— that might have been easier somehow, because then he wouldn't have been there long, alone with his thoughts, his body stiffening up where he lay and his breathing getting shorter and more laboured. It was no good to think about it. Life ended suddenly sometimes; if it wasn't a stray shot off a hillside, then consumption, or the plague, or nothing discernible at all. Harper had known many men die soldiering, often in strange lands, where the people spoke French and who knew what else. But what comfort was it to die on English soil when you were this far from home, from help, from consecrated ground? If you mouldered in a forest, you mouldered in a forest. There would be no marker of you for anyone to pause over and remember. For all the difference it made you might as well be in France.

They had not so much as prayed over him. Well, that put the lie to that, then, didn't it?

He thought of poor Francis Alwood, vanished from the back of the line in this place that had seemed to terrify him into gibberishness. The woods around them now were quiet—not unusually so for a forest, it was true, but there was something unpleasant about it nevertheless; it felt like anything could be disguising itself under the faint whisper of wind and drips of recent rain from branches. The few quiet creaking sounds could be tree trunks, or they could as easily be something else entirely, moving around them or alongside them, just out of sight.

He shook his head a little to clear it. It was no good losing his nerve now, when he most needed it about him. He flexed his fingertips, as much to prove to himself he still had control over them as anything else, and positioned himself towards the back of the group, the better to keep an eye out for Cadwell and Davies.

It could no longer be called a line; they walked in a clump. The few of them that had tried to keep hold of their pikes as they came into the woods had long since abandoned them. Byrne had the banner, still, but it was slung across his back in two pieces rather than raised. For all purposes they were not soldiers at the moment and could not be: if a waiting ambush had found them like the one from the previous day—only a day ago—they would hardly have known what to do.

It was self-preservation, Harper realised. Or something like it at least. The strength they still had was best saved for keeping moving, for keeping your mind on the way ahead, and not thinking about what was beyond it. Maybe that was why Davies wasn't fighting back, was acquiescing quietly to his fate: he didn't want to be left behind. Not that it would mean death, exactly, nor that death was what frightened Harper—but devouring. In Davies's place he might have done the same thing.

In that light, Richard Jessop was the bravest among them. It was a shame that whatever had been following them had apparently not been put off. He didn't know how he knew, but he did.

Lord, preserve us in our hour of need, and forgive us the transgressions that brought us here.

The captain was looking at him, but Harper avoided his eye. It wasn't that he thought it was right, what had happened, what Thatcher had managed to instigate. It was just that there was bad luck at the back of the line, and worse luck stringing along in its wake. And he wanted that barrier, albeit only one person deep, between him and it, for as long as he could have it.

It was not a brave thought, but then he was not, in his heart, particularly brave. Most of the time he'd made peace with the fact, but there was still sometimes the sting of shame when he thought about it directly.

The woods were more open here; where earlier by the stream it had been thick with bushes, almost so much that they were being steered in a particular direction, now the trees were spaced more widely apart, and more light could get in. It was a relief, in a way—and now also that the rain had eased up there were small patches of blue sky overhead, moving quickly as if in a strong wind, although such a wind could not be felt in this relative shelter. This was more like the woodland he recognised, the kind you got further south or even in France. Underfoot there was grass, in places, and he could hear birds—that at least was a good sign. Better than the morning, at any rate.

A little voice in his head said: *And which woods are we in? Because, like you said, it stands to reason—* But he didn't want to have those thoughts. He wanted to have different ones.

If one took all the messiness and fear and all else out of it and just focused on where they were, and the feeling of walking, this was nearly as pleasant as soldiering got. His boots were falling apart and wet through, but when did anyone have boots that weren't falling apart?

Given the state of the sky, at a guess they were going roughly north-west. And at least, if something *were* following them, they would have more of a chance of spotting it now that the light was better and the trees were a bit more open. There were no further obvious footprints like the ones they'd seen a few hours ago. He looked over his shoulder again, squinted behind them, but saw nothing.

"What's the matter?" said Cadwell, quietly.

"Nothing, I think."

"Hmmph. I just wondered if you... Well. No."

"Spit it out, man."

Cadwell cast a glance forward to see if they were listening in at the front. But nobody turned around. "Lost, aren't we? S'what comes of following someone with no sense of direction. Which way would you say we're going?"

"North-west."

"My gut tells me we're going south. I keep an eye out, you know."

"We're not going south," said Harper. "We'd be out on the hill again by now."

"I know that," said Cadwell. "And it keeps moving. We're going round in circles, we'll be wandering around for weeks at this rate."

"Nonsense, we'll be out in four days no matter what direction we walk in, as long as we keep walking in it."

"You tell yourself that, Mister Harper," said Cadwell, and he yanked on the rope with Davies attached to it. "Pick the pace up, old man. Don't make me leave you behind."

"You could let him go," said Harper, gently.

But there was a glint of something in Cadwell's eyes, and Harper thought briefly that it was unhinged. "I want to get out of here. I don't want to go back in. You understand. I just want out of here, that's all."

He wanted to say something, to ask if Cadwell too thought there was something else here with them, or whether Harper was imagining things and there was something wrong with him after all. But afterwards he could never remember if he had asked the question, because that was the moment that, further up the line, Jack Onslow collapsed.

There was an odd localised shimmering where Onslow stood, a suggestion of movement and perhaps a change in the quality of light, and it looked as though he was attacking Kilburton—who made a strangled noise and hopped with his long limbs out of the way. And then Onslow was down, with barely an audible thud. If he hadn't been near the front of the group, he might have gone overlooked.

For a moment no one moved, and they were mostly drawn to Kilburton's movement. Then, "Ambush!" yelled Taylor, and they scattered for cover.

Nothing happened. The body of the fallen Onslow lay where it had dropped, and did not so much as twitch.

Ames said, "I didn't hear a shot. Why was there no report?"

Taylor said, "A bowman. It must be."

Bill Stiles lay on the path they had made, curled tightly into the foetal position. He shook silently.

If there was a shooter, of arrows or ball shot or whatever else it could possibly be, they did not strike again. Harper had no choice, or so he felt—he crawled out on his hands and knees towards Onslow. If it was an arrow that hit him, there ought to be something that could be done for him, or at the very least they could get some idea in which direction the assailant was hiding. Was it the soldiers from yesterday? Surely not.

He was halfway out towards Onslow through the long grass when he heard a scuffle behind him, and Thatcher swore. "Oh no you don't. Cadwell, I will gut you." He had caught the captain, twisted his good arm up against him and slammed him against a tree.

"I'll shout," hissed Davies. "I'll tell it where we are."

"It already knows where we are."

But Harper was more interested in Onslow and not getting shot than in seeing which of them would prevail— assuming nothing got to them first. He made it to Onslow almost without any of the rest of them noticing him, for they were all intent on the fight, or else staring around looking for the shooter who must surely make themselves known soon.

Jack Onslow lay in a pool of blood—almost too big a pool, in fact, for one hit by a piece of shot, and at any rate he was definitely dead. His face was gaunt and waxy, and his eyes were bloodshot, and... Then Harper saw it and involuntarily flung himself backwards. "Kilburton." He gestured the man over. "What did you see?"

"I didn't see anything, I just—"

"Did you see *that*?"

For half of Onslow's stomach looked like it had been blown away, his innards spilling out of a gaping hole in his leather jerkin. Harper felt his stomach roil and he turned away, to where Thatcher and Cadwell seemed to have subdued Davies. There was no shooter, no bowman, no anything. From his brief look, Harper guessed a cannon could have done it—if it were extremely lucky, impossibly lucky. And then they'd all have heard it.

Maybe he remembered it wrong. He'd seen *something*, at least. Maybe there had been a sound after all. But the blast of a cannon?

Kilburton said, "Is that... a toothmark?" but Harper didn't turn around. If he looked again, just yet, he might never move from the spot. He realised now that he could smell it. Blood. Offal. He thought of Jessop, sitting quietly at the foot of the ash tree. He wasn't that far back, after all—a couple of miles at most. When was it better to just give up?

"Where?" said Taylor, quietly. Harper forced himself to look again at the body.

"There," said Kilburton. "Do you see? It looks like a clean cut."

"I don't know how you can tell under all that—"

"Shut up," said Harper.

It was even worse now that he knew what he was going to see. Onslow no longer looked like a person, but an effigy dressed up like someone Harper had once known, a scarecrow spilling its straw over the ground. No different from any other battlefield, any other field.

Out of the corner of his eye as he turned, he swore he could see ghosts.

The rest of the men were coming over, Thatcher loping towards the knot of men gathered around the body, his attention diverted, and Cadwell and Davies following along in his wake. When he got close enough to see the pool of blood, his whole gait changed—he seemed to shrink an inch or two, although his pace didn't falter. "Who did it? Who saw it?" He rounded on Kilburton. "You were next to him—what happened?"

But Kilburton only spluttered. "There was nothing—I didn't—"

The shimmering again came before Harper's eyes, off to one side in the middle distance, and he jerked his head around to look at it—noticing as he did so that Thatcher had angled his head that way too. It was a trick of the light, though—there was nothing there, and now he looked again at Thatcher the man's attention was focused back on the bleeding-out body in front of him.

"Well," said Thatcher, and he seemed to have reached some kind of resolve, to have gathered his strength. "All I know is, whatever did this, it would never have found us, never have known we were here, if it hadn't been summoned." He swung around, and his gaze fell on Bill Stiles, still curled on the ground a few feet away. Harper for his part felt a sudden stab of foreboding—his eyes flickered to the restrained Captain Davies, and they made eye contact for half a moment before Thatcher lunged.

He had Stiles by the throat before anyone could step in, not that any of them would. Stiles himself was not resisting, had ceased to resist many hours ago. "You brought the Devil on us," said Sergeant Thatcher. "You said its name. You brought it here. You're in league with the Papists and the Devil!"

Bill Stiles was gasping for air; he seemed to have forgotten that his arms and legs worked, and scrabbled ineffectively at the ground around him and at Thatcher's forearms.

The rest only watched, like they were rooted to the spot, like they were incapable of doing anything to save the boy being choked to death in front of them. Kilburton looked relieved, now that the pressure was off him, and someone else had drawn the focus of Thatcher's ire. Charley Ames's expression was one of wild glee, the recklessness of one whose senses were not where he'd left them. And in the middle of it all, Sam Harper was cold. He shouldn't be— he hadn't been, up until now, or had not thought he'd been. He could smell Thatcher's fear and something about it was indecent. He was like an animal trying to fight his way out of a trap, and Stiles the unfortunate creature he'd caught. There was nothing Harper could do, and somehow it felt natural that it was so.

He turned to walk away, at the same time as Captain Davies said, "That's enough, Thatcher." He spoke in such a tone of voice that Harper was sure he had slipped his bonds, was back in control or at any rate would be. But the captain's hands were still fastened behind him.

It had worked, though, for Thatcher's grip had involuntarily loosened, a learned response to a direct order before his brain kicked in. That was Thatcher's problem, Harper thought: he should never have been promoted to sergeant. Into his head, unbidden, the thought came that Davies had trusted him, and now there was no use trying to do anything to help. It wouldn't work. *I know how this will end*, he thought, *and if Davies has gone, I'm next.* And he kept walking, slowly, slowly, his shoulders stiff and his heart like a lead weight.

From behind him, the irregular thumps of a good kicking, and the high-pitched sound of Cadwell saying, "Thatcher! Thatcher!" over and over, like a child wanting his mother's attention. Harper didn't turn around. He took his pipe out of his pocket with trembling hands, and wiped it off on the front of his trouser leg.

He was searching around one-handed in his coat for his tobacco when something in the forest caught his eye. It was a structure—far off in the distance, but definitely man made, and the first sign of life he had seen in here. Squinting through the trees it looked like a hut of some kind—surely nobody lived here, in this place where the trees moved, and the mist hung low, and men came to die? But it certainly, from this distance at least, looked like it.

Harper turned around and stumped back to the dregs of the company. "Someone's been here."

Where he'd left them, only chaos. Now the captain was the one curled on the ground, blood streaming from his nose, his arms at a strange angle and his hands still bound and limp. Thatcher stood over him, kicking him like a man with many years' worth of grudges to get out of him. Behind him, barely two yards away, Onslow's body still lay in its dark pool.

Something in Harper's chest twisted uncomfortably. "Is he dead?" he said, quietly.

"Does he look dead to you?" Thatcher wiped an arm across his mouth which was flecked with spit. He was foaming at the mouth like a rabid dog. If the rest of them weren't injured or terrified or some combination of the two, perhaps they'd have done something other than standing frozen.

Harper thought it best not to push his luck, or make any sudden movements. "There's a dwelling out that way. Maybe whoever lives in it can help us get out of here. Leave him," he said, indicating the prone Davies, "and let's go to them."

Thatcher narrowed his eyes.

"What if they're the devil worshippers?" said Ames. "Or witches?"

"They're not witches," said Harper. "Pull yourself together."

"That you know of," said Ames sulkily. But he consented to go because everyone else was going, and because it meant leaving this spot where so much violence had already befallen them.

They did not bury Onslow, partly because it would have taken too long, and partly because they were exhausted; but instead they took the rings from his fingers and the boots from his feet—which were in fairly good nick, so one went to Ames and the other to Byrne. They took his comb, and his eating knife, and the contents of his coin purse, which was nearly empty. The purse itself was thick with blood, such that nobody wanted it; the hole in his side was enough to put them off rummaging too thoroughly through the rest of his possessions. Then they slung his body under a bush, and covered it with ferns, and said a prayer over him.

Kilburton and Cadwell dragged Davies upright—he seemed more dazed than anything—and leaned him against the foot of a tree. Then they returned their attention to the rest clustered around Onslow. Davies lay there, his eyes half-closed. He was breathing heavily.

Harper went over to him. He still hadn't managed to have his smoke. "What did you go and start that for?"

Davies tried to crack a smile, but his voice was thin. "Stiles is just a lad. My Johnny is probably the same age."

"I suppose so. Well you've learned your lesson now, haven't you?"

"Aye. It won't last, though."

"You're not moving any time soon, old friend."

The captain lifted himself up a few inches on his elbows. "Oh, I'm not as bad as all that. I'll catch you up."

"I'd like to see you fight someone now, you stupid bugger." They had been travelling together for near on a decade, one way or another. Harper thought of Jessop, propped up against a tree, alone in his last vigil; of Onslow, ripped apart, or as good as. Who was to say Davies's chances were better than Harper's?

He glanced over his shoulder. The rest were picking up their things, getting ready to go. "Here," he said, and he pulled out his own pistol, and his little box of tinder, and in a swift movement thrust them into Davies's hands. "Give it my compliments, if it finds you first," he said.

Davies transferred the gun to the inside of his coat, but he made no other gesture of recognition. His eyes, at least, seemed a little brighter.

They were a motley group who moved on towards the little hut in the woods. For a start there were now only nine of them. More than a few kept glancing back over their shoulders, as the sitting figure of Captain Davies receded into the distance, watching them go. Harper did not glance back.

They didn't need to walk long before the little hut became visible through the trees. No light came from it, and nor did anything seem to stir in places near to it. But it was, undoubtedly, a place where a person had not too long ago been living. Getting a little closer enabled them to make out an earthen mound, about six or eight feet high behind the hut—it was a charcoal heap; a charcoal burner lived here. In the middle of the forest in general that was not so strange, but this forest in particular was more of a conundrum. There appeared to be no path leading up to the little clearing—for both the hut and the heap were situated in a small clearing, presumably also cleared by a man—and that lack of path was odd. How did anyone get a cart in to take the charcoal away? And yet here it was.

It was the end of the afternoon, and the light was just beginning to fade. They edged forwards towards the clearing.

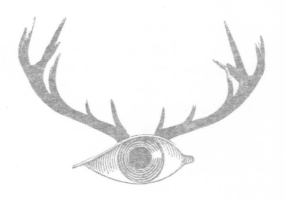

CHAPTER ELEVEN

A Fork In The Path

FOR A WHILE a kind of paralysis settled over the remains of the expedition. Sue took the last set of batteries out of the GPS unit and put them back in again, trying over and over to get some kind of life out of the thing. It had no effect whatsoever, and served only to make her more frustrated, until Kim muttered, "For Christ's sake," and made her put it away. Every mobile phone they had on them was unresponsive, not that they would have been any use without signal in this ridiculous place. The rain subsided quickly but even so, they were soaked through and numb and bewildered. And Helly was still dead.

Her body lay very close to where she had fallen, rolled over now onto her back. Her face was still streaked with mud and blood diluted by rain water. The rain had stopped now, but she was still wet, her hair plastered to her head where the hood was thrown back.

What were they supposed to do now? What *could* they do? Just leave her lying here in the thickening mud and the brush for animals to find? And besides that they were lost, and had no link to the outside world, and no one was expecting them back for a whole week.

Technically, the final decision about what to do was Alice's. She was ostensibly the leader of this expedition. Now she was very quiet, wide-eyed, and she seemed to somehow have retreated into her own head so that nothing outside it, not the cold or the wet or anything else, was able to reach her.

*　　*　　*

THE PERSON WHOSE main job here was to ensure the safety of the others was Kim, and in a cruel twist it was Kim who had been closest to Helly when she... when it had happened. Now Kim played the whole thing over in her head, imagining sounds or movements under the grey rush of the rain, anything that might help her understand what had actually happened. Because what had happened was this: Kim had put the hood of her waterproof up so that it obscured her peripheral vision. There had been a flash of colour—of what colour, she could not with hindsight say. Helly, very slightly ahead of her had stepped without warning six inches up into the air—stepped like she was going up a set of stairs, unless Kim had got it wrong now that she was re-imagining it over and over. Or maybe she hadn't risen into the air at all and even that was a twisting inside Kim's own mind. But it would account for the thud, which was what she remembered most clearly. Helly hadn't pitched forward. She hadn't tripped on her crutches or on anything else. If anything she had been pulled backwards, as if something unseen had caught at her yellowish hair, pulling her off balance that way—although of course she had had her hood up too, so it couldn't have. And she didn't pitch backwards very far. She fell to the ground with a thump, where she stood, tipping back at the last second, bashing the back of her head on a rock she had just stepped over. That was where most of the blood seemed to have come from. That and, inexplicably, under her fingernails. There was nothing here that should have been able to kill her, and yet she was dead.

Had she tripped on the rock? But Kim was so sure she had seen Helly out of the corner of her vision, or as much of that as she had under her hood, rising half a foot into the air. She was convinced of it. Now, of course, she didn't want to ask the others in case they thought she was mad. And yet... she ought to have been able to do something to help. Anything. But it was too late now for that.

* * *

NURIA STOOD A little way off. Her face was as neutral as it had been for most of the day, but she trembled and would not look at any of them, nor even in the direction where they stood, grouped together. Her breathing was shallow. She had met Helly Wheeler for the first time less than a month ago. The idea was that after this expedition they would never have met again. In her mind that thought kept slipping against the reality of it. She kept dissolving into abstractions, memories, like when you're so tired that you go cross-eyed and it's almost easier to stay like that.

Detached, she thought. Apart from the rest of them. This was not a *normal* way to respond. And she hated herself for it.

Dr Christopher was a lost cause. Nuria could see her already getting itchy feet. She wanted to go further into this forest, and the scary thing was that it was only *this* that had jolted her enough that she could see that it was a terrible idea. Nuria was not given to shouting. She kept her opinions to herself. But even she could see that the only course open to them now was to get out of here as soon as possible. They couldn't, surely, stay here much longer. There was no possible benefit to waiting.

In her everyday life, Nuria Martins ran marathons. It cleared her head when she found herself drowning under the weight of her thesis. Now she itched to run. To run away, but also just to run. And yet she could no more do that, just abandon everyone here and sprint away by herself, than she could bring herself to pipe up and tell the rest of them what to do. They didn't need another opinion thrown into the mix, another opportunity for an argument. Alice alone could cause enough chaos that arguing with her would slow them all to a standstill, which was the worst thing that could happen now. All Nuria had to do—the best way she could help—was to keep her head down and go where she was told.

Back by the rest of the group, Sue was clenching and unclenching her hands without seeming to be aware that she was doing it. Her breathing came quick and ragged, as if she was trying to take deep breaths and at the same time not to sob uncontrollably. When she caught Nuria's eye she looked away with something like guilt, and pushed her hands into the pockets of her coat. Nuria saw that she had the GPS unit tucked in one of the pockets, as if she couldn't quite bring herself to let it go, not just yet.

* * *

THE CONCLUSION SEEMED to rise to the surface as having always been there, rather than as something that they formulated. They couldn't stay here forever. And they certainly couldn't split up. If anything else happened, someone would be left alone. And it seemed now more than plausible that some other misfortune might engulf them; it seemed likely. It seemed somehow only fair that they should suffer. If everything suddenly now became easy, then *that* would all have been for nothing.

There was a red line, horizontal or near enough, across Helly Wheeler's neck. It wasn't deep, or it didn't look it, but it still wept blood from the cut which was angled upwards, as if something had swiped at her from a height of five or six feet. It hadn't, that was the thing—Kim and Sue and Nuria had been close enough to Helly that they would have seen anything that had got close enough to cause it. There had been nothing. Nothing visible had touched her, so nothing could possibly have done so—except that she had stepped a little way into the air, and stumbled, and crashed awkwardly and improbably onto that rock.

There must be some explanation for it. But there was a high chance they would never find out what it was. If they couldn't stay here they would have to leave, and there was no way to drag Helly's body with them. They would have to leave it here, and mark the spot, and hope that no animals interfered before they were able to return with greater backup.

That was the conclusion everyone had by and large come to by the time the paralysis started to wear off. It was beginning to get dark proper, or it would do imminently—now it wasn't just rainclouds making the sky so dark. Nobody wanted to say aloud that they didn't want to camp right next to a body, so by common consent they packed up their own things ready to leave. Not knowing what else to do, they covered her body over with ferns, and left a makeshift wooden cross as a marker—although Helly wasn't religious; it just seemed like the right thing—and around it they wound a few twists of yellow high-visibility tape. Dividing up the belongings in her backpack was the worst bit, and Kim took the lead as the person most used to the idea of doing it; the heavier things had already been divided among them when Helly had turned her ankle, but it wouldn't do to leave all of her personal belongings here. Helly had a husband, and a daughter. Kim had met them. They would want whatever they could have, whatever remained of her.

They could put it off no longer. So much of this had happened in wary silence, or monosyllables, in the hope that they could put off making the final, prickliest decision. Kim in particular did not want to have to decide which direction they would go in next. It would please nobody, and more to the point it was impossible to tell which way was the right one to go in. If she'd had any confidence this morning in her navigation skills—or any of the others'—then it had long since evaporated.

Like it or not, she would have to start the conversation. "Right," she said. "Which way are we going?"

Nuria busied herself with the waterproof shell of her backpack.

"Forwards," said Alice, predictably. "We'll never get out of here at all if we don't keep going in the same direction."

"Absolutely not," said Sue promptly. "We're turning around and going back the way we came. We know that part is safe." Alice tried to say something but Sue kept talking over her. "No more exploring. I don't want any part in it."

"Don't be flippant," said Alice. "I'm trying to find us the best way out of here. And besides, you've had the map."

Kim tried not to visibly wince.

"We're going deeper in," said Sue, and her voice was a little bit lower now—she sounded dangerous. She was putting the warning signals up. "I tried steering us east to where the fence ought to be, but every time I try there's a patch of bracken we can't walk through, or a bog, or you see something off to the left. We've been heading north-west and that's further in."

"You can say it," said Alice. "I know what you're trying to say even if the others don't."

Kim interjected: "That's enough. We all know we need to work together to get out of here."

"Do we all know, though?" said Sue, and the danger was unmistakable now. "Or does Dr Christopher here have something else in mind?"

Alice said, "I'm not going to dignify that with an answer." She turned away. Next to her, still bending over her bag, Nuria flinched.

"Is it or is it not true, though?"

Kim said, "Is what true?"

"That we're getting closer to Corrigal's Nest?"

Alice froze for a fraction too long. "We're nowhere near the Corrigal's Nest. Not that I know of, anyway. How could we even tell?"

Kim said, "Sue, you can't accuse her of—"

"I'm not accusing anyone of anything. I'm just asking if it's true that we're getting closer."

Alice said, quietly, "We must be, I suppose."

"That's why we have to turn around and go back. I'm not going anywhere near it."

Alice said, "What are you afraid of? I thought you were far more sceptical than that."

"You think I'm superstitious? I'm just going by what I see. Trees that disappear. This piece of shit." She waved the GPS unit about.. "It's already... We're already... What do *you* think is going on?" It was an accusation.

"I think," said Alice, "that the best way is to keep going. You can go your way, if that's what you want to do, and everyone else can decide if they agree with you. But I really think..."

"You're going to get us all killed."

"Are you saying," said Alice, "that this is my fault?"

"Nobody's saying anything," said Kim. "We're just trying to work out which way we're going to go. We all want the same thing."

"I'm really not sure about that."

Alice said, "Do you really think I want to go somewhere I think is going to be dangerous? I'm trying to find the easiest way out of here, and I think your way is going to take us much longer." Her face was very red. "We don't even know," she added, "exactly which direction we came from. Going back—or trying to—will put us exactly as much in the dark as we're in now. Only this time we're going somewhere we know these kinds of—unexplained events happen."

"We're getting closer to the Nest," said Sue. "Surely you can see that. What do you think is going to happen?"

"I've no idea." She sounded like an adult talking to a child mid-tantrum. "What do *you* think?"

"Helly would have got what I'm talking about." Sue appealed to Kim. "Surely you can see that something is very wrong here. Unexplainably so."

"I guess so. I guess so, yes. But it's not a five-hundred-year-old monster, Sue; even Helly—"

Sue threw the GPS unit on the ground in frustration. "I know that! But clearly *they* were scared of something. Something environmental here is scary. And we're going towards it, and this idiot wants to go towards it, and you want to keep walking!"

Nuria by now had straightened up, and was wearing the determinedly neutral expression of someone trying their utmost to mentally retreat somewhere else entirely. She brushed off the front of her trousers, and when they all looked at her she made eye contact with nobody.

Sue said, "Let's take a vote. Forward or back."

"Forward," said Alice.

"Kim?"

Nuria said, "I'll go with Alice."

"We're not splitting up," Sue told her.

"Forward, then." Nuria was still wearing the faraway

expression, still irritatingly inscrutable. Still, in Sue's obvious opinion, a complete pushover. Proof you could be extremely clever without needing common sense or to understand how the world worked.

Kim said, "I'll go with Nuria. Forward."

"Are you joking?"

Alice said, "You wanted a vote, Sue. You can keep the map if you want. When we get out we can recruit some more surveyors."

Kim wanted to tell her to shut up, that she was making it worse, but there was no point. Someone had to be the designated adult here. She was supposed to have shared the role with Helly. She turned away, so the rest of them wouldn't see the misery in her face. Poor Helly. The shock still seemed to occupy the back half of her brain. She wasn't feeling anything properly at the moment—she could barely feel her own fingers. But that was normal in situations like this—Kim Macleod knew someone who had lost a member of his party on Everest, and he'd said something very similar. She could feel cold water in one of her boots. It would do them good to get walking again.

And so with regretful looks back at the place where the body of Helly lay, they made to leave. Sue was silent for a while, which at the beginning seemed to have the character of a sulk—but after a little while she seemed to have given herself some kind of pep talk about professionalism, because the further on they went the more notes she took on their navigation, and the more she went towards the front of the group to take up her old place in the lead.

It was definitely beginning to turn dark now, and without saying anything about it to anyone Alice was sure she saw something out of the corner of her eye—a movement, a flicker of change. Her gut told her it wasn't human, or even animal—more like the flickering of a computer screen, a landscape superimposed on another one. A tree had disappeared, or reappeared. Maybe Sue had been right all along, although then again, maybe not. They just couldn't pass up the chance to walk through here; surely no one in their right mind would pass up that chance. She wondered idly which version of Moresby Forest they had buried Helly in—the real one or the not-real one. Either way, a horrible thought.

Nuria stayed at the back, her face in shadow, her cold hands shoved into her armpits and her shoulders hunched, as if she was trying to fold herself into the smallest possible space.

They would stop soon. They couldn't keep going much longer. It had been an eventful day—too eventful. For most of them it was a strong contender for the worst day of their lives, and Helly Wheeler was dead.

CHAPTER TWELVE

The Charcoal Burner's House

NINE MEN CREPT towards the little clearing with the hut in it, as the day edged towards twilight. Sam Harper stayed to the back of the group. He kept turning around to check behind them—Davies was far out of sight by now, left propped up against his tree, and although that stung, he wasn't what Harper was looking for. Something had been light for a moment and then wasn't again, like the reflection of sunlight on water. There was no water, of course; they had left the stream far behind by now. Maybe that hadn't been such a good idea after all, but it was by the by. His eyes were playing tricks on him, probably, but at any rate it made the hair stand up on the back of his neck, and he looked back, now and again. Like Lot's wife, tempting fate.

As the ones ahead of him approached the clearing, Byrne said to Stiles, "Do you know who lives here?"

But Stiles shook his head. "I've never heard of anyone living in this place at all." His voice trembled but he seemed now to be trying to pull himself together.

"Strange spot for a dwelling," said Taylor. For some reason they were all keeping their voices low. It was only the home of a charcoal burner.

"Go in ahead," said Thatcher to Stiles, and pointed his pistol at him to push the boy forwards. But perhaps Stiles was braver than they had given him credit for, or perhaps he wanted to put space between himself and the rest of them, because he nodded once, and went forward alone.

The rest watched as Stiles made his way up to the clearing, putting more weight on his right leg than on his left, picking out a path between scrubby patches of bracken and ferns. It was barely two hundred yards away, maybe even less than that. When he reached the edge of the clearing proper he paused and looked around, then beckoned the others forward. They edged closer.

"Is anyone there?" he called out in a reedy voice, when he was only a few yards from the entrance to the hut. He didn't sound like the rest of them, Harper noticed: he was leaning on his accent, the fact that he was from this same county. There appeared to be no answer, or at least none that was audible to the assorted onlookers. But whatever Stiles had heard—if anything—did not seem to dissuade him: he went boldly up and rapped on the wooden door with his knuckles. The sound of it echoed slightly, or maybe it was just incongruous and they were listening out for any least sound from that direction.

The door itself was not barricaded, but nor did it creak when it was opened. He called out to them: "It's alright!

You can come, it's empty." And they did, moving toward him without any longer troubling to be quiet.

The little hut was furnished in such a way that it appeared to have been inhabited, and not too long ago: there was the remains of a burnt-out fireplace with an axe and a couple of logs left next to it, and on the opposite side what was either a bed or sleeping place and bedraggled blanket of woven wool, and a wooden bowl and spoon. A tin billy can lay next to the door, with an inch of scummy water in it and a blackened bottom. It had clearly been used, maybe a few days ago, but not much longer than that.

Outside, Byrne was looking at the mound where the charcoal was burnt. It was covered in a thick layer of earth, from which some fragments of browned grass still drooped. He poked the end of his sword into it and it came away covered in black. There was charcoal in there, for sure, under the covering of packed earth. Someone had built the pile with considerable skill, and by the feel of things it was still warm. In which case, where was the charcoal burner himself? No good charcoal burner left his pile unattended. Not—given the state of the billy—for up to a week.

Beyond that, the clearing was practically bare.

Emboldened by Stiles's success, Thatcher elbowed past him into the deserted hut. It was cramped and dark, and had the chilliness of a place not recently lived in. There was no smell of bodies, nothing to suggest in what state, or for what reason, the inhabitant had left. He knelt down by the bed—although it could barely be called a bed, being more like a wooden pallet. It was old-fashioned, but who was to say what people slept on in this part of the world. Maybe civilisation hadn't reached this far north. He spat into the middle of the floor, and the gob lay there, on the packed earth, winking in the little light coming through the door.

His curiosity was rewarded, in the end: there was a little hollowed-out section underneath the pallet. You could see it if you nudged the musty blanket to one side. Inside was a small object, wrapped around with some kind of dark material. Thatcher was alone in the hut; none of them had dared come in after him, so he scooped the little bundle out. It was a moleskin, and inside there were ten misshapen little copper pennies, each no bigger than a fingernail. There was a chunk of amber, maybe an inch and a half from end to end, with a dead fly suspended inside it, wings halfway aloft; and a fine comb made of bone that had a couple of teeth missing at one end. And under all of it was a rosary, with uneven beads that seemed mostly to be made of fired clay, although there were two little freshwater pearls on it near the cross, which was made of bone.

Thatcher picked up the rosary between thumb and forefinger, his sense of foreboding returning. Rosaries were for papists, and no papist would suffer a pack of Parliament's men in his home unless he could help it. It made sense that whoever lived in here was a papist. No true Christian could stay here amongst whatever stalked these woods; any inhabitant must be under the Devil's protection, and to Thatcher's mind that could only mean one thing. A man wouldn't leave a rosary unless he was expecting to come back for it. He scooped up the little coins and pocketed them. Then he turned back to the door, holding the rosary as if it were contagious. "Harper! Get over here."

Harper appeared in the doorway. "What's going on?"

Thatcher waved the rosary at him. A few of the little

beads clinked against each other. "No friends to be had here after all. I should have known."

Harper pushed his way into the hut, more to block the rosary from the view of the rest than for any other reason. "Do you think they're still here?"

"Could be," said Thatcher, and briefly Harper saw again that fear which seemed outsized, the fear of a man who had seen or connected things the rest of them hadn't. He might have had sympathy for Thatcher if he hadn't seen him break Captain Davies's ribs.

"Well," he said, "we can either stay here and wait them out, or we can get out of their way."

"Aye, wait for them to come and shoot the rest of us down where we stand."

Harper was looking around the bare little room. "All two dozen heavily armed men who live here. Right."

"It doesn't need two dozen of them if they have the Devil himself with them."

"Have you met a Catholic, Rod? Since you were a boy? Pull yourself together." And he turned around again, to go out into the clearing, where the air smelled less stale and he wasn't in such confined quarters with Thatcher.

The other sergeant watched him go. Harper could feel his eyes on his back. He half expected Thatcher to say something else, but was grateful when he didn't. Harper, for his part, would put money on nobody living here any more.

For a while they had got their hopes up, that someone might have been able to give them directions out of here, or at least a little food, or some reassurance that it was possible to stay alive in this place for any length of time.

But it wasn't true. It wasn't possible after all. Something—something that mattered—slipped.

"What's in there?" said Kilburton, who was still poking around the perimeter.

"Not much," said Harper, and kept walking.

"Is there a body?"

Stiles said, "No, there's no one in there. I told you."

"Well then. Are there any supplies? Anything to drink?"

Harper said, "Go in yourself, Kilburton, if you really want to know. I'm not stopping you."

But Kilburton frowned. "What did he show you?"

Harper said, "He can hear you, you know. Go on then, ask him yourself." He went across again to the charcoal pile. That there were people here at all was a miracle, no matter what kind of people they might be. If it were the shack alone, he might have thought it was built by someone passing through, here a few weeks at most before moving on, but that didn't account for the charcoal. None of it accounted for the charcoal.

Something caught his eye, halfway distant in the trees, but when he looked again, it was gone. He studied the distance, thoughtfully, before realising—he had never smoked that pipe, in the end. He took it from his pocket, and held it in one hand. "Over here," he said to no one in particular, turning away from where he had been, off to the other side of the clearing.

"What is it?" said Ames. His hand was on the sword at his belt.

There was a noise from inside the little hut, of a flint being struck. Then the door opened, and Thatcher stumped out, followed by a wisp of smoke.

"What are you doing that for?" said Cadwell, and it was this that seemed to make the rest of them cotton on, and recoil.

Thatcher held up the rosary again, and this time all of them could see it. "Devil house," he grunted. "Must be. Only way you can live in this place." He took a few steps out from the doorway. The unmistakable crackle was audible now behind him; the walls of the shack were made of little more than sticks, they wouldn't last long. "We're moving on now," he said brusquely. "It'll be dark soon. We're not staying here."

"Perhaps we should wait," said Taylor, "just in case they come back."

"Do you see this?" said Thatcher, and he shook the beads. "I'd take no help from a papist if he offered it me, it'd be like making a deal with the Devil himself, if the Devil doesn't make his own self known. To be here after dark? They'd slit our throats as we slept, we'd do better to—"

There was a deafening crack, and he crumpled where he stood. At first it looked like whatever had hit him had come from inside the shadowy little cabin, and Harper could have sworn he saw the shadow of a figure behind Thatcher in the doorway, obscured or nearly so by smoke. But the next moment it was gone again, and besides, he knew where the shot had really come from. Alexander Davies could not quite stand upright; he had found a stick to lean on, his face was agony overlaid with determination, and his own blood still crusted his neck and exposed forearms. His aim was as good as it ever had been. He stood at the edge of the clearing now, the pistol in his outstretched hand and the smell of gunpowder hanging in the air. The shot had hit the sergeant square in the Adam's apple. None of this taking chances with breastplates. Thatcher fell sideways against the smoking door frame, and moved no more.

"If anyone wants to stay with the sergeant," Davies whispered, "he can make himself known."

There were not enough of them left for there to be uproar, and besides, they were too exhausted by now. For a moment there was only silence, and the crackling of the fire, and a hiss of steam as it swelled towards the shack's makeshift roof. Then Ames dropped his sword. "I just want to get out of here. Please. I just want to leave this place." And he too looked young, or else new to soldiering, and to such frequency of violent death.

"Alright, man," said Davies. "We'll move on, if you're with me. Has anyone got a drink?"

"Cadwell has rum," said Harper. He was still holding his pipe.

Cadwell had turned white, but he composed himself and passed his flask over with shaking hands. "Only a drop left, sir."

The captain took it, and took a swig. Thatcher's reign had lasted, at most, half a day.

The flames inside the shack had reached the roof now, and the wet wood fizzed thickly as thick black smoke mingled with steam. The fire did not falter, though—it must be too hot in there. Either way there was no saving it now. They pushed the body of Rod Thatcher as far inside the burning shack as they could get him before the heat overcame them. There would be more rain soon, besides which the light was thin and fading fast. They couldn't stay in this cursed place. Who knew what might approach them in the dark, how the landscape might change around them if they were forced to remain here for another night. They left the blazing shell of the unknown charcoal burner's home, and struck out again to what was probably the north.

As for Davies himself, it seemed to Harper that something had got hold of him. He had seen men get up and walk after having the shit kicked out of them before, but that and the shot wound from the day before had effected some kind of transformation on Davies. He had exacted his revenge now; and it appeared as if the rest of the men faded almost to a pinprick in his mind. What was left? Self-preservation? It was hard to tell. Harper had known the man many years and had never known him to be like this. He was paying more attention to the woods than to them around him, or even to his own injuries. He squinted into the far distance, barely aware of the rest of them or even his own body, painful and bruised though it must be under his coat.

Thatcher had seen things here that the others had not. He too had insisted that they not stop, that they keep going. Admittedly, Thatcher had been less clever and more likely to lash out than Davies. If anyone should be in charge here, Harper thought, he was glad it was Davies. Yet. He was holding something back, where he hadn't been before. Harper couldn't even tell what gave it away, but he knew it.

And there was something else, too. The feeling that they were being watched was stronger now—he felt it on the back of his neck. Maybe it was because now he knew for sure that there had been someone else in these woods, that it wasn't completely without people. It was more complicated than that, surely. Harper's gut told him so, though, and in any other circumstances he tended to trust it.

They walked on, and the smell of smoke clung to them.

CHAPTER THIRTEEN
The Second Night

THE TWO HISTORIANS, the surveyor, and the remaining park ranger set up camp in a sheltered part of the wood, halfway up a slope, in an area they were pretty sure they hadn't walked through before, and which was therefore probably somewhere to the north. It was a despondent group and a shell-shocked one that finally sat down in the chill mist to eat some hot food. They ached from carrying all their things over such a distance. Nuria needed fresh blister plasters. Their clothes were still damp with the rain from earlier and the mist that still, strangely, hung about the forest, obscuring their view and preventing them from any kind of competent navigation. The GPS unit still showed no signs of life. It was as if they were the only people left in the whole world. And there were four of them, and there should have been five.

Alice Christopher felt the exhaustion settle over her of having cycled through such a range of emotions in one day. Even now, she was sorely tempted to carry on in the direction she had originally intended, at the very beginning of this whole expedition—which was, as Sue had correctly guessed, towards the Corrigal's Nest, or the direction she believed it to be in. She felt guilty about that, too, although less guilty than she perhaps ought to feel. And awful though it was, she was almost sure they were getting closer to it anyway, whether they intended to or not—it was the path of least resistance in this place of unnaturally muffled light and sound. The whole wood was still reorienting itself around them, manoeuvring and shifting them to move in the direction it wanted. The land was alive, the forest itself could think and feel and, in its own way, communicate. No wonder she was a little nauseous. It was basically seasickness.

She sounded crazy. She knew that whenever she voiced her real ideas about the wood they sounded crazy, and that everyone around her had secretly thought so for years, which was why her promotion had been blocked and her colleagues thwarted her at every turn. But sometimes that was just what the truth looked like—or curiosity, at least. Other people could not be expected to understand. There was something about this place that had drawn her to it, some spark of inexorable attraction that didn't affect everyone, only a select few. Maybe the Davies company were among that few, the ones for whom the slight unreality or off-kilter-ness of the place was an enticement, a thing that called out to them, as much as it was a place of immediate escape from that ambush on the hill. Maybe the Moresby family were the same. Deirdre Ellison was, for sure: Deirdre was the one who had pointed it out to Alice. And everyone else's reactions to Deirdre had been how she knew that not everyone got it. For Alice, it was the same as it had been for Deirdre. Curiosity drove her. Pure, distilled curiosity. When it came down to it there was no pursuit in Alice's mind higher or more necessary than the pursuit of knowledge, and this knowledge in particular. Even if she was wrong. Especially if she turned out to be wrong.

The mist in the growing dark was eerie and strange. It seemed heavy somehow, a curtain that ought to be falling to the floor but instead was held up by some unseen force. She peered into it. It was hard enough to count the trees already, and without even the camera to help them, how would she know when she woke up the next morning whether they were the same ones?

She wasn't so dogmatic that she hadn't even imagined herself being wrong. It could yet be the case. But as soon as she had set foot in this wood she had known that there was indeed something not quite right about it, and now, after more than a day of being within its borders, she was sure: there were two forests, and one of them kept flickering into sight—not even on the edge of her vision now, but sometimes right in the middle of it. A darker forest. Fewer oak trees and beech, and more dark conifers, more evergreens. Gaps—interestingly, she thought—in the fog. The second forest was clearer, if only they would allow themselves to walk in it.

That was, in a way, why Helly Wheeler had died today. They had chosen to walk in the obscured forest in the hope that they could get home through it. If they'd chosen the second one they'd have been able to see where they were going. If they walked in that wood they would be able to see all of it. They'd be able to understand. They'd be, almost certainly, she thought, safer.

They were all looking at her. Alice jerked out of her train of thought. "What? Oh. Thank you." And she took the mug of tea that Nuria was proffering. "I was just thinking about Helly."

Sue said, "We're all thinking about Helly. Aren't we?"

There was a long silence while they drank the tea. And then Alice said, "What was it? Did you see it?"

Kim shook her head. "There was nothing there."

Sue said, "That's not possible."

"Did you see anything?"

Sue thought about it. "No. But I wasn't looking. My hood was up."

"There couldn't have been anything. Not without any of us seeing it."

Nuria said, "So she tripped."

Sue gave her the dirtiest look. "Oh yeah. Tripped and slit her own throat. She must have been running with scissors."

Kim said, warningly, "Sue."

"But," said Alice, "it must have been something. There must have been something there."

"What are you getting at?" said Kim.

Sue said, "Oh no. No. No more ghost stories tonight. Not after everything else that's happened today."

"I'm not suggesting ghosts. That's bedtime stories. I just think... about the second forest."

"The second forest…?"

Nuria stood up. "I'm going to bed. I'm tired." And she went off to where the tents were set up. She could hear Sue behind her saying, "What do you mean, the second forest?" before she unzipped her rucksack and rummaged around as loudly as she could so as not to hear any of the rest of the conversation. But the tone was enough. She knew what was going on out there, or at least she knew enough that there was no way she wanted anything to do with it.

Nuria was a listener, who preferred not to process her thoughts out loud if she could help it. By and large she was an optimist. She would give people the benefit of the doubt. It had got her most of the way in life, and then it had got her here.

Alice Christopher was her second supervisor. She had a reputation for being driven, as one who could tell if you hadn't done your seminar reading at sixty paces. Nuria had been taught by her as an undergraduate, and on the basis of that and their overlapping interests had asked her to supervise her doctorate.

She had been warned off Alice several times. Apparently several members of the history department had clocked Nuria as impressionable and easily hooked in to a hare-brained scheme. Maybe she was. They said Alice was full of big ideas and some of them were off the wall. They said to take her advice on reading material but not on research topic. To always ask for help if Nuria needed it, if she needed to say no to something. That one in particular had got Nuria's back up because it felt like she was being infantilised. Early on she felt like she was turning down far more than she agreed to—conferences and papers and digs and side projects. There were always more than she could handle, anyway. But now it was four years later, and somehow without realising it here she was, here she had got, six weeks before her final hand-in date—six weeks! What was she thinking!—and in a tent in the rain, lost. A woman had died, and here was Alice fucking Christopher, shooting her mouth off again with impossible theories.

Nuria should have known. She should have been well aware right from the word go that she should never have come to Moresby Forest, not with Dr Christopher, that there was no possible way for this to go well. But it had been four years, and Alice had toed the line. She had been considerate. She hadn't asked too much. And Nuria had been curious to finally see the place. It was close to her research, too. It was a place with significance to her. And so she had given in.

All along, Alice had been working up to it—it had always been Alice's goal to come out here.

Now Nuria wiggled her way into her sleeping bag and felt miserable. She could hear Sue outside, the only voice that carried, saying, "You can't be serious." Then Alice said something inaudible, and Sue was half shouting: "The 1731 map is horseshit. It's three centuries old!"

Nuria rolled over on her hard bed mat. She knew that Alice wasn't thinking about the rest of them, and hadn't been from the start. This was Alice's expedition in the sense that the history was her speciality, she had secured the funding and had chosen the research aims, but it went further than that. All of this was an excuse—four other people, including Nuria, were an excuse. They were only here to give Alice the pretext to be here herself. If Alice Christopher was thinking about anyone other than herself, it wasn't any of the people on this trip with her. She didn't care about any of them beyond that pretext. She never had done.

It occurred to Nuria that Alice might be unhinged. She couldn't be of sound mind. This wasn't something a person of sound mind would do. Everything everyone had ever warned her about Alice was true. She wasn't right in the head.

Lying in the darkness on the cold earth, Nuria felt a wave of despair. She ached all over. She was freezing. Her unfinished thesis weighed heavily on her mind, crowding out some but not enough of her other thoughts. She wanted a hot shower and a conversation with someone who wasn't any of the people out *there*.

Outside around the campfire whatever ill-advised conversation Alice had started was returning to normal volumes. Alice and Sue were talking, although it was harder now to distinguish tone or to make out what they were saying. For a very brief moment, watching the spots which swam in front of her vision in the darkness of the tent, Nuria worried that Alice might somehow have convinced Sue of her stupid theory. It wasn't possible, of course. Sue would cut straight through the bullshit.

Would Kim? Yes. Probably. Surely. Any reasonable person must. But this was an odd place, and the events of the day, right from waking up and finding that such a huge tree had gone, played tricks on a person.

The oak tree. How did you explain the oak tree? You didn't. You didn't explain any of what was happening here. You trusted in your gut, and in the physical laws of the universe as you knew them, and you shut up and kept your counsel until you could get out, and then you consulted someone who knew what they were talking about. There would be an explanation in the end, surely. There had to be. Not even in the sense that if the tree didn't fit with the rest of the world then it would be bad—what had happened had happened already, so clearly it could fit, somehow or other. The alternative was too terrible to contemplate.

The red-tinted flash of a torch through the canvas of the tent. Then footsteps coming over: someone was coming to bed. It turned out to be Alice—she fumbled about with the zip for the outer tent, and sat in the half-open doorway for a good couple of minutes before moving. Nuria held her breath for a while, pretending to be asleep, wondering what Alice was thinking about while her emotions still coursed through her, feeling like a pushover. She was. She was a pushover. There was no changing it.

Finally the rummaging in the outer tent started up again, and Alice came into the main tent.

"Are you awake?"

Nuria said nothing.

Alice sighed, and wiggled her way into her sleeping bag without saying anything else. After a little while, Nuria heard a muffled sniffling, but she still didn't move and it soon subsided again.

She slept badly. The wind whipped up in the trees around them, periodically, and Moresby Forest whispered its secrets in a way that, in Nuria's half-awake state, sounded almost like people. She didn't hear Kim and Sue go to bed for a long time, although at some point they must have done.

Twice she believed she heard the voice of Helly Wheeler outside the tent, but both times she concluded that she had imagined it. Fretful rain fell onto the tent and she found herself playing Helly's last moments over and over in her head, and no one could sleep well after that.

Next to her, Alice tossed and turned, and it was hard to tell whether she was awake or asleep. And outside, Moresby Forest just existed—as it had done for centuries before they had come anywhere near it, as wild and inscrutable as it had ever been.

CHAPTER FOURTEEN

Decimation

IT WAS THE middle of the night, and of the remains of the company, half were asleep.

There were only eight of them left now—there had been twice as many as that the night before, after they had been forced to abandon their comrades on the side of Sibbert Hill. Byrne and Cadwell had taken the first half of the watch, which was by now close to ending without any apparent incident; they huddled around the embers of the fire, shoulders uncomfortably hunched against the damp chill. Cadwell in particular had volunteered for first watch as a show of goodwill and deference. Captain Davies himself had been uncharacteristically lenient since the incident outside the deserted hut—perhaps because there were few enough left that to mete punishment on the rest of the mutineers now would be too much for any of them to countenance—but, after all, who knew how long it would last. Right now, they were survivors, all of them—uncertain though it still was what exactly they had managed to survive.

In the low light of the fire, Sam Harper smoked his way through two pipes, as slowly as he could make them last. Finally he sat motionless, watching the embers flicker and die down, thinking about the men they had lost.

It wasn't just the ones who'd perished in the last two days, although there were enough of those—Willis and Onslow and good old Jessop, Blashford, Shepherd, the rest. Watch enough friends die and something in you scarred over, so that it wasn't that it didn't hurt, more that it hurt in a different way. One loss reminded you of all the others, toppling back through the years until you wondered how you could possibly still be here when none of the rest of them were.

The wind whispered in the trees in all directions, and the air smelled of woodsmoke and mud. He couldn't sleep now, even if he'd wanted to.

Next to him sat Bill Stiles, his knees up under his chin, his toes poking out of the front of his falling-apart boots. Stiles was different from the others now, now that Alwood was gone. He was the only one from further north than Colchester, for a start. Last week when he had joined up to come north with them, he had been excited, and so had Alwood. A chance to do their bit, to make use of themselves in these strange and dark times, to stand up against the despots and the traitors that roamed the north. So much for that. They'd not even been much good as guides, in the end—both boys had barely left their village before, never mind gone forty miles north. Someone had to be excited around here, for the march and the cold and the hunger would wear you down eventually, even if you'd not seen so much as a skirmish yet.

Their dream died faster than most men's did, even. No one had much hope of glory after a few weeks' marching, and it had been less than a week since Bill Stiles and Francis Alwood had joined up, and already Alwood was dead.

Harper cleared his throat, and the three around the fire with him all twitched like they were reaching for their weaponry, until they saw it was him who had made the sound. None of the others lying around them moved at all, although Harper wondered how many of them were actually asleep. He said, gruffly, "How are you keeping, son?"

The ends of the fire were reflected in Stiles's eyes, and in the tears travelling silently down his face. He didn't look up, and made no move to wipe them away. "Been better." He sounded like a boy whose voice was still breaking, trying to be gruff. Surely he wasn't that young?

Harper had done this before—had been be the veteran who sat with the younger man through his first experience of loss on the battlefield, but this wasn't like that. Those times, he might say, it's what we all signed up for; you're tougher for it, even if you don't feel like that now; don't let their deaths be for nothing. Now he said, "We should have listened to you, eh?"

The captain must be asleep, after all. If he'd been listening, Harper would have known.

Stiles said, "It wouldn't have made any difference."

"You might as well tell us what we're facing, then. We'll need all the help we can get tomorrow."

The watch, Byrne and Cadwell, were definitely listening now. For a while Stiles said nothing at all, then he wiped his eyes with the heel of his hand. "You want me to say its name."

"I'm not as stupid as all that."

"Because I won't."

"I know. What kind of thing is it?"

Stiles said, "I only know the stories. There used to be a witch in the woods. They say she made a pact with a beast she found here, which has its lair in the deepest part of the forest, and now nobody comes out alive. They call it the Nest."

"And the witch is the... what did you call it?"

He flinched. "No. The witch was Essie Moresby. The— That's the beast, and it's been here longer than Christendom."

"The wood is named after a witch?"

"Her family. Some people say it was the Devil himself she met, but in this county no one says that. We know it was here before the Devil ever was. They say the witch still walks the place, and feeds men to it when they enter her path."

Byrne said, in a low voice, "The hut, this afternoon. That wasn't hers?"

"Essie Moresby lived hundreds of years ago. If she lives here still, I can't think she has any need of charcoal."

"Then who lived there?" Byrne was more musing than expecting an answer.

Harper said, "I bet men come through this way all the time, one way or another."

"And stay alive?"

Cadwell said, "I'm glad we didn't stay there past dark."

"What do you know of the beast?" said Harper, not to be dissuaded.

Stiles looked uncomfortable, but at least now he was no longer crying. He was twisting his hands by his sides, into fists and out again, and didn't seem to notice he was doing it. "I come from two days' ride to the south. I know it by repute, that's all. My brothers would tell me, there's a forest to the north with a creature older than Christendom in it, if you don't shut your mouth we'll take you there and leave you. You know, it'll drag you to its nest and then you'll be sorry. For a summer when I was a boy they'd tell me everyone who left the village was going to Moresby Wood, whichever direction the traveller set off in. They did it to scare me, and it worked. We all know the place, that's all. There was a witch used to entice men in, and they would see her in Tapford long after she ought to have been dead. And men disappeared here, now and again— my father once knew a man who went this way and never came back. Sometimes someone says they've been in here, and come out untouched, but all of them are liars. Mostly people stay away. We shouldn't have come here."

"And do you think," Cadwell said, very quietly, "we're going to get out again?"

Byrne said, "You shouldn't ask that. It's not fair."

Stiles's expression was of abject misery. "Since we've been in here, I've had this feeling in my chest, of ropes around it squeezing it tight. And I can hardly breathe."

"That's not monsters, lad, that gets us all sometimes," said Harper.

"But what if it isn't?" said Stiles. "What if..."

"Trust me. That's part of the bloody awful bit of soldiering, that's part of you becoming a man." He appealed to Byrne and Cadwell, who each nodded seriously. "And you got beat up pretty thoroughly earlier," he added, "which can't have helped."

Cadwell said, "It's rum that makes it ease up. Or better if you can find it. Not much else to be done for it. That happens all over." And he handed his flask over to Stiles, who took it with shaking hands.

"It's easier," said Harper, more to himself and to the fire than to any of the others, "if you're with your rightful company. Good men. Worth more than gold. You find yourself some good men, you stay with them. Do right by them. Most important lesson you can learn."

They switched watch after that, waking Ames and Taylor and Kilburton and leaving them to sit up in the darkness. Harper lay awake, staring at the remains of the fire, thinking about witches and shadowy creatures and what might happen if such things really were in their midst. A decade ago, he might have been confident in his ability to remain strong in the face of moral adversity, but that was a young man's conviction. He no longer had that—he had spent far too long as a soldier to believe in his own moral fortitude in a situation he had not yet experienced.

Now, too, there was something else—something he had wanted to find out and which gnawed away at him. And it was this: when Jack Onslow had been killed—that is, when Jack Onslow had died, Harper had been behind him in the group, facing toward him. If the creature had been there, it stood to reason, then Harper would have seen it. So what had he seen?

He tried to remember anything at all. A flash in the trees, off to one side, or right next to Onslow's head. The curve of a claw from nowhere, or a suggestion of dark matted fur. He could convince himself it was true, and then a breath later that he was making it all up. Whatever he had seen, it was too bogged down now in what he *ought* to have seen.

The important thing was what to do next, and Harper had no idea what that might be. This, as it happened, was the main reason that Thatcher had been an idiot, with his entire bloody afternoon of half-hearted mutiny—nobody would trust him to steer them through a situation in which their immortal soul was at stake and the normal way of things could not be relied on. That was all anyone could want in a leader, at a time like this—someone to make the decisions when they were hard, and not to be manifestly stupid about it. Davies was beaten to a pulp now. Harper had never taken him for a coward before, although maybe that was what losing half your men in one ambush did to you. It was sad, what had happened to Thatcher—like shooting down a rabid dog. He'd rather follow Davies, though. Rather that than do nothing.

Had Harper meant for Thatcher to die, when he'd slipped the captain his pistol? He hadn't meant for any of this. It had worked out for the best. That much was probably true.

It was too complicated. He had talked big talk to Stiles and the others about being a man, about comradeship, about doing the right thing. When it came down to it and he felt the shadow of Death brush past him like this, all he really wanted to do was follow someone else. Let someone else decide. And hope that that someone else knew what he was doing.

IT WAS AS well that Harper didn't know that Captain Davies was awake, had been awake all the time, could not sleep for the pain in his shoulder which now mingled with the bruising in his ribcage and made him feel like he was on fire. Davies lay in the darkness, pretending to be asleep, and he heard all that they said about witches, about that discomfort of being a soldier which happened to us all, sooner or later; he heard it all and it settled on him like a layer of earth, like a dead man being buried. He had the strongest feeling that he was going to die in this forest.

Earlier today when he'd been sure that he was about to die, he'd more or less assumed it would be by the hand of Rod Thatcher. The fact that it wasn't ought to have been comforting, and yet somehow he still couldn't shake the notion that he'd never be anywhere outside of this place ever again.

So that changed things. Davies stared up into the sky, where there ought to have been stars through the treetops. There were none, only the suggestion of moonlight under thick cloud.

He wasn't afraid of dying. A lot of soldiers were—for some it got better the older they got, when they realised that the situations they found themselves in couldn't be much worse than whatever the next life held for them. For others it got worse, and as the years went on they grew more desperate and clung on to life at any cost. That had been Rod Thatcher's problem. He'd got too desperate. But Davies knew better than Thatcher—that if you wanted to take command, it barely mattered who you were, or what you did with it half the time. It mattered that command was taken, that *someone* took it, and didn't let it go. An office was immortal in a way that its holder never could be—the gap a man filled lived on forever, even while the man who had filled it perished. That was a comfort of sorts, a continuity.

He had felt like he'd been living on borrowed time since the age of about fourteen, since he'd watched the first man who was kind to him in the army be cut down on the battlefield. In the not quite two decades since, he had taken risks he probably wouldn't have otherwise taken and they had so far served him well. It had never felt so clearly like a premonition of the end before. The fact was, though, that God would know if he left these men he was responsible for to their deaths. If his time was coming, he would know when it was.

It was in that frame of mind that he dozed, in the end—the sleep of a man who had thought before that this sleep might be his last, and who had long since come to terms with it. It was never exactly comfortable, but given that he was more bruise than man at the moment, being comfortable with the near future was probably not even possible.

He slept, and those around him laid out on the ground slept too, and above them a strong wind blew up and died down just above the level of the treetops, and the cloud cover moved along without ever really coming to an end. Near dawn, the woods gave the slightest shiver, and became damp without it precisely having rained, and all was quiet, and all was still. The first light began to creep through the trees.

The previous day, Davies had woken to shouts of panic, and disbelief. This time, he almost believed he was back there, where the giant oak tree had been, with half a dozen more of his men alive and the chance to do the whole day over. He opened his eyes. It was starting to get light already, in the diffuse way of a foggy morning. And then he turned over, towards the rest of the group, and saw the bloodbath.

The last watch of the night—those three men, Ames, Kilburton, Taylor—were all dead. They were not where they had been sitting before near the fire—they were maybe ten paces off, as if they had gone out to investigate something. Which they should absolutely not have done without either leaving one man behind or waking the rest up; they *knew* this, and now here they were all laid out. Drenched with blood. Unmoving.

Davies scrambled to his feet, and as he did, a man howled in anguish. His first thought was that it must be Stiles, but it was Byrne, sprinting towards the bodies, then kneeling over the fallen Taylor with his hands covering his face. Who else was here? Stiles, Cadwell. Harper—oh, thank the Lord, Harper was still alive. And that was all.

He went over and Cadwell and Harper followed him. It looked for all the world like the dead men had been attacked by a wild animal of some kind—something with gigantic claws and a powerful set of jaws. A wolf? But there must hardly be any wolves left in the wilds of England. And the ones there were, hunted for food. They did not leave their quarry where it lay. The bodies of the three soldiers had guts spilling from them—it looked like Kilburton had put his hands up to protect his face and there were slashes all down his forearms. There was blood everywhere, spattered outwards away from their little encampment four or five yards or so, but it looked more like it had been sprayed from the bodies by a strong wind than that it had been tracked there by another creature.

Davies said, "Did anyone hear anything?"

They all shook their heads. Byrne was crying. So was Cadwell, now, although he tried to hide it, and Stiles was a lost cause. Only Harper seemed to be keeping his composure, and he looked white as a sheet.

The sergeant said, flatly, "This doesn't just happen and we don't hear it all of five yards away."

Cadwell said, "Keep your voice down. What if it's still about?"

It was this more than anything else that spurred them to action—for how could you tell after all where something was, when it was silent and unseen. Davies put his hand to the forehead of Charley Ames; the dead soldier was still slightly warm. Why hadn't the beast gone for the sleeping men who were right there next to him? Had it been scared off? Surely not. What little he could comprehend didn't bear thinking about, and the rest was enough that he couldn't pause to think twice.

They gathered their things up in their hands. Harper pissed on the fire. Nobody suggested stopping to bury the bodies, or to so much as say a prayer over them, although Byrne in particular looked regretfully back at the body of his fallen friend. Now they were only running away, as fast as they could go, away from they knew not what. The direction didn't matter, if any of them cared to guess which direction they were going in, which for the first while none of them did.

The first hour after they woke up was a solid little closed bud of fear, but it couldn't stay like that forever. After a while the fear took on a different character; they started to ask themselves if they were still being followed and realised there was no answer. Whatever had killed their three comrades had been so quiet—it had been more than quiet, it had silenced the space around them in a way that wasn't natural, no matter how you tried to look at it. It was demonic, or it was old enough that it didn't have to behave by civilised rules. From that there came a different kind of fear, one that grew and flowered and looked for the light. They didn't know where they were—it must have been early still because the light was thin through thick clouds and it was hard to see which way the shadows fell.

They walked now because staying still was worse. Their things were slung haphazardly on their backs—or what was left of their things, what they had been able to think clearly enough to grab before they had bolted. Now they were five men on the run, only five, out of so many, scrambling through woods and fleeing from who knew what. The rest were dead, and no one would ever see them again.

All that remained in the head of Alexander Davies from the night before was the knowledge both that he could not run and that he was going to. Not for his own sake. Barely for the sake of the poor saps left with him. Now it was because everything burned away in the end, and what was left was not people or names or even feelings, it was the holes they fitted into. He was a captain, and the captaincy would remain. And now he was prey, too, of something or someone—and so he would stay that course to the end as well. The men would do what they could and he would do his best for them. And all that would be left in the end was the holes into which they had once fitted.

CHAPTER FIFTEEN

Into Two Forests

IT FELT AUTUMNAL now. When the four remaining campers woke the next morning there was no denying it. The air was cold and crisp and the ubiquitous mist hung low around their tents. The sky ought to have been much clearer than it was given how much the temperature seemed to have dropped in the night—as it was, there were occasional glimpses of blue, under clouds fast moving but thick, and nothing more. There was evidently more wind than there had been the previous day, and mist or no mist, it set the treetops whispering. The GPS unit, on inspection, still did not work.

None of them had slept well. Every little creak or shudder of leaves had felt like an invisible threat heading directly towards them. Besides that, Nuria had definitely left at an opportune moment the night before; the discussion that had followed her retiring had dissolved swiftly into an argument that despite Kim's best efforts she had not been able to resolve before they went to bed. She had lain awake as Sue seethed, wondering about what the hell she had got herself into. This expedition, and this place, were not as Kim had been led to believe.

Now she woke to find herself alone in the tent, and for a second panic erupted in her mind—was she the only one left? But no, Sue was awake and had got up already: she was outside, trying to poke the remaining embers of last night's fire into something that could be reused.

Kim scrambled up and joined her. "Let me," she said, with the easy confidence of someone who had poked a lot of bonfire ashes in her life. It was difficult this time; the wood they had was damp, which presumably meant it had continued to rain overnight, or else that this mist had been settled for a long time. The air outside the tent was sweet, and Kim could almost convince herself that she smelled something rotten in it, although whether it came from anything in particular was impossible to tell.

They heated water and made cups of tea, which at least on a superficial level improved matters. It was something warm to hang on to, at least.

They were starting to run low on water. They'd not brought much with them, having intended to filter their own from the river. You couldn't get away with that in a lot of places these days, but since Moresby was so pristine and untouched they had thought that it would save them carrying too much, make them more manoeuvrable, to collect their daily water as they went along. Now that seemed like a mistake. Sue in particular seemed reluctant to drink the water they'd collected, as if she didn't want to take anything from the land itself if she could possibly help it. That had surprised Kim when she had first noticed it, but the more she thought about it, the more she thought she understood. It was not that Sue believed all the stories *per se*—more that she thought they had to have come from somewhere. Maybe some of the superstitions responded directly to things true but as yet unexplained. Was that not how plenty of medicine of the Middle Ages had worked, after all? You did not have to know exactly the mechanism of something for it to be effective.

Sue was quiet this morning, speaking in monosyllables and only when addressed, and not meeting Kim's eyes. It was as if she had given up on the long-held scepticism that had led her to deny that anything supernatural was going on at all here—it wasn't right at all to be admitting it, Kim thought, but what other choice did they have?—and now something in Sue had shifted irreparably. Moresby Forest had taken something from her, and what was left was smaller and less certain. Kim found herself wondering: was this what had happened to the Davies company too?

It was churning her up inside and there was no one to discuss it with. After last night, Alice was off limits.

Nuria emerged from her tent next—her eyes were puffy, like she had been crying, and again she wouldn't meet Kim's eye, or respond to her attempt at a "Good morning!" She wandered off into the woods a little way to perform her ablutions, and Kim felt a wave of hopelessness, of helplessness—at least when you were climbing a mountain, you felt like you were part of a team, your group all pulled together to triumph over adversity. Here went nothing.

"You're a good woman," said Sue, somewhat unexpectedly.

Kim coloured. "I'm doing my best. Most we can do at the moment."

Sue finished off the last of her tea and looked around.

Alice was still in her tent, Nuria a little way off. "You don't think these are extraordinary circumstances?"

Kim frowned. "Well, obviously, but why should that matter?"

"When do you think it becomes every man for himself?"

Ah. "Not at all, for me. This is the point of my being here, to look out for all of you. I don't intend to stop."

"It wasn't your fault," said Sue gently.

Kim twisted her head, and looked over towards the tents. "It wasn't hers, either." She wasn't talking about Helly, but about Alice. Sue might have said something in response, but the front flap of the second tent opened and Alice herself appeared.

"Is there any hot water left?"

Kim said, "Enough for a cuppa," and went forward to take the mug that Alice proffered. She didn't want to look Sue in the eye.

*   *   *

IF ANY OF them had thought that Alice would have been given a wake-up call by that argument the previous night they were entirely mistaken: having articulated her case in front of an audience, it now seemed to have solidified in Alice's head into something that, in her mind, could only be the truth—a truth that was evidently too hot for the likes of Sue Aitken to handle.

Alice still held in her pocket the little fourteenth-century coin they had found in the charred remains of the hut. It was proof of something, or that was what it felt like—proof that people had either lived here or passed through, and more recently than the fourteenth century, given where they had found it. Alice was a historian, which meant that part of her wanted that connection to people over the centuries, people who would never and could never meet and yet still had something in common with each other. Now she had that feeling of connection, and she was clinging to it.

The trouble was that she was more connected to those imagined people than to the ones in front of her. Her mind was somewhere else. None of them could reach her. Kim handed the mug back, now with a teabag floating in it, and Alice was already distracted, already elsewhere.

Nuria came back over. When she was back within earshot, Sue said, "Now we're all here."

Nobody said anything.

"I decided last night," said Sue. "After our *conversation*." She leaned on the word. "I'm going back the way we came. You don't have to, none of you have to do anything—and of course I'm not in charge here. But I'm not going another step forward."

Kim said, "You can't go back alone."

"If I have to, I have to. I've made my decision."

Alice said, "But look, Sue—all the trees are here that were here last night."

Sue looked like Alice had just thrown a brick at her. "See? That's it. That's why I'm going back. You've cracked and I'm not going any further just because you tell me to. My job was to check the accuracy of the maps. Fine. They're not accurate. I can't do anything more without a lot of backup and some instruments that actually work."

Kim said, "We'll be—"

"We won't be out faster this way. She's lying to you. All along she's been lying to you. There's something not right about this place, and even if it's not some kind of, some kind of fucking portal to Narnia or something, it's enough that the whole place has been cordoned off. It's dangerous. I'm not walking towards it, and I'm certainly not because *she* told me to. We should have gone back yesterday, if you ask me."

Alice said, "In case you've not noticed, Sue, I've not been in charge of direction since yesterday morning. I thought we were already trying to leave?"

"Don't pin this on me. How many times have I said we should be trying to retrace our steps?"

Kim said, "It's more dangerous if you go alone. It's safer to stick together."

Nuria said, "Sue. Don't do this. Please, don't do it."

"Then come with me. You won't, though." She rounded on Nuria. "You certainly won't, you're so far up Dr Christopher's arse that you won't even challenge her when she's got a woman murdered."

Alice said, "You think that's my fault? You think I did that to—"

"Of course you didn't," said Kim.

"I was ahead of all of you! It shouldn't have come for Helly, it should have come for me! I was the one it should have taken!"

"We all just need to calm down…"

"No," said Sue. "I've been very calm for very long—"

"You've just accused me of murder!"

"Shut up," said Kim. "Both of you. You're impossible. When things get stressful this is what happens. Save the talk 'til we get out of here. You have to, or we won't. And in the meantime, we have to pull together."

Sue looked stormy. Nuria looked like she was about to cry again.

"Great," said Kim, encouragingly. "Let's pack the tents up, then, and get ready to go." She caught Sue's eye. "I don't know which way we'll go," she said, in the steadiest voice she could manage. "But I just need you to not talk, and to pack the tents up. Alice and Nuria, you take the other one." Sue tried to say something but she said, "Shelve it. Just for ten minutes. Shelve. It."

They took the tents down and packed up their bags. Between the low-hanging mist and the stifling atmosphere, Nuria Martins felt like she was going to choke. She could feel the choice approaching her with the speed of a train, whether she wanted it to or not. She was moving slowly, as slowly as she could possibly go. There was a lump in her throat. Alice was shooting daggers at her with her eyes, and she could barely breathe.

"Okay," said Kim—again with her most patient voice, before Sue cut in.

"I'm going back. You can't change my mind. I'm sorry, Kim, I really am."

"You believe in the Corrigal?" said Alice, with the merest hint of sarcasm. Nuria flinched.

"No. But there's something going on here and we have no chance of understanding it. I don't want to go anywhere we haven't gone already, even if it ends up taking us a few hours longer to get out. It's enough that I don't want to take the risk."

Alice nodded slowly. "But definitely science, is what you're saying."

"For god's sake," said Kim, "can you stop trying to bait her? Wait 'til we're out of here. We'll be out today. It's not that far."

Sue said to Kim, "Are you coming back with me, then?"

"Not I," said Alice, airily. "I'm going forwards."

Kim was sagging around the shoulders. "I don't know," she said. "I still say we'd be mad to split up. It's just common sense."

"It's terrorism," said Sue. "She won't go back."

"You started it."

"Please!" said Nuria, putting her hands up to her face. "You're acting like children!"

Sue rounded on her. "Are you coming, Nuria? Do you honestly believe we'll get out of here the way *she* wants to take us?"

"I'm right here, you know," said Alice. "And I have a name."

Nuria covered her eyes. "I don't know. I don't. I suppose… I'll go with Alice."

Sue made a noise of contempt.

"What if we're really close to the boundary? I just think we shouldn't give up on—"

"Sure. We're probably half an hour from the car right now."

Nuria said, acidly, "I don't do things because *you* tell me to, either. Please. I just want to get out of here. Isn't that what we all want?"

"Is it?"

"It is what I want," said Alice. "I'm not actually doing this *just* to wind you up, you know."

"Oh," said Sue, "but you are doing it to wind me up then."

"For god's sake, Sue!" said Kim.

Alice said, "I know this is bad. Believe me. I wish… we had all been able to get out of here yesterday and none of this had happened. And I do feel responsible for Helly, I do, and I'm sorry. But I really, truly believe that forward is our best way out of here."

Sue was shaking her head. There was a glint in her eyes that might have been the beginning of tears. "I believe that you believe it. But I just can't do this any more. We shouldn't have gone this way in the first place. It was a stupid idea. I should have gone back yesterday when I wanted to, and you should all have come with me. But now we're here, and we need to do the right thing."

"Is that splitting up, though?" said Kim.

"If you want to go on without me, go on without me."

Kim appealed to the others. "I can't go on without her. One alone in here is just asking for trouble."

"Don't, then," said Alice. "If you think it's right to go back, then go back. You can take the 1960s map if you want, I don't think it'll do us any good."

Nuria said numbly, "You're going back? Both of you?"

"Come with us," said Sue. "You don't have to stay here."

"Then I'd be alone," said Alice, "and Kim would come with me, right?"

Kim didn't say anything, but shook her head.

"Alice is right," said Nuria. "I wish it wasn't true, too.

But we can't go back, even if we want to. You've tried navigating in this place. We're already lost. You'll only end up going the wrong way again."

Alice was nodding now, as if Nuria had said something incisive in a tutorial. "That's what I'm saying." Nuria shot her a look.

"I guess that's that, then," said Sue, and she picked up her rucksack and slung it, in an ungainly movement, onto her back. "I think we'll take our chances just like you will. And the best of luck to you."

Kim's face was a picture; she looked like all of this was tearing her apart. "You understand, though, don't you?" she said to Nuria.

"I get it. Do what you have to do."

Kim said to Nuria. "You're going to be okay?"

Nuria met her eye, because she was supposed to, and that was how this went, to the extent that anything like this was supposed to happen at all. "We'll be fine. We'll see you out at the end, anyway. It might just take a few more days for some of us." She didn't believe it. It was hard to tell if Kim did.

They all picked up their bags, and stomped out the fire, and Sue and Kim went back the way they had come from the previous evening—or the way they thought they had come from, at least—and Alice and Nuria went in the opposite direction.

And all was quiet again in the woods, at least for a little while. Alice wanted to say something, to thank Nuria for showing this faith in her even when she might not have strictly deserved it, but Nuria didn't seem to want to talk and so she said nothing.

Nuria's stomach was a ball of cold iron and anxiety. She had made the wrong decision. They would never make it out of here. That was how a large part of her felt, and yet she had studied the maps, she knew that this forest could not possibly be so large that they wouldn't come out of the end of it sooner or later. Alice knew it better than anyone and if she said they were going to find a way out, they'd make it out eventually, despite Nuria's misgivings. She held back her tears out of sheer, desperate professionalism, and when Alice sped up again and strode forward Nuria followed along in her wake, and tried to let the loneliness and fear stream through her and disappear off in a trail behind them. Whatever was going on, she had no power over it. All she had to do was keep going, keep her head down, go where she was told.

If there was some kind of supernatural creature or pagan monster stalking them through Moresby Forest, it must be able to smell them a mile off. If that was true, it would certainly know where they were by now anyway. But that was the least of Nuria's problems.

Alice up ahead had her right hand shoved in her pocket. She was on the alert, looking from left to right all around them as she steered their course to the north.

"North-east," Nuria called out. "We ought to be steering more to the east." When Alice turned around she pointed further out to their right. "It's more that way isn't it? Unless I've lost track."

"North-west," said Alice.

"Is that not further in?"

Oh no. Oh please no I was already regretting this...

Alice pulled her hand out of the pocket of her jacket, and

held it out. In her palm was the little fourteenth-century coin, misshapen and tarnished but still recognisable, the head of King Edward still unmistakable for people who had seen it before.

"What about it?" said Nuria. Her mouth was dry.

Alice's eyes were bright, as bright as they had been when the five of them had first set foot inside the boundary of Moresby Forest, two days ago. "Don't you see what this means?" And she held out the little coin, as if she was expecting Nuria to take it.

Don't do this to me, please I'm begging you. Nuria's own hands were shaking. But instead she said, "No."

"Come on," said Alice impatiently, as if Nuria would be excited too if only she understood what was going on. "Edward III. This coin clearly belonged to Robert Moresby or his family. It's an incredible discovery."

"That hut wasn't fourteenth century. It couldn't possibly be."

"Exactly!" said Alice, ignoring everything about what Nuria was saying except for the words themselves. "This is your area of expertise even more than it's mine! Isn't this exactly what you came here for? And here's a piece of direct, actual evidence—not only that the Moresby family were here in the fourteenth century but that they weren't the only people! This is a breakthrough! We can't leave now."

"You're not listening to me."

"Well then, what?"

"People have been here recently. Maybe all the archaeology is gone."

"That's not it," said Alice, and there was no use arguing with her. "It's my theory. About the woods, and how it's actually several different woods, and that's why all the stories half-match like they do. Well, you weren't there last night, but—"

Nuria said, "I know your theory. You think the oak tree confirmed it, don't you?"

"Well, what do you think?" She didn't wait for Nuria to answer. "It's a point in its favour, surely though? I know you want to explain it some other way, but it can't be done. I've been trying for years and years and it just doesn't add up. It never did." Now she had noticed Nuria's expression. "Don't look at me like that. I'm not mad. I know they thought I was, Kim and Sue, but you understand. You've done the research. Nuria! Look at this coin!" She was proffering it now to Nuria, who took it from her with great discomfort.

Nuria held the little coin between finger and thumb. It was still warm.

"We've got to go further in," said Alice. She had managed to curb the desperation in her voice. She sounded, disconcertingly, like she was suggesting a logical course of action in the circumstances.

And after all what was there to do now? What choice did Nuria Martins even have any more? The others were far too far away now, so there was no longer any real chance that she could turn around and catch them up.

Overhead, the canopy of trees seemed to be bearing down on them, steering them forwards. Out of the corner of her eye, something flickered, or moved. When she turned to see better what it was, there was nothing there.

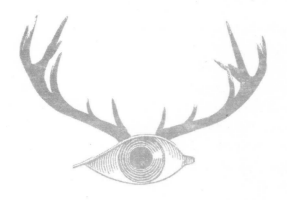

CHAPTER SIXTEEN

The Deserter

IT WAS A few hours into the morning of the third day, and Sam Harper felt like he had been inside this forest for weeks. He was beginning to forget what a blue sky even looked like, or a horizon not covered over by trees as far as he could see. Harper had grown up on the Kent coast. He was used to seeing the sea, the comforting edge of the world that it represented every day of his life, the solidity and distance of the horizon. Nothing could hide next to that; here, there could be anyone or anything yards away in any direction.

He had his pipe out while he walked. He and the captain had made the mutual, unspoken decision that the best way to deal with the present predicament was to smoke their entire remaining supply of shag. Harper wouldn't have done it if Davies hadn't started first –

the smell of cheap tobacco probably followed them half a mile back in the direction they had come from, just in case any wandering devils had happened to lose track of them.

But since he wasn't the only one, he wasn't going to object to it, and the tobacco surely helped to calm his racing heart and his nerves which were in shreds. Five of them left, and three more of their comrades left to rot where they lay or be eaten by animals. He wouldn't have thought himself capable of leaving men like that, not even anywhere close to a battlefield. And yet the fear had been real, and there was nothing any of the survivors could have done for them.

He thought again of Richard Jessop, biding at the bottom of that tree the day before, watching them leave him behind with drooping eyelids and blood still oozing from his chest. He'd had the stink of death about him already, poor Jessop. Maybe they all did.

There was another odd thing out here: they'd not seen a single living deer since they'd entered these woods. There had been that carcass, of course, with the slashes of some great claw down it, but otherwise not a pheasant, not so much—not that he'd been looking terribly hard—as a rabbit. They'd heard birds, of course, but they must have been good at hiding, because he'd not laid eyes on one. That being said, if he were a bird he'd not want to get too close to this horrible lot either. Sweet Jesus, how were there only five of them left now?

If he got out of here, he'd be glad to head north. He hadn't thought he would be—marching towards a place you were going to fight in was never much fun but it was at least easier than the battlefield itself—but Harper preferred the overwhelming clamour, the physical exhaustion, even the smells of war to a place like this. Here, the mists and the shadows blended into each other so that it was hard enough to tell which was which, and you could make out and distinguish the breathing of every single individual you travelled with.

They walked faster today than they had the previous day; there had been more injured men to slow them down then, and now they were fewer and fitter—and also more set upon keeping moving. They were heading what was probably due north, or near enough—they hadn't found the river again since veering away from it yesterday morning, and navigating by the sun was still a fool's errand in weather like this.

By and by, there was a faint sound off the way ahead of them, off to what was probably more or less the north-west. It was a crackling, as of something moving through the undergrowth, and five men stopped dead in their tracks.

There was nowhere about them to hide, no trees easily climbable, no clear direction in which they might be able to sprint. Captain Davies drew his sword, and Harper couldn't help but respect the man. He reached towards his own, for whatever good it would do, and there they all stood, rooted to the spot, waiting for whatever they had heard to come to them.

They heard the sounds of it getting closer before they saw any physical sign of it—whatever it was, it was not troubling to keep itself quiet. That was a good sign; it wasn't stalking them, at any rate, and it might not even know they were there. Harper relaxed his hand on the hilt of his sword, and saw Davies do likewise. And then there was audibly ragged breathing, and the creature in the distance swore quietly, and Byrne said, "I know that voice."

Davies said, "What?"

Byrne broke away from the group, plunged forward through thick fern, and a moment later called back, "Get over here! Now!"

He had found one of the men who had deserted in the night—he'd found Roberts. Against all the odds, it was one of their own, alive, in this place that swallowed men whole.

Roberts looked bad. He looked like by rights he ought not still be alive at all. There were gashes across his face as if something had clawed at him—his right eye seemed to be so full of blood that it trickled down his face like tears. His left arm was gone completely from about the elbow downwards—though it was hard to tell the exact point of the amputation. When he saw Davies and the men approach, his gasping sobs descended into groans that made Harper suspect he had several broken ribs under his leather jerkin.

Byrne got to him first and knelt down beside him, wiping the blood off his face with a scrap of rag. Roberts was still gurgling sobs as he registered their presence above him.

Catching up, Davies said, "Roberts. Roberts! Where are the others, man?"

It was hard for Roberts to even speak. Harper said, "Who's got water? Anyone?"

Cadwell passed his skin forward; there was not a lot left, but Harper unstoppered it anyway and Roberts tried in between slack-jawed grimaces to gulp some of it down.

"Where did the others go?" said Davies irritably. "And how did you get here at all?"

"Can't it wait, sir?" said Byrne, but Harper shook his head.

"I doubt it. Come on, Roberts. You can do it."

"There was something... The trees... kept moving... in the distance... I tried to get back..."

"The trees kept moving?" said Byrne. "The oak tree?"

Harper said, "That's not what he's saying. Haven't you seen it too?"

"What about the others?" said Davies sharply. "Are they out there too?"

But Roberts could not or would not say. It was hard to blame him at this point. A little bubble of blood came out of the corner of his mouth and popped pathetically, spattering onto Harper's hand which still held the empty water skin. "Where are the rest of you?" he gasped.

What could they tell him? Harper said, "It got them." And Roberts said nothing, but Harper thought he understood. His shoulder sagged a little and his ragged gasping calmed.

"Go slowly," said Davies. "Everyone give him some room to breathe." They all moved back a pace or two.

Through eyes still bloodied and half closed with pain and fatigue, Roberts tried falteringly to tell them what he could. "There's something out there. The watch ran. I... woke up—tried to go after them, but I lost them. I came back but you weren't there. All round that tree, you'd left without me."

His voice was getting slurred now. A chill breeze spread over where the little group knelt.

Harper felt something constrict in his throat.

"Don't go in," whispered Roberts.

"In where?" said Davies, at the same time as Stiles's eyes widened.

"The cave..." Roberts lifted a shaking finger—on his left hand, and they all grimaced and tried not to imagine where his severed right hand might now be—and pointed away from them. Blood spattered the ground behind him in that direction; Roberts had dragged his way laboriously here with the last of his strength. The trees were too thick to see if there was a cave beyond them, although it did appear that after a few dozen yards the way curved downhill again.

Stiles said, very quietly, "What's there?" and the dying man looked at him. Roberts was young, twenty or twenty-one at most. He might have been Stiles's older brother—in the weeks past they had got along well enough, had similar enough taste in jokes.

He said, "I don't remember. I'm sorry." He was blinking blood from his eyes again, and it was indecent to watch.

Harper felt that knot in his throat tighten. He couldn't look at any of them. He couldn't breathe.

Cadwell said, "Whichever way we go is in, isn't it? There is no out, or away."

"I mean it. Don't go inside. Whatever's in there, it's worse than this." Roberts tried to lift his head a little and winced, and saw his own right arm again and seemed about to retch—except that he had no strength left with which to do it.

There was only stunned silence, as he bled out onto the ground in front of them. After a while he said, "Don't wait for me. Try to get out of here." But none of them moved.

Byrne said, "We'll wait for you." A sort of fatalism had settled over them now, the last five men and this one other who shouldn't by rights have made it even this far.

"I remember something," said Roberts, and now his eyes were fully closed. He was starting to slur his words, so that they had to pay attention to really be able to tell what he was saying. "I think. In the trees, or maybe in the… Very dark eyes, like the spots when you blink by candlelight."

"I've seen it," said Stiles. "It's true. What you say is true."

Cadwell said, "Behind the line, when Alwood disappeared.

It was there."

The creases around Roberts's eyes and nose were caked with rusty brown. He had stopped shivering now. "I thought so. Promise you won't—you won't… go… in."

Byrne took his hand, and rubbed the back of it with his thumb. Maybe his mother had taught him to do it.

If any of them had been looking around them in the trees of the middle distance, they might have seen that flickering, once or twice, as if the trunks of far-off trees were the flames of candles, casting light intermittently on whatever they were near to, and occasionally lighting up something completely different. They would have seen the greenery grow and shrink before their eyes, sometimes far, sometimes closer, less like trees themselves and more like the reflections of trees on water. And maybe if they had seen those, then the ground beneath them would have felt less solid, more changeable, or negotiable, and they would have caught sight maybe two or three hundred yards away of the mouth of a cave in the woods, flickering in and out of sight, just every now, every then.

But they were all looking elsewhere, attending to their dying friend. The only one who might have seen anything was Captain Davies. And if he did, which was far from certain, he said nothing.

And that was the end. Harper found that his mind was roaming, trying to keep him as far away from the present as it could manage go, and he was pulled back in only by Byrne leaning forward and closing Roberts's eyes for the last time. The rest of them had their hands clasped together in front of them, as if in prayer, and they were looking at Harper like they were expecting him to follow suit. If Roberts had had any last words, he hadn't heard them. The other woods were right there, and it was much easier to stay in them, and hard enough to come back, even if only for a short while.

He bobbed his head respectfully, and cleared his throat to reassure them that he was still here among them and hadn't yet disappeared entirely. It seemed somehow unfair to try and bury Roberts when they had left the others where they lay this morning—not to mention the men still mouldering on the side of Sibbert Hill from two days before. Not that any of them really had the strength left to do it. Death had followed them around in the last few days, and it was only now that they were starting to be able to put some kind of face to it. A shadowy face, with eyes like the dark spots you see when you're trying to block the rest of the world out. Whatever Roberts had seen, and whatever sliced him up so thoroughly, he would see it no more.

"I can see the cave," said Davies. "Which of you can see it too?"

They all looked in the direction Roberts had pointed. It was, through the trees, a smooth hillside—and then it wasn't, and then it was again.

A forceful sound, and then spattering beside them. Bill Stiles had thrown up.

CHAPTER SEVENTEEN

A Familiar Place

ALICE CHRISTOPHER AND Nuria Martins, crashing their way through the depths of Moresby Forest as it had always been ordained that they would do. Breathing the same air as the quarry whose stories they sought—now not only the elusive company of Captain Alexander Davies, but also that fourteenth-century family of whom they had only heard second or third hand. The Moresbys had been here too, six hundred years ago, the only recorded people in a thousand years to have survived inside these woods for any length of time.

Of course, now it was clear that the Moresbys were not, in fact, the only people ever to have lived in this place. The little hut seemed to prove that, apart from anything else. But whoever the hut had belonged to, they had left so little trace of themselves that they might as well not exist.

Were they still in the woods somewhere? What had they even been doing here in the first place?

All of this served to galvanise Alice. What if there was a link to the Davies group in here too? Moresbys or no Moresbys, that was really what she was interested in, the thing she most wanted to know. What if it turned out that there was more to be known about the Davies group, and people alive who knew it? There were answers here. There had to be. And she was so tantalisingly close to them now, that it could only be a matter of time before she made some kind of huge discovery. She would answer all of the questions; she would amaze everyone—she would be the one to solve this impossible puzzle, to prove everyone wrong. Everyone who'd had no faith in her, who'd denied her funding, a platform, an opportunity to prove herself. She walked faster, with purpose, casting about in all directions for the answer that had to be coming.

Nuria could see all of this writ large on Alice's face, and it didn't give her any confidence at all. She too saw the implications of what they had found, and saw that they were fraught with danger, that they led as far as a cliff over which she could not see. That was what Alice was striding towards with such haste and enthusiasm. They were going to pitch themselves over the edge if they weren't careful, and if they hadn't already done so.

This place was not of nature, and it became more unnatural the further into it they went. Before, there had been sudden gaps in the mist or else flashes of colour where she least expected it. It had made her feel sick. Now there was more of it, though—enough that she could see what was happening. It was the wood itself, or rather it was both of the woods, splintering through each other, appearing and disappearing without warning. Dark fir trees replaced deciduous ones, only to disappear again, like a page in a book turned over too quickly. Glittering sunlight appeared in two square feet of ferns up ahead, and was gone again. One tree became a sapling, then immediately returned to its full-grown size. It was no trick of the light. That much was certain. There were two woods here, or even more, overlaid on top of each other, and it would be completely crazy to imagine if Nuria didn't now see it with her own eyes. She had to watch where she was putting her feet, because occasionally the gradient of the ground would shift without warning, and every time it did she recoiled and nearly lost her balance, and something dropped again in her stomach. The further they went, the more she felt lightheaded, with each footstep unable anew to precisely estimate the weight of her own body. And the intermittent sunlight sparkled and the nausea trembled in the back of her throat.

Occasionally the flickering would subside, and she could almost manage to convince herself that it hadn't happened at all, that it had been her imagination, gone wild from fear and lack of sleep. And yet whenever it happened again, in that moment it somehow felt right. If you walk somewhere long enough, that place makes its own kind of sense. Foul weather walked in long enough feels like it covers the whole world. This was the same.

The wood curved around them, forming and reforming, shaping and reshaping, changing just enough to left and right that it narrowed the options of the directions they could walk in. If the direction was imposed on them, though, all their considerable forward momentum came from Alice, or so thought Nuria, except that as soon as she thought it she realised that the terrain wasn't exactly flat—it went almost imperceptibly downhill. They were tipping forwards. Just a little.

A thick carpet of damp leaves coated the ground, obscuring the extent of it, springy when they walked on it and crunching quietly underfoot. Once she had noticed it, though, it became much more difficult *not* to notice, nor to feel propelled forward by something, or hurried along.

That implied intention on the part of the wood—on something's part, at least. Of course there was no such thing. But whatever was going on, surely the right thing was to turn around and go back the opposite way. That's what all the others had done. Whatever this was, it was getting worse the further they went in this direction. The response to that should not be the one Alice was exhibiting. That was how you got yourself killed.

They were heading towards an epicentre, and it wasn't hard to work out what that was. The monsters people had feared in the seventeenth century, in the fourteenth, were real, even if they were nothing like the stories made them out to be. There was no Corrigal in here. No creature called the Corrigal existed. It was only the wood, cramming two of itself into too small a place, falling apart at the seams, pouring itself into a space where it could not fit. The legend of the Corrigal was only a way to understand that. So what did that mean about its nest?

"Doesn't that make sense too?" she said to Alice, trying to keep her voice steady—it was wavering so much she feared it was unintelligible. "It's like your theory, except it's worse, and we shouldn't be trying to walk into it. Please, Alice, let's not—"

But Alice's smile only grew, and her eyes shone, and she said, "I knew you'd see! Think of the papers, Nuria!"

"We won't get to write any papers at this rate," Nuria said, and she held up the little coin which she still carried. "Isn't this enough? For the first time at least? We could try sending the coin for lab analysis, then come back."

Alice faltered, or Nuria thought she did. "We can do all those things, I suppose. No. They're important, I know they are. But you know how long it took me to get here the first time—what do you think our chances are of getting to come back? We have to take this opportunity while we have it."

"But I don't want to," Nuria said. "I want to go home. I want to finish my thesis. I want to see my family again." She wanted to ask, *What if we can't find our way out*, but one look at Alice's face told her what the answer would be. "You don't care, do you?"

Alice put a motherly hand on Nuria's shoulder. "Don't lose your nerve. It's going to be okay. We can find out together."

"You aren't listening to me."

"I am, and I know you're scared. I understand. But anyone could read books in a library, and we're the only people who could possibly discover the answer to the mystery of this place. The only people in all of history!" She tilted her head to one side. "It's hard, I know it is. But we must make the most of the lives we have."

Nuria shrank back. "I want to see my mum again. My little brother. I just want to go home."

But Alice had no siblings, and Nuria knew for a fact that her mother had died ten years back, and even if neither of those things had been true she would still not have listened, would have kept walking forwards, even as Nuria tried to get her to slow down.

The forest around them flickered again, not just up ahead but around where they stood, and a little way off to the left.

Alice said, "Did you see that?"

"See what?" said Nuria in despair.

"It was the oak tree! The one we camped under the other night! I swear it, I'm not kidding. It was definitely there. Wait, hang on. Let's see if it comes back." She flashed Nuria another smile. "Maybe we'll know where we are after all."

Maybe they would. Maybe they'd spent two days walking in circles. But Nuria didn't hold out much hope.

They stayed there for thirty minutes or so waiting, eating cereal bars and watching for more changes. But although other parts of the wood much further off appeared and were gone like bizarre flashes of lightning illuminated them and then hid them again, the huge oak tree did not reappear. More and more Nuria felt like the ground was tilted at an angle, or else that they were circling some gigantic plughole, round and down, their hopes of making it back out diminishing by the minute.

After a while, Alice got itchy feet and suggested they move on. Nuria hoped beyond hope that she was joking. She was not. They started walking again, and Nuria felt the freezing, silent tears fall down her face and wondered not why but how she was managing to do this to herself. It was colder now, especially for so early in the year. She found herself starting to shiver.

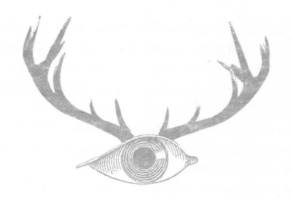

CHAPTER EIGHTEEN

The Mouth Of The Nest

THE MOUTH OF the cave had not appeared to be very far away when they had all been crowded around the fallen Roberts. They didn't know why they had all decided to go to it, except that it was by silent consensus, and if any man had another suggestion he didn't make it known. But as they tried to make their way towards it, it turned out to be further away than it looked—or at least it took them a long time to get not very far in its direction. True, they were slowed down by Davies and Stiles, who were the ones with the most significant injuries, but even for all that their progress was slow. The cave itself was extremely well camouflaged, which was to say that Harper found he could see it only a fraction of the time—not more than occasional glimpses, in fact, of the place where a shadow and an overhang suggested that the mouth of a cave might be. If there hadn't been periodic smears of blood or bashed-up and trampled greenery that marked the path that the injured Roberts had taken,

he might have been quite easily convinced that they were going in the wrong direction. But there was no mistaking it: even if that little overhang that he alternately could not find and then spotted again was not in fact the entrance to the Nest, the trail of blood told no lies.

They were further impeded by the fact that the clouds were threatening rain again: in the last hour the sky had darkened although it could not be much later than midday. At any moment Harper expected to feel the first fat raindrops on his face. They would be soaked again, sooner or later—as soon as it came.

They were definitely heading towards the Nest of the Corrigal now, there was no trying to deny it. If he'd thought they had a chance of getting out of here alive, he might have wanted to, but as it was he found himself strangely resistant to the idea. If they could find whatever the creature was—for a creature he now very much believed there was—that had been stalking them, then maybe they could kill it or at the very least maim it so that its chances of killing more unwary folk were lessened. The thought came into his mind from nowhere, and as soon as it did he realised how stupid it sounded. To kill something centuries old? Maybe not, after all. But he at least wanted to lay eyes on it, to know for sure what it looked like.

He said to Stiles, "It definitely knows we're here." As soon as the words were out of his mouth he realised that nobody else had been talking, that he had broken a silence that was nearly complete—only the faintest breeze, the dullest footsteps, and Davies wheezing quietly, trying to keep the pain of walking to himself.

Stiles nodded.

"So there's no reason for you not to say its name, and tell us everything you know. However little. What do they say in the villages?"

Stiles said, "I suppose." He sounded tired.

"Say the name," said Davies.

Stiles stopped walking. Really, they were hardly closer at all to the entrance of the cave. And yet where was the spot on which Roberts's body lay? Way back, surely. "Must I say it?"

"Yes. Go on. That's an order."

The trees seemed to hold their breath.

"What will you do," said Stiles, "shoot me in the head?"

The captain stared at him. Then, "No. Let's keep moving."

Byrne said, "What Roberts said, did that match up with the stories?"

Stiles said, "You must understand, no one comes out here. No one that I ever knew of, and I don't know anyone who ever did. They told the stories to scare us out of coming in here. I don't know if they were true. My uncles all swore by them, but…"

"There must have been someone here," said Harper. "Did they come from the north, whoever stayed in that place?"

"It's no one from round our parts or that I've ever heard of, they wouldn't dare. That's what I'm trying to tell you. We all know you shouldn't ever come this way. But who knows what they tell each other in other villages. The only people I've ever heard of living here are the Moresbys, and that was three hundred years ago."

Harper cut in. "What happened to them?"

"All I know is, they went into the forest, or so we were always told, because Robert Moresby wanted claim some of the land for himself. They were supposed to have all died in here. Except for Essie, the daughter. And that's just what I... Robert Moresby was supposed to have burned charcoal."

Davies sucked air through his teeth. "That's a mighty coincidence."

"I know, but lots of people do in these parts. I've been thinking about it. We'd know if there were still Moresby descendants—they'd have to come out of the woods occasionally, wouldn't they? Even to sell the charcoal?"

Harper said, "And you didn't think that was worth mentioning?"

"To Sergeant Thatcher?"

Byrne said, "I want to know what happened."

"I'll tell you what my brother told me... The story is that something happened to Essie Moresby. The darkness got to her, and her father killed her to stop it spreading. Then the plague came, and the mother was taken by it, or something worse. And after that whenever the Moresby men came out of the wood they seemed changed. Their eyes were darker and their arms were longer, and they breathed like the plague had found them and yet didn't die. They say Essie Moresby met something in the deep, dark woods, and that she talked with the old gods, and whatever it was spoke to her convincingly enough that she sacrificed her family to them one by one. And in the end the only one they ever saw again was Essie, and she was a witch."

He was looking about to left and right now, and his face was very red. Was it the effort of walking? Some of it, at least.

"You don't believe it, though," said Cadwell.

"My brother never believed it. The story changes when you get older—they tell the little ones a monster got the Moresbys, then when you're a bit older they say it's the plague that got them. Then when you're nearly grown, they tell you they invited the evil into their hearts, and finally," he licked his lips, "finally your father sits you down and tells you it was true the first time, that whatever is in this place is a monster and it'll devour your soul because it knows where you are the moment you set foot in here and the witch'll tell it to. My brother never believed them, but we all thought he was showing off. And, look, weren't they all right? Such an old story and it was right all along."

"And the creature is… it?" said Davies. Harper realised he wasn't saying its name either. So much for bravery. They were still clambering over rocks and wading through ferns but seemed to be getting no closer to the little outcropping. A thought gripped him: maybe this wasn't where they were supposed to be going, after all. He faltered.

Stiles said, "You can feel it, can't you? Something's got inside your head. I think it got to Francis when we were still out on the hill." He sounded more regretful than anything else now, and a little resigned.

Harper said nothing, although a sliver of doubt crept into his mind. The thoughts, after all, didn't feel terribly characteristic of him.

"Don't let it win." Stiles's footing seemed surer now; it sounded as if he was repeating something that had been told to him. "Let it crack its teeth on you, and the spirit of the Lord run through you."

Cadwell and Byrne both crossed their arms.

The rocky outcrop was closer now—they were making progress after all, it was just that they were in a particularly overgrown patch with a hidden slope in both directions. The marks made by Roberts coming in this direction were still occasionally visible, which meant that they were definitely going the right way, but Harper found himself wondering again why Roberts had chosen the path that he had. Something gets into your head, maybe. And sends you down and up a hill? Well then.

He found that it was easier to keep knowing where the cave was if you didn't try and stare right at it or keep your eye on it, for if you did then the landscape around it would seem to pulsate, to grow and shrink and twist, and the ground beneath you would start to feel like the swell of an ocean. And if you didn't blink for long enough it would be worse, for just on the edge of your sight the shadows began to grow and—he blinked. Gone again. It was better that way. Better to cast about, not to look too hard at any one thing, to keep a general idea of everything around you to either side. If that meant you had to search for the cave again every now and then, so be it.

Next to him Davies was frowning. His breathing was heavier, and his gait grew more and more lopsided as the way turned uphill. He must be in some considerable pain now. There was nothing to be done to make it better. They had long since finished whatever drink they had left. By and by the air smelled damper, muddier, and the threatened rain began to fall intermittently but heavily. Still they walked on.

When finally they came to the spot with the outcropping of rock, they saw immediately—and almost to Harper's surprise—that they had come to the right place. It was smaller than the height of a man—maybe four feet high and six wide, with a little cavern back behind the opening that went into the side of the hill. Of course, they could only see that when they got close to it: from the approach it looked pitch black in the spattering rain and the little remaining mist that shimmered around it—like the spots you saw behind your eyelids when you closed them, or like the socket of an eye, protruding from the very rock. Empty, of course. Harper thought, *Is that where I have to go, if I want to see it?*

It wasn't that it looked at all dangerous—on the contrary, in fact; in the rain it looked perfectly normal and rather cosy, the sort of place you would absolutely choose to shelter from the elements if you found it inside an ordinary wood. But they were on their guard, besides which there was a thick smear of blood at one corner of the opening, sticky and browning, that could only have come from Roberts. The remains of his missing arm were not anywhere obvious.

Byrne said, hesitantly, "He said not to go in."

"There's nothing in it." But Davies still did not make any movement to get closer to it than ten feet away.

Cadwell shivered. "With respect, sir, if Roberts said don't go in, I see no reason to doubt his word."

Byrne said, "He did seem like he knew what he was talking about." He was looking at the bloodstain again.

"I'm going in," said Davies. He was looking at the bloodstain too. "I won't make you if you won't follow me. Do whatever you have to do. But I'm going in there."

"Why?" said Byrne.

Davies hesitated. "I want to know. And besides, I can't walk all the way out of here, look at me." Even under the rain, he was sweating.

Harper thought of Jessop again, and of Thatcher saying "Who's with me?", and knew in his heart that he would be following the captain in.

Cadwell said, "They won't believe that when we get to York." They stared at him.

"Well then I don't know what I can tell you. Will you come with me?"

Cadwell shook his head. He looked like he might be about to vomit.

"Billy, I'm not going to make you. You've been brave enough."

Stiles looked guilty. Relieved.

"Harper? Byrne?"

Byrne was rubbing at the stubble on his chin like he thought it might come off completely. "I don't want to go in there." There was a whiff of some smell from the entrance to the cave. It was damp, mouldering, earthy. Like mushrooms left too long for eating.

"Harper?"

Nothing but the drip of rain, and a silence that stretched out a moment too long. Then, "I'll come with you."

He wasn't expecting Davies to show such relief, but there it was. They had travelled together a long time now, fought together almost as long. "Are you sure, Sam?"

He wanted to say, *it's not for you. Not really.* I just want to know… what it was I saw. If I saw anything at all. "I'm sure."

"Wait," said Byrne. "We should eat something, before you go."

"Have you got anything?"

But none of them had any more. What little food there had been had been left at their makeshift encampment in the morning. There was nothing left.

In the end they shook hands awkwardly, and the three who were staying behind looked more shocked than the ones who were leaving.

Harper couldn't feel his fingertips. If anyone had asked him he would have told them he was going by his instinct, but it wasn't strictly true. His instincts were telling him that this was the end of something, that he was walking into an ending in an attempt to—what? To catch sight of something invisible? To understand?

It was easier to think of it as a duty, in the depths of this dark and dangerous place. A duty to try to find out, to bear witness to something that had brought with it death, and no explanations. He didn't think he'd have had the guts to do it if Davies hadn't volunteered first, but now that the situation presented itself, he couldn't very well refuse it.

The cave looked small, nothing to be afraid of, it didn't look like it was big enough to contain any surprises. But that was no guarantee of anything. There was a whole hill, and more, that could be in there. For all they knew, it might lead into the depths of Hell itself. Well, he would find out soon enough, wouldn't he?

The captain went first, stepping over the threshold like he was stepping onto the deck of a boat—gingerly, checking that the ground beneath him wasn't going to immediately give way. And it didn't, because it was only a normal little cave like you'd find on the side of any number of hills, so he brought his other foot in too and put his weight carefully down. It was fine. Two days ago he'd not have bothered to be nearly so careful. He looked to left and right, and then ducked his head under the entrance way and did it again. Then he said, "Ah, I see how this is."

There was a tunnel in the back of the cavern, off to the right. It was strange that it couldn't be seen from the outside because further in it was plain as day, sloping gently downwards in a sort of corridor. He took a few steps towards it.

"Here," said Cadwell to Harper, and he handed him a stub of tallow candle, maybe two inches thick and three tall, with the wick carefully pinched out.

"Where did you get this?"

"A church near Coventry. But you'll need it more than we will."

Harper took it for the gesture it was. He cast about. Every stick on the forest floor was soaked through and useless, but between them they had flint, and tinder, and after a little fumbling the stub was lit and burned with a tall, smoky flame.

Then he set foot over the threshold into the cave. The candle sputtered in his hand—some inconsistency in the wick. And almost immediately he felt the panic settle on his shoulders. There was a hissing in his ears, which might have been because of the candle and the rain, or might have come from inside his own head.

He looked across at Davies for reassurance, but Davies was already using the meagre light from the candle to squint further down the corridor of rock. It appeared to be natural, occurring from a faultline in the hill rather than being obviously carved by men.

"Godspeed," said Sergeant Harper, and the little group saluted him.

"Go well, man," said Byrne.

"Still sure about this?" said Davies.

He wasn't, not at all and increasingly so. But he went anyway.

CHAPTER NINETEEN

Over The River

IT WAS UNSEASONABLY cold now, especially for the beginning of September. Nuria was not dressed for it, and not even the warmth generated by walking as swiftly as they were could compensate for it. There was a chilly wind that seemed to run right through her thin knitted hat and made her feel like she had wet hair. She was not used to it and didn't like it—it made it harder to think, and Nuria's brain was working on overdrive right now.

She had lost count of the number of times in the last few hours that she had asked Alice to stop, or slow down, or at least just consider the possibility of turning around and going back, and coming back another time. Sometimes she must have just had the conversation in her own head, because Alice was nearly ten yards ahead of her a lot of the time, and she didn't pay any mind to Nuria or her discomfort. She wasn't arguing back any more, or even giving lip service to the fact that Nuria had addressed her.

A couple of times—and this was the only way Nuria had yet found to get Alice's attention—Nuria had halted altogether, forcing her supervisor to stop and turn around.

"Why are you back there still?"

"Because you're not listening to me at all! Why are you charging off like this? You didn't when the others were with us."

And Alice would look briefly guilty, and Nuria would say, "I know you don't think so, but I really, really think we should turn around and go back. Sue was right."

The second time this happened, Alice rolled her eyes. "We can't go back now. I mean we physically can't. Two forests, you see! Even if we could get out of one of them, we're too far into the other now for it to work."

"Please," said Nuria, desperately. "That doesn't make any sense. I know your gut reaction is very well developed, but mine is telling me to go back." But by that point Alice had turned around again.

She said over her shoulder, "It'll be worse if we split up. Come on, we're close. I can feel it."

And that was that. She marched on, and Nuria's options were to stay behind alone, or to be carried along in Alice's wake. There were blisters on her heels, and she was silently crying so much that her nose was stuffy and her eyes ached. But what choice did she have? She limped on, at as fast a pace as she could manage, knowing as she did that she was trying her supervisor's patience enormously. Nuria was supposed to be handing in her thesis in six weeks. That was in another world, but still some part of her was convinced that she couldn't afford to alienate Alice now.

The two woods—for there were indisputably more than one of them—were changing. Nuria was scared to blink in case something changed irrevocably while she wasn't looking. It had been less noticeable before, when the superimposed places had the same kind of greenery in them. Now they were significantly different, and the weather was different between them as well. In one half, the oak and beech and holly that she had got used to over the last couple of days were still muffled by thick fog, that occasionally descended into spitting rain on her bare face. In the other, those trees gave way at some point in the morning to tall evergreens, less regular than the planted forests of such kind that she was used to seeing in Britain but nevertheless leaving much more room to walk. That was the reason—more than the changing gradient of the path, which seemed to have flattened out in both cases—that she had to watch where she was putting her feet. It was easy to walk into things that appeared and disappeared out from underneath her. It went beyond hallucination, and at any rate she and Alice were seeing the same things, at least when Alice paused for long enough to describe what she saw.

The evergreen forest was chilly—it was the one of the two that was noticeably colder, and looking up, Nuria could see a few patches of blue sky. A frigid wind blew in it—the most disconcerting thing was the wind appearing to rise and drop as the forest blinked in and out—and there were patches of bright sunlight scattered to left and right. By contrast the deciduous wood was quiet and dark. It smelled peatier, and the mist hung through it, so that patches of fog lit up with an eerie glow where shafts of sunlight must be further off.

To look at Alice, you might think that navigating these two places was second nature to her. Certainly she had got very good at it very quickly, and now went on ahead, dodging between the flickerings like she'd been doing it for years. If Nuria had at all been paying attention, rather than trying desperately to keep up and not plant herself face first into the endlessly shifting earth, she would have seen that it was harder than it looked. Alice dodged and weaved, trying to keep to the evergreen sections as much as possible. Nuria was doing the opposite herself: sticking to the fog-filled deciduous parts that were more familiar to her, that seemed to have more of a connection with home.

Not even Alice could deny that, however fast they were going, making progress was exhausting. After an hour and a half, they were forced to stop, panting, red-faced from the increasingly blistering cold.

"Do you have any water left?" she called back to Nuria, who now was quite some way behind. Nuria said nothing. She repeated the question: "Do you have any water?"

Nuria said, "I don't know. I'll check," and refused to do anything more until she had caught up with Alice completely. A little, turned out to be the answer, and between them they drained the rest of it, standing awkwardly in a ten-yard-wide sliver of cold, barren fir trunks, flanked by elm trees barely visible through a sea of white mist. It made a kind of corridor pointing them forwards, but then there was a fork like lightning and the corridor moved, facing ahead to the right diagonally from where they stood, and once again they were blasted by chilly air.

"What do you think is going to happen?" said Nuria.

Alice frowned. "What a strange thing to ask. I don't know, but the whole point is to find out."

"That's not the whole point of this at all. We've not found any evidence of the Davies group and we're not going to. They were never here."

"Which here?" Alice gestured around them.

"Here. This far into this wood. Either one. And even if they had been here, we're not going to find any evidence of them if you keep running off."

Alice said, uncomfortably, "I just want to know what's going on."

"But I'm here too. You're only thinking of yourself."

"That's not true at all."

"Well, you're not thinking about me, anyway."

"I just have this feeling that we're going to find something really important. And if we do, it's going to be in this direction."

"You always tell your undergraduates that intuition isn't research. I was one of them, remember?"

"Good to know you do listen to me sometimes, after all."

"But this is just your intuition. It's not evidence. We're looking for the Davies party and there's no evidence they ever came this way. I think we need to do this better. Gut instinct isn't enough. Not when the forest keeps doing *this*,"—she waved at it—"and we're completely lost, and everyone else is gone."

Alice said, "I hear what you're saying, and I'm telling you, I have been working up to this for twenty years. Twenty years of having people laugh in my face, cut my funding, snigger about me behind my back. But I was right. And soon I'll be able to prove it. Not many people do anything for twenty years straight. I'm not leaving until I have answers."

Nuria bowed her head and reminded herself: six more weeks. Six weeks until her thesis was done and defended, and then she'd never have to talk with Alice again.

They went on. At least it was a little bit slower now. But that was alright, that was marginally better, because at least Nuria wasn't alone and running to keep up. She was sore all over. Her bag was far too heavy. And now that they were definitely out of water, she was thirsty. She had a couple of paracetamol if the worst came to the worst—that would help her keep walking if she ended up desperately needing it, but it could only take her so far.

She thought about how she would get back, if she needed to. She had no idea which direction they were walking in. To be fair, she hadn't been very sure of that for most of the time they had been inside Moresby Forest; stronger personalities had taken control of the single dodgy compass, the worse-than-useless maps, the GPS unit which might as well have been a brick from the start. To begin with, she had been content with that. On any normal expedition it would be fine, a reasonable division of labour, nothing to get worried about. The day before yesterday she hadn't *needed* to know exactly which way was north and which was south at any given moment. Now it mattered much more, and she had no way of finding out: even in the parts of the wood where the sun shone through the high-up treetops there were not enough patches of sunshine, or enough shadows, for her to detect the direction they were coming from. They could be walking any which way. They could have been spiralling in on some fixed point all along and Nuria would have no way of knowing.

Nor would Alice. Was that more or less comforting? It was hard to tell.

Then they heard, under the pitter-patter of intermittent wind and drizzle, the sound of running water. It was not too far off, although it was hard to tell direction in this strange and roundabout landscape. The noise, when they identified it, seemed to cheer up Alice a whole lot.

Its source turned out to be a little creek running directly across their path, from left to right. When they had come across it before, the river had been a good six or seven feet across, which meant that this must be significantly further up towards its source: here it was only two or three feet wide. When they came right up to it, they saw that it was both deep and fast flowing, and had cut down into the ground a long way, four or five feet in places.

"Fantastic!" said Alice, and she beckoned Nuria over, and slung her bag over to the far side. "We can refill our bottles here. That'll make everything much better." She hopped over the water in one movement and bent to start rummaging in the pockets of the rucksack.

Nuria had got to the point where more than anything else she was relieved to have a chance to stay still, to get some water, and to put some fresh plasters on her swollen and shredded feet. She approached the little gorge but did not cross it, dropping her rucksack on the near side where she stood. It was a wide patch of deciduous woods; the closest flickering here was nearly fifty or so yards off. She sat down heavily.

Alice climbed down the side of the narrow gorge, managing to cover the palms of her hands and the knees of her trousers in thick gritty muck. "Pass your bottle down?" Nuria threw it, and she caught it, and when she bent down to fill it up the top of her head disappeared from Nuria's view.

It was only when Nuria sat down that she was hit by the full force of how tired she was. It wasn't just the exhaustion of walking, but of the last few months of intensive work, the last four years of sleepless nights and working weekends and listening and nodding and offering to take notes. She should have known better than to agree to come on this expedition. It had been supposed to do her some good, to get her out of the four walls of her office or even the university library. But even that had been someone else's suggestion that she'd acquiesced to, someone else's idea that she'd been talked into helping with. Even while she was packing she had felt in her heart that it was a mistake. She had too much to do. And now... an ordinary mistake might have cost her a couple of weeks of sick leave, a month or two of deferment. This was different.

She rummaged in the side pockets of her rucksack and found the little cardboard packet of paracetamol. There were six left—she'd given the rest to Helly. There again was that stab of regret in her chest.

"Have you got that water?" she called out.

There was silence for a second except for the sound of running water and gently rustling leaves, and then Alice's head appeared. She was pale, and for the first time today Nuria thought she actually looked worried. "Nuria. I'm... I don't know what to say."

Nuria's heart suddenly plummeted in her chest.

The gorge came up to Alice's shoulders at the point where she now stood, which was balanced precariously against the mud wall so as not to be swept away by the flow of water. She bent down again, then straightened up and placed an object about the size of a fist, very carefully, up onto the bank next to Nuria. It was obvious immediately what it was. Soaked through and with a thin coating of pale grey muck lay the little GPS unit. The last time she had seen it, Sue had been holding it in both hands like a talisman. Now the screen was cracked and blank, and when Nuria snatched it up and turned it over she could see that the back panel had come off and one of the AA batteries was missing.

She scrambled to the side of the cut and looked down. The water was clear, bubbling over pebbles the colour and size of horse chestnuts. There was no other evidence that anyone had been here.

She said, "Was this down there?"

"Yes. I just found it at the bottom."

"Sue wouldn't have let this out of her sight. Even if she dropped it in she'd go down and get it back. Or Kim would."

Alice screwed the lid back onto the bottle of water that she was holding. "Let's not jump to conclusions."

Nuria tried to laugh, but it came out as a kind of shriek.

"Are you joking? Are you winding me up?"

"I just think—"

"You stand right there, and *you* tell *me* not to jump to conclusions? No. No, I'm sorry, I can't do this any more."

"I'm just saying, they might not be dead. There's no evidence—"

Nuria's voice was rising. If Sue and Kim were still alive, they could probably hear her a mile away. "There's no evidence for anything here! Not one thing! And yet here we are, and here I am, because I wanted to give you the benefit of the doubt, and I didn't want to believe Professor Bell when he said you'd never cared about anyone other than yourself in your entire life."

"Alastair has had it in for me since day one," said Alice, hotly.

"And you know what? He was right! He was right about you, all along, and if I'd listened to him I'd be in a warm library right now, finishing my thesis—which you've also never given a shit about in three and a half years—and three good, brave women would still be alive!"

She was breathing hard, and there were spots in front of her eyes. Alice looked like she'd been slapped, and for a second Nuria felt a twinge of panic—had she gone too far? Despite everything, Alice still loomed large in her head, a figure of authority with blazing eyes and a razor-sharp bite. After all this, a figure to be appeased.

Then Alice said, "You think that's my fault. You're just like the rest of them."

"Do you feel no sense of responsibility at all?"

"You're calling me a murderer!"

Nuria shook her head. "This is exactly what I'm talking

about. You go after your obsessions, and they're all you can think about, and as soon as anything doesn't go your way it's every man for himself. You just completely abandon us, and it's more fool me for coming all the way out here with you, and being loyal, because when it comes down to it you don't care about me and you never have!"

Alice had scrambled back up onto the other bank. She said, "I thought you of all people would understand," and her voice was quiet and level. "None of the rest of them have any idea what it's like to spend your whole life chasing after something you know in your heart is true. To have them tell you time after time that you're taking it too seriously, you're pushing for it too hard—of course I'm pushing hard for it! In the end, knowing the truth is the only thing that matters. It's what everything else is for. Alastair has never sacrificed anything important for knowledge in his life—look at him. He wouldn't know what it *meant* to make sacrifices for your work. And the rest of the department are the same, all of them. I thought you got it, Nuria—you had the drive, the tenacity. You asked the right questions. I thought you were different. But you're just like the rest of them."

It would have broken Nuria once. She was here because she had wanted to support Alice, to impress her, to show her that Nuria was serious about her study. The knowledge that she would have been so easily bruised, that a week ago Alice Christopher telling her "I thought you were different" would have haunted her, made Alice's words feel more calculated than they almost certainly were. And yet now, Nuria found that she didn't even care. Alice Christopher's professional respect was the least of her problems. "Maybe," she said. "Maybe they don't understand you. But you don't understand them either."

"Oh, sure!" said Alice. Her arms were crossed tightly across her chest. "They care about knowing things, they're academics. But would Alastair Bell have ever seen anything like this? No. He wouldn't have the balls. He'd be running back to some cosy dig in Wiltshire before you can say the boundaries of human knowledge. Because he doesn't *really* want to know. Not properly. And you know what?" she added, buoyed along now by her own mounting outrage, "he'd have got away with it, too! He'd have gone prancing back to the Arts Council the next year, and got the same old pat on the back, and they'd give him all the titles and the grants just the same! Because it's not about the thirst for knowledge, and it never has been."

"Three women are dead! And you're grinding your axe about not getting the Winstone Grant?"

"It's not about the Winstone Grant! It's about all of them, every single one, going back years and years. And it's not even the money that matters, it's the respect. When you put your finger on something that's true, and not just true but *fascinating*, and you're just dismissed, again and again, and they don't even listen to you. I was younger than you when it started, and I've fought it my whole career. It was much worse than it is today. You'd understand if it were you."

"It is me and I don't understand," said Nuria coldly.

"Fine! Fine. That's how it is, then. Apparently. You just stay here and make your own way back. I had to get myself everywhere on my own, maybe it'll do you some good to as well. But aren't you curious? Not even a little bit?"

"I was curious at the beginning. Just not enough to get myself killed because I can't go back and wait a few more weeks."

"A few more weeks? Do you know how long it took me to get this expedition? Two and a half years. I was asking for this twenty years ago, when I was still a postdoc. I have done risk assessment after risk assessment, filled in form after form, I have sucked up to endless old men in ways you can't even imagine, and finally I got the go-ahead for five people. Have you ever done a research expedition with five people before? Eight? Anything less than half a dozen specialists? I am never going to get to do this again. It's my only chance, and it's all I have. It's all I'm ever going to get. So you can come or you can stay, whichever you like. I hoped you'd come, but..." She blinked. "Just don't tell me to go back, because this is the only chance I'm ever going to get, and I'm not going back now, for you or anyone else."

Tears were running freely down Nuria's face. She could feel them frigid on her hot cheeks. Alice was perfectly still.

"Three women are dead. You're going to die in here. We're going to die in here."

"I'm not going back. Not now I'm this close."

"Then," said Nuria, "you'll have to go without me."

A pause, while it sank in. Then Alice scrambled to her feet. Her face was completely blank, but her hand with the bottle of water in it shook. Nuria flinched, but Alice tossed the bottle across the gap next to her.

"You were a good student," she said. "I'm sorry I probably won't get to see your viva." She didn't wait for Nuria to say something back, which was probably just as well. Then she slung her bag onto her back, clipped it up, and stomped off. Onwards. Forwards. Alone.

Nuria was left alone at the top of the cut through which the little stream flowed. Water soaked into her trousers where she sat on the sodden ground. She had taken her boots off to replace the blister plasters, and had not yet put them back on. Her socks could not possibly hold any more water now, and her feet were numb with cold.

She curled up in the foetal position, as the woods flickered around her, and closed her eyes. She stayed there for a very long time, while the broken GPS unit lay inert beside her.

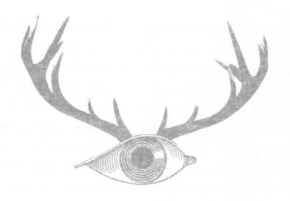

CHAPTER TWENTY

The Corrigal's Nest

CAPTAIN DAVIES WENT ahead, as the way into the cave curved downhill. Leading the charge, as Harper thought of it, although it was only the two of them. Harper was the one who held the candle, so Davies was striding ahead into darkness and his own shadow. As they went downhill, hearing the *drip-drip* of moisture on the floor and smelling cold stone, and air which had not been breathed for a very long time, the ceiling did not narrow but instead opened up over their heads. The shadows grew longer and taller, and the candle smoked up in Harper's face and into his eyes.

There was a turn in the tunnel, quite sharply to the right. As they rounded it, a gust of wind came from behind them, and the candle winked itself out. The tip of the wick glowed for a longer time than he expected, and he didn't pinch it out, but waited for it to disintegrate and dim of its own accord.

The smell of old tallow and smoke followed them down, down, down.

They walked side by side in the darkness after the candle went out, because the tunnel was now wide enough to accommodate it, and it was the easiest way of keeping track of each other. The way continued to slope downhill, but the path was not uneven—not even up the sides. Harper kept his right hand to the wall, brushing against it often to make sure he wasn't losing sight of it. Presumably Davies was doing the same on his left. And on they went, at a slow, regular pace.

It went on, the passage, for a very long time. There were no forks or breaks in it—at least not to Harper's side, and if there were any to the left then Davies didn't mention it. Harper found that this didn't worry him—even if they ended up very far underground at a dead end, they could always turn around and come back, even if neither of them seriously believed it would come to that. After a while in the darkness, their eyes became accustomed to it, and not long after that, the first wave of intense worry hit Samuel Harper, and his vision responded to it by rebelling, and exploding into acid colours. Oranges, greens, the dark reds on the back of your eyelids that usually mean you've closed your eyes in bright sunlight. He wouldn't have been too disconcerted by it if his eyes had been closed, but they were wide open, and the colours didn't look like such he would expect from a dream, or even a vision. He knew what something brightly coloured looked like when it was superimposed on his sight—like the ghost of the candle flame when it had been snuffed out in the wind. This wasn't that. This had depth, like ribbons of air in bright colours stretched out ahead of him and painting themselves up the walls, soft and undulating like smoke, merging into each other in weird and unexpected patterns but otherwise undeniably, somehow, real.

"Do you see this?" he whispered, and that was how he noticed that his mouth was extremely dry. His voice sounded quieter than he had expected, and more echoey. Maybe the ceiling above them was higher than he had realised. It could very well be true; he had no real way of knowing. At any rate, they weren't going to stop and explore.

"What *are* they?" came back Davies's response, which led him to believe that they might both be seeing things, but that they were not necessarily the same things.

But that was alright. In a perverse kind of way, that was comforting, because it meant the colours and the smoke weren't real after all. He didn't have to pay them any mind if he didn't want to.

It wasn't that he just watched them as they went past, but that was certainly one of the things he was doing while his mind wandered elsewhere. That was the way of walking, however. For Harper, at least. He thought more about life and the nature of Christendom while his feet wore through the soles of his boots than at any other time. Usually there were others around to pull him into conversation. The rhythm of the marching order was predictable and familiar, not always comfortable but to be depended upon whether you wanted to or not. This was not that, but it shared some of the same cadences. He felt it the same way in his legs, across his shoulders. Colours fluttered about him and he walked through them without feeling them touch him, and his boots took him forward.

"Why did you come here with me?" said Captain Davies, breaking the quiet. Some of the coloured smoke receded from Harper's vision.

It took him a short while to answer. "I wanted to see it. I thought maybe I could find out what it was." It sounded insubstantial, now he said it out loud—as insubstantial as everything else in here, except the slight crunch of earth underfoot and the rough wall against his fingers. "I suppose… going where you go hasn't steered me far wrong over the last few years, either."

He heard Davies snort. "I don't suppose I shall ever get out of here alive, so the chances of you doing it aren't much higher."

"Well then. Why did you come down here?"

Davies said, "Fate, I think. We've been circling this place ever since we came into these woods. No matter what way we've been thinking we're going. Longer, maybe."

"Longer?"

"The company on the hill. Do you remember what any of them looked like?"

Harper shook his head to clear it, and the shadowy lights swirled. "Dark red coats. Their arms were blue and gold."

"But faces. Any of them?"

"None."

The captain said, "We were meant to come here. And if I… do what we're meant to do, then maybe the others can get away. Maybe it'll follow us instead of them."

"You think there's something following us?"

"Can you not hear it behind us? It's been here since the candle blew out."

It was true—after they subsided into silence again Harper took to listening hard. There were other noises under the occasional dripping, and the sound of his own footsteps and breathing. Harper had never been much of a hunter—he was not even any good at fishing, and the thrill of the hunt that so often got talked about was alien to him. In the past and as he was growing up he had been more likely to be acquainted with poacher than with hunter anyway, and joining the army had hardly done anything to redress that balance. Still, he was not likely to notice any of the little signs of nearby life until someone else pointed them out, and so it didn't surprise him in the least that he hadn't heard the quiet footfalls behind him, that set of hints that told Captain Davies—by far the more experienced at spotting such things—that they were not alone down here.

His immediate urge was to stop and turn around, but he didn't. Nothing that would set it off. But what was it? What did it look like? Was this how Francis Alwood had felt, at the back of the line the previous morning, waiting for something he could not see to reach out and silently grab him?

"It doesn't understand English, surely," he said, in a half-whisper.

"I shouldn't think so," said Davies.

"Are we going to fight it?"

"It would get us long before we managed to round on it, in this place," said Davies. "We'll keep going, see how far we can get. Give the others as much time as we can."

Something that had fluttered around his chest now settled. Yes, that was what they were going to do. Maybe the others were even now fleeing, taking this chance to get away which was afforded them by a sacrifice that was still taking place. A sacrifice. Put it like that, it seemed almost noble. At least one of them had intended it that way. Perhaps, if the others did get out, they would tell people that Sam Harper had been brave too.

But now he knew it was there, the anticipation surged through him, and the bright-coloured smoke in front of him got paler, with sharp glints of silver in it. He came to feel like what he saw was in some way a representation of how he felt, which was all well and good except that it wouldn't do if anyone else—or any*thing* else—could see it, and besides which what could that vibrant green possibly tell him about anything?

His fingertips were completely numb, he noticed suddenly. And not only that, but his cheeks were burning with the cold as if it was the middle of winter as opposed to the beginning of the summer. Presumably that was a result of being so far underground, but the most disconcerting thing was that he hadn't noticed it at all until now. His left hand had a thin layer of wax on it where he still gripped the stub of candle; it had moulded itself to the shape of his fingers but now felt brittle in the chill air. If he'd been able to see anything at all, he expected that he would have been able to see his own breath rising in a freezing cloud in front of his face.

Thank God that he was not alone. He couldn't have stood to be alone, not with whatever it was closing in behind him. Now he was very aware that this place was essentially a grave, a place you would walk until you could walk no further and then died where you landed. He would be here forever and never see the sky or his family ever again.

Whatever was behind them gave no clues to its size or its intentions. The steps were light and long and regular, as of something tall and unhurried and loping, with plenty of time to spare. Not the steps of something which had made this place, so much as which had found it and explored it and colonised it for its own purposes. The Corrigal was of this place but not the master of it, a cuckoo in the nest that bore its name.

That was the truth as Harper now came to understand it, and he carried the truth with him under this pitch black and unknowable mountain.

CHAPTER TWENTY-ONE

The Charcoal Burner And Essie

ALICE CHRISTOPHER, WALKING through a pine forest alone at twilight. She had slowed right down since Nuria had stayed behind by the bank of the little stream. She was not quite sure why, except that it was more difficult to get anything done without some kind of accountability, no matter what you were trying to do. Company made everything easier to stomach. To begin with she had been in shock—she had pushed Nuria to do her best work before now, and Nuria had always stepped up and put the effort in; besides which her mind had always been open and her ideas interesting, which was what had made her such a pleasing student to supervise. Alice had not thought that Nuria would hit her limit in the middle of an expedition, never mind one so novel and so relevant to Nuria's own thesis. Perhaps, Alice thought, the mistake was doing this so close to Nuria's thesis deadline. It was maybe not so surprising that she might crack under that particularly hefty combination of pressure.

It was just a shame, that was all.

Further on, her disappointment and shock turned to anger. This place was astonishing and fascinating, and Alice had given every possible indication of what she had expected from it, and it wasn't just Nuria who had let her down, it was every single other person that had been involved in this project from the word go. They had not listened to her, or they had disbelieved her, called her a crank, tried to discredit her or short change her in terms of manpower because they didn't think she knew what she was talking about. Her proposal had been rejected no fewer than five times, and in the event, they'd given her a third of the budget she'd asked for. Nobody in the department had thought she had a chance in hell of finding anything, and after all that, Alastair Bell had even tried to dissuade Nuria from going. She ought to have expected it by now. If experience had taught her nothing else she should have learned by now that academia was, for her at least, not collaborative. She could do it alone, she could find out the truth and pour all those hours into doing so entirely on her own, or she could do it not at all. She would have killed a man, in a manner of speaking, to have the kind of trailblazing mentor that she'd been to Nuria. A strong female figure, with grit by the spadeful, clear of vision and more inclined to face down unwarranted criticism than to run from it. Someone whose example she could follow. But Alice Christopher did not get any of that; she had to do it all alone and that was the only way it could ever be.

And that made this triumph more bittersweet than it ought to have been. She was here, wasn't she? She was in this place, finally, entirely under her own steam and despite all of them telling her she couldn't. It was a victory, but it was a victory that she celebrated alone, exhausted, abandoned, untrusted, and most likely with her entire career in tatters.

She had not always been like this, was the most gutting thing about it. Once upon a time, she had had a colleague. Someone to look up to, who had supported her. Deirdre Ellison was a light in the darkness, a free thinker the likes of whom didn't come along very often. She had in fact been more influential on Alice's thinking and her approach than either of them had ever fully been able to appreciate. Alice Christopher was not the first person to suspect that something was deeply wrong in the depths of Moresby Forest, nor even to begin to feel her way around the nature of it. To begin with, this had been Deirdre's obsession, not Alice's—the deserter's narrative, the local legends, the tantalising, oblique references in half a dozen other unrelated sources, the lack of physical evidence out on the hill. But the more Alice had seen of the mystery, the more she had turned it over in her mind, the more it had gripped her, and she found she couldn't let it go. She had to understand. There had to be a way. Deirdre would have cheered Alice on.

The two-woods theory had been Deirdre's. A long shot to begin with, based on the information they could gather. Then, privately, between the two of them, the only thing that made sense.

It had all gone wrong, of course—Deirdre had wanted to come out here to do exactly this, and she had never managed it. She had been planning an expedition of her own, on which Alice would have been her research assistant, nine months after she had finished her own PhD.

"You mustn't listen to the rest of them," Deirdre had said. "The decisions of funding committees bear no relationship to the real world as it is, so when it comes to the truly strange none of them have any idea what to do with themselves. If your department can't even ask the right questions, which they quite clearly can't," she had added acidly, "then what are they going to do with the answers?"

She had been dead right, of course, and Alice had carried that with her ever since. The man who had hit Deirdre with his Ford Escort, going at eighty down a country road at dusk, hadn't walked away from the accident either. He had been paralysed from the neck down. That made it a lot harder to be angry with him, although Alice still was. They had cancelled the expedition, which had been difficult enough to organise in the first place, and the department had instated the Deirdre P. Ellison Fellowship in Early Modern History. They had given it to Alastair Bell, then fresh out of his first postdoc spot, over Alice—Deirdre's own student. Alice had never forgiven him, and she didn't think she ever would.

Now she walked these woods alone, the only person with the courage and determination to have made it this far without blinking, and to make it all the worse she had been right all along, and so had Deirdre. There were two forests here. Something unnatural was going on. The maps from 1966 were all laughably wrong, and this species of pine ought not exist in this part of the country. Now that she knew she was right, they ought to be able to get on to the plethora of new and far more interesting questions that opened up. But here she was, alone, her research once again buried by the inadequacy of others.

But she was here, at the very least—she was inside Moresby Forest. The further she went, the more she was distracted from the sense of injustice, of loss, by the sense of wonder she had felt on that very first morning when they'd stepped past that chain-link fence and turned away from the boundary. Being in the middle of here, now, for the first time ever, was like nothing else she'd ever experienced. There were other historians who were fixated on a specific place, or event, who made their life's work out of that one thing. Alice felt now that this must be how it was for them when they stood on a street or the deck of a boat or in a house that meant so much to them, and felt the electricity of hundreds of years of history linking people to people to people on a single spot. The fewer the people on that spot, the stronger the connection seemed to become, and there were few enough that had set foot inside Moresby Forest in the last thousand years that it was almost possible to name all of them. Where in the rest of the British Isles could that be said of? Or even the whole world?

What would she do if she found the definitive proof she had been looking for, that the Davies group had come this way? The odds were, honestly, against it, but what if she did? It was only now that she was really daring to think that far ahead, and of course the plans had changed so radically in the last forty-eight hours that it was hard to really know what to do for the best. She had no idea exactly where she was—and no map, not that it would be much good anyway. Preoccupied though she was, Alice Christopher was not unaffected by what had happened to the rest of her team. She regretted it, of course she did. But her mind was elsewhere.

She was exhausted, though. As the afternoon drew on and twilight began to approach, she didn't know why she was still bothering to hold off the tears since there was no one else here to see them. Her whole body ached; Alice was not exempt from the blisters that had plagued Nuria. Her back and shoulders were sore from the too-heavy bag, her thighs and calves from having walked too fast in the afternoon in an effort—she supposed—to outrun Nuria's second thoughts. That had been her attitude to her own feelings for so long that it hadn't even occurred to her that it might not work with everyone else's too. She had a headache from not drinking enough, on top of which she had spent two days freezing cold and as often as not soaked to the skin. She'd catch the flu if she wasn't careful.

Stopping was out of the question, though. She would keep going until her legs could carry her no further. The flickering of the woods had subsided somewhat; there weren't nearly as many patches of deciduous trees any more, and she walked almost entirely in the wood without mist. The ground was softer in this wood, the soil a darker, richer brown. It sank under her feet, squelching like a thick layer of peat. In the early evening, this wood was getting darker faster, the light turning golden sooner and the shadows lengthening further than they did in the places where it was strained through fog. If she had to guess she'd say that this place felt older than the other one. She wasn't a botanist, so wouldn't like to speculate on how old, specifically, but—

There was something there, way up ahead. For a moment, Alice was sure she had imagined it, she was seeing bright spots in front of her eyes. Then it was there again, a tiny spark of orange a long way off. In the semi-darkness it was hard to make out who was there or even how far away they were, but indisputably there was someone. Someone else was inside Moresby Forest, and they had lit a fire.

Her first thought was that it must be one of the others, but Kim and Sue were gone, and Nuria had long since left her in the other direction. She wouldn't have come somewhere this old, anyway. So it must be someone else, who wasn't troubling to keep themselves hidden. The only thing to do was to walk in their direction—if not to speak to them necessarily, then at least to find out who exactly they were and how they had got here. What were the chances that everyone in this place was lost? *Don't answer that.*

The little fire was a very long way off, and for a while she wasn't sure if she was getting much closer to it or if whoever was next to it had just built it up to a good size. It took her twenty minutes of walking and trying not to limp—why was it that when you admitted the existence of blisters they immediately got several times more painful?—to make out any of the details. A small campfire, smoking and crackling amongst the trees with what was presumably quite damp wood.

As she got properly close she could see that there were two figures sat around the fire. There was no sign of a tent or of backpacks or anything like that—just two people next to a little fire, on which a lidded pot sat. They were not dressed like anyone she had seen before, and Alice was not sure if she was hallucinating, or dreaming, or if maybe, just possibly, against any kind of logic, she had found some of the people she was searching for.

She hadn't. One of the figures was small, small enough to be a child, and had a dark-coloured blanket wrapped tightly around them. The other figure was a man, skinny, and not dressed like a soldier. It didn't make sense. But then nothing about this place made sense.

They were, equally obviously, not dressed like people from the present day. No brightly coloured waterproofs, no camping equipment. The figure wrapped in the blanket had braids down their back—a girl. Well, that settled it: no women or girls had been travelling with the Davies group. The skinny man wore an old-fashioned leather jerkin, and a close-fitting cap.

She ought to be surprised, but she wasn't. It occurred to her that she had left the little coin back with Nuria.

She was still a way off, and debating going right up to them, when the man lifted his head. "Thou in the woods! Walker. Come closer."

Alice froze. He wasn't even looking at her, but some way to her right. Then his head turned slowly, and he looked straight at her.

His accent was strange. She couldn't pin down where it was from. There was no hiding now, however, and nothing about him seemed particularly threatening. On the contrary, it was comforting to see anyone else out here at all. She advanced in their direction.

The girl was staring at the fire, and did not look up when Alice approached. She was wrapped tightly in her woollen blanket, and she could only have been eleven or twelve years old. The man was, closer up, probably only a couple of years older—still a teenager, although he had managed to grow an impressively full beard for his age. It was his eyes that gave him away. He reminded Alice of some of her students—guarded, more content to be watching from the edge, and in fear of being called upon to answer a question. He frowned as she came into the circle of firelight.

"Who art thou? We've not seen thee before." The words sounded *off* somehow: they got his meaning across, but the way he spoke gave the impression that the words themselves were unfamiliar to him. Like phrases in a second language. Or maybe he just didn't speak very often.

"I'm Alice," said Alice. She felt the heat of the fire on her face, and faltered—it was only now that she realised how much she was already tensed up with the cold.

"Alice," he said, as though it meant nothing to him.

"Dr Alice Christopher."

His face was still blank. "Well thou had better sit down, then, Dr Alice Christopher." He watched her as she slid her backpack painfully to the ground and rotated her sore shoulders experimentally.

"Are you Robert Moresby?" she said.

The girl staring at the fire didn't so much as twitch. The firelight was reflected in her eyes, and on top of the fire the lid of the pot rattled and shuddered: whatever was inside it was boiling.

"No," said the man. "Robert was my father. I'm Geoffrey. And that's Essie. She can hear thee but she won't talk. Pay her no mind."

Alice wanted to ask if Essie was alright, but it seemed rude to talk about her while she was sitting right there. Besides, the girl was more disconcerting than anything else, so Alice tried to settle herself down in such a way as to keep her within sight. "Of course. What—can I ask—what happened to your father?"

Geoffrey Moresby didn't say anything. The fire crackled and the pot on top of it shivered and chattered. A faint gust of wind set the trees whispering.

"I'm sorry," said Alice. "I shouldn't have asked."

He looked up at her sharply. "Thou can ask what thou likest. There's more askings than answers in these parts. Whence came thou?"

Alice said, "I'm looking for the company of soldiers. Captain Davies's men."

"There were some soldiers. Which ones?"

"Which have you seen?"

He leaned back, and stretched his feet out towards the fire. His boots, she noticed, could barely be called boots— they were more like scraps of rotting leather. "They burnt our home. By the grace of God they didn't find Essie, although she saw it happen. She hasn't been the same since. We didn't have much, but you can't trust soldiers. Couldn't in our day, either."

Alice said, "How long have you been here?"

He smiled, like he knew the answer to a riddle he wasn't about to share. There were dark rings around his eyes, under streaks of muck. "A very long time, child. A very long time indeed. And then again, no time at all."

She nodded, to show him that she knew what he was talking about, and because the word "child" had been calculated to make her feel small. She must be at least twice his age. "Which woods do you live in?"

This seemed to confuse him. "They're all the same woods. They've been here longer than we have, and they'll still be here after all of us have crumbled to dust. Well, except Essie, maybe. She might yet outlive all of it."

"Where I come from, they tell stories about her."

"Do they, now?"

Essie made no sign that she was listening. The light still reflected in her dark eyes. If it weren't that she occasionally blinked, she might have been a statue.

"In the stories she's older, though. How old is she?"

"Twelve," he said. "And she wouldn't hurt anyone, if that's what is said."

"What do you mean," said Alice, "the same woods?"

"The nature of this place is beyond our ken, no matter how far we bide in it. I see thou hast come from the young part. Thou may yet be able to return there."

But Alice shook her head. "No chance of that. I'm here for good, or until I find answers, at least."

He did not seem sympathetic. "I've seen your like come through here in my long years, and each thinks that he can see some kind of truth obscured to the rest of us. Essie and I have been here longer than most. I tell thee, there is no why, not that could fit in any one man's mind. My father thought he could do it, and he was a good man, brave, and canny. If he couldn't find answers to his questions then none can."

Alice said, "At least tell me this: what is the Corrigal, and how did it come to be here?"

"The Corrigal has been here longer than us, even; she was here when the woods had not yet grown. But none of this is the doing of the Corrigal. She knows no better than the rest of us. She was caught here even before man set foot in this place, and she was chosen to live long like the rest of us prisoners."

"What chose her?"

"The wood," he said simply. "The wood is both captor and gaol. That's all there is to it, as far as I can see. No monsters or demons, no great spirit that giveth and taketh away. God's grace can't reach in here, it's beyond His sight.

The only thing that endures is the wood, and we in it. Now, if Essie be believed, she says the wood doesn't know what it's doing, only that it's folding in on itself."

"What do you mean?" said Alice to Essie, but Geoffrey Moresby said, "She won't say. She's listening to it." He poked at the fire with a stick. The pot fizzed. He pulled his sleeve down over his hand and took the pot off the flames.

"There are some who pass through here and won't eat with us because it's like stealing from the fae folk. Wilt thou join us?"

Alice said, "If you don't mind." She reached into the pocket of her backpack and pulled out two Kit-Kat bars. "And these are for you. Then it's an exchange. You're not fae folk, are you?" she added, because anything could be true inside this place.

"I'm not," he said, "but I cannot speak for Essie." But his eyes sparkled and she guessed that meant that he liked her. He filled her tin camping mug with some of the contents of the pot—it looked like stewed rabbit and what might have been lovage—with only the merest flicker of curiosity. Here was a man who was used to being around things he had no hope of understanding. He took the Kit-Kat from her and, upon being shown how to unwrap it and snap the two sticks apart, chewed it thoughtfully. In his place, Alice would have been asking all sorts of questions, but Geoffrey Moresby asked none.

The little girl who was Essie did not move. She seemed uninterested in the food, and untempted by the Kit-Kat, but only blinked a few times in quick succession and continued to stare at the embers of the fire.

"She distrusts strangers," said Geoffrey, seeing that Alice was looking.

"I can imagine." Alice took a bite of the stew. There was no salt in it, but she supposed that was par for the course in here. Other than that it was good, and she apparently hadn't realised how desperate she had been to eat something hot. "Who else has been through?" she said. "It can't just be you two still here."

He said, "I think it must be us alone. And the Corrigal. The soldiers are long gone, all of them that we've found. It's hard to say, because things don't happen in the order they should." He paused. "Know thou Lamont? It's been so long. I remember not his first name. Little man."

"I've never heard of a Lamont."

"And Wood. Alwood. Good name for this place. He was scared of Essie, we had to ward him off. Never saw him again."

"I think he was one of my company!" she said. Her heart was suddenly beating very fast. "What did he look like? Were there any more of them?"

"Not with him. I recall no others."

"Any women?"

He shook his head. "Not to my mind. There don't tend to be many women come to this place. It's too dangerous. Excepting thyself, of course."

Alice said, "If they didn't come by you, where would they have gone? On to the Nest?"

"The Corrigal's never nested there," he said. "She's always known better than to get too close. And we never have—only bad things can come of that place." He cleared his throat. "That was where my father was going, the last either of us saw him. We're not fool enough to go after him and he wouldn't have us make his mistakes over again. Thou canst go there, if thou wish. It's hard to avoid in here—if you want to stay away you have to make sure to leave every road it tries to set you on. And I would commend thee to do that if thou hast any thought to live."

"I'm not sure that I do," said Alice, quietly. She was looking at the girl in her blanket again. "I came here to find out about the Davies company. And I think I have to finish that. I have to get to the end."

"I tell thee, thou shalt find no answers here." He took another mouthful of the stew. "Time works not like it ought to in these woods."

"No kidding. I saw the hut, and the charcoal pile. It looks like you only moved out of it a few months ago. Maybe a year."

He looked very tired. "Was it that long ago? They smoked us out. But if not them, it would have been something else. There's no stillness to be had. If thy intention is to try to stay for a while, thou wilt find the truth of it too."

They sat there in silence for a while, eating, while the little fire crackled in front of them. At one point, Geoffrey put another handful of sticks on it, and it shot sparks and crackled loudly before settling back down. Still the girl Essie didn't look away from the fire. Now and again, under the woollen blanket, Alice saw movements as if Essie was slowly clenching and unclenching her hands.

Alice herself could feel her own heart beating in her throat. The soldiers had been here. She was going in the right direction. She was *right*. The stew was bitter and it stuck to the roof of her mouth, but she had no appetite for it. She was thirsty, but could barely swallow. Darkness fell properly.

In the end, she left alone. She couldn't sit still, apart from anything else, and she worried still that if she got comfortable she wouldn't be able to get going again. Geoffrey didn't seem to be surprised that she was moving on, nor to have any inclination to dissuade her. He helped her get her bag back on, and when she walked away it took a few minutes for her eyes to readjust to the new darkness.

Away from the camp fire, it was freezing, and for that reason alone she almost regretted leaving them. Her breath rose in the air ahead of her, although it was harder to see it now: the sky was cloudy enough that no light from moon or stars could make it through, even accounting for the tree cover. But there was very little in the world—whichever world that happened to be—that mattered to her any more. She walked on.

CHAPTER TWENTY-TWO
Downhill And Downhill

IT MUST BE the middle of the night now. Surely it must be. But Alice could not see the face of her watch to check. Somewhere in the depths of the bag she still carried on her back, there was a dynamo-powered torch, but she was loath to try and find it lest it attract the attention of some unnatural creature lurking in the area. When it came to it, she was probably incapable of the manual dexterity required to open the bag and rummage around in it. It must now be below freezing temperature, and when she walked she could hear every so often a crunching underfoot, as if of frost on the ground. It wouldn't surprise her. Wherever she was, there was no chance that it was September any more.

For a long time, she had been cold enough that her shoulders had felt like they were seizing up, but now she wasn't even shivering any more. She was outside her own body, carried along by it and aware of it mostly in the sense that she could hear her own footsteps. She considered dumping her bag somewhere, but whatever remained intact of her mind told her this would not be a good idea in a few hours. Things were changing, frequently and erratically– she ought to be expecting them to change, in ways she could not yet predict. There was no chance she would be putting up a tent any time in the immediate future, but after that, anything could happen.

She was not mad. That much was still important to her, that despite everything she was still making decisions based on the evidence, that even here in the middle of everything, in the very eye of the storm, Alice Christopher was still trying to be a scientist. Trying to work out the truth.

It was difficult, though. This was without doubt the most difficult thing she had ever done or would ever do.

There was moonlight, diffused in places by thin cloud but still bright enough to see by. As she staggered forward, aware of her own body and its limits and the noise she could not help but make, she saw off to one side a clearing, in which there was something hulking and huge.

She stopped. Her own breathing was loud in her ears. It was not the oak tree that she was looking at—that much was obvious, even from this distance, even with the trees between her and it. Moonlight glinted off dark fur, off lean, powerful legs, off curling tusks. It hadn't seen her. It was crouched over something, busily attending to it in some fashion that Alice could not make out from here. She heard what it was doing more than she was able to see it, in the silent depths of the wood—a crackling and tearing and open-jawed chewing. It was eating. And then it straightened up to its full height and Alice saw that it was twice the height of a man. More.

Something caught her eye, lying on ground by the creature's giant back feet, now illuminated by the thin moonlight as the beast stepped away from it. A flash of fluorescent pink, such as might make up the fabric of a woman's waterproof jacket. Half-obscured by muck and who knew what else. Alice registered this, had only a brief second to do so, before the gigantic beast moved.

The Corrigal was in no hurry. It was idling, nosing around the earth. Its shape was similar to that of a bear or perhaps a wolf, although it was leaner and bigger than any bear she had ever come across. What creatures from the British Isles' distant past might have recognised this beast? How good was its hearing? Its sense of smell? These were all things she couldn't possibly know. She covered her mouth with her arm and tried not to move.

Suddenly it put its head up, as if it was listening for something, and its whole demeanour changed. It tensed, and the moonlight glinted off what before had seemed from this distance like fur, but now shone almost like polished leather. Then it looked towards her, and for the first time she caught a glimpse of eyes, which in the low light were only black, deep, expressionless. Alice felt something shift irrevocably inside her—it wasn't looking at her and yet she felt the force of a thousand years of seeing, of knowing. This was the primeval hunter, the killer that stalked these woods and struck without warning. It understood this place the way no others could, by sheer reason of having been here so long, and whether it was trapped or not everything else that wandered across its path was its prey. What was it? And where had it come from? None of that mattered. She looked into its eyes and understood: for the Corrigal—and for Alice too—there was no past and no future. It was a creature of *now*,

and *now* was all that there was.

It moved with uncanny but practised stealth out of the far side of the clearing, and then she couldn't see it any more.

She thought she had forgotten to breathe, and now it came in great ragged gulps, sharp and painful in the freezing cold air. And then she had fallen sideways onto the ground, her body no longer under her control. She was dry-heaving, although nothing came up, and even as she tried to be quiet, there was nothing she could do but stare ahead, carried along by the agony in her throat, her lungs, her diaphragm, and the emotions coursing through her like crushed glass.

At length they subsided a little—enough for her to quiet her own breathing, to still her chest, to try and regain her control. She lay there, now aware that she was shivering, that her hair was wet, and that she had seen something no person was meant to see. Already it was becoming difficult to picture the beast's dimensions, what it actually looked like. When she tried to recall, it grew larger and larger in her mind's eye—she closed her eyes for a second, but the images came unbidden, and she tasted acid in the back of her mouth. So instead, she looked back to the clearing— saw the fragment of fluorescent pink and almost lost herself again. No. If ever she had been strong enough to check what that was attached to, she wasn't any more.

Maybe she would die in here after all. Of the hundred ways she'd imagined her death in this wood, the Corrigal loomed large. But she couldn't stay here. At length, she struggled agonisingly to her feet, and shuffled forwards.

Eventually, the way began to slope quite steeply downhill. She had to keep her hands out in front of her, and in places scramble down on her hands and knees. The thin pair of fingerless gloves she wore were completely useless; when she used her hands to steady herself she felt only shooting pains all the way up her forearms to her elbows.

This was where her instinct kicked in, this crawling along in absolute darkness. If she tried to think about what she had just seen, she would fall down and never get back up. Then she would have ended up with nothing—as opposed to this, which was intensely painful and disorientating and humiliating, but at least it was *something*.

It felt as if the whole forest was caving in on her. Down and down she went, with no concept either of how far she had gone or how far she had left to go. The sky held no clues; there was no sky, there was only this ancient forest folding itself in over her head, pushing her further down, suffocating her.

There was not enough feeling left inside her now for there to be anything like fear. She had seen the worst of this place, seen how it could creep up without warning if it wanted to. It was hard now to picture anything except the black sockets of those eyes—the rest of her memory of the beast kept slipping from her grasp. All her previous suppositions had been stripped away, everything she had believed or thought she knew, and now most of her senses were gone too, and all that was left inside her was a cold numbness.

A day ago, two or three days ago, she had been full of determination and enthusiasm. Both of them burned brightly. She had still felt them a few hours ago. Now she could have screamed, and it wouldn't have meant anything, not in the end. Another person would cry, but the very thought that that might apply to Alice did not even occur to her.

It had also not occurred to her until now that, having gone downhill so steeply, the sound of the wind rustling through the trees had died off. There was no wind at all, and the air was completely still. But the first she noticed of that absolute silence was when it was no longer there.

It took her a minute of standing still and straining her ears to realise what she was hearing, and even longer to ascertain its direction. But it came from directly ahead of her, and although it was very faint, there was no other sound save her own breathing to disguise it.

She could hear running water.

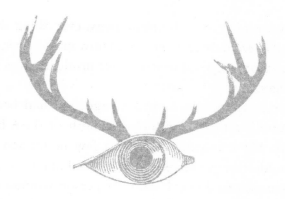

CHAPTER TWENTY-THREE

Harper's Last Stand

THE CAPTAIN WAS gone. Harper became aware very suddenly that he was alone—and not only that, but that he had been walking alone for quite some time. An hour? Three hours? A day? However long it had been, he and the captain had lapsed into silence long before it, and the two of them had walked together many miles, and now he was continuing by himself. It was so cold that he had stopped shivering and now just ached, dully, everywhere. The path—because it was a path, he knew instinctively that it was and that he was intended to follow it—still sloped gently downwards, so that he must have been very far underground by now.

He tried to remember what had happened to Davies, if anything noticeable *had* in fact happened, but there was nothing he could recall, not a moment of sudden movement nor even so much as a time when the footsteps had died away in one direction or another. Whatever had happened, wherever the captain had gone or not gone, it had happened without Harper noticing a thing.

In some ways it was not terribly surprising to him. He had been walking—and this he had been aware of for a significant amount of time—with his eyes scrunched up against bright pink and green and orange lights, the hues of which he had never seen so vibrant before and which were almost blindingly bright. For a while without him even noticing it that brightness had been the only thing he could fit inside the whole of his mind; it was all-consuming and it blocked everything else out or overpowered it. His feet moved without him consciously telling them to; it was only now that he had somehow come to his senses that he realised how extremely cold he was, and that he was aware of the sound of his own footsteps. Alone. Or maybe not quite alone after all.

He knew, in some sense at least, what had happened to Captain Davies. He wasn't sure how he knew, or even what it meant, but he had ascended. The Corrigal itself, or whatever was following him and had been since they entered the tunnel—entered the land, to be truthful—was not itself the Devil. It was as Stiles had said—that the Corrigal was very old, had been in the forest long before the Devil had got here, and when he said that the captain had ascended he did not mean to Heaven, so much as he meant that Davies had gone on somewhere in a way that neither Harper nor the Corrigal had achieved. It was the only way Harper could make sense of any of it. Davies had gone or been taken, and would move on to the next place, and Harper would remain here, alone, without friendship or responsibility, descending into the darkness where lived and lurked whatever had killed the rest of his companions.

It was no use asking how he had got here or how it had come to this. Men had asked him before and he had never been able to answer them. You were where you ended up, that was true of all men, and he was no better than anyone.

All time was folded in on itself, and this place was both an infinity and the tiniest pinprick. He couldn't pray, because he was deep under the weight of a mountain and God couldn't hear him, let alone reach him.

He had felt before, at times in his life, that he was in a place where God couldn't see, and every one of those times had felt different from the ones that preceded it. Once in France. Once further east, but he had not known where more accurately than that. Both of those moments stood out in his memory as the most hopeless he had ever felt. But at least, on both of those occasions, even if the Lord had been absent Harper had not been completely alone. True, in France half of his company had been idiots who could barely be trusted to find their own arses with both hands, but they had shown courage in the end and Harper was not the only one of them who had lived to fight another day.

Lucas Blashford had been one of them. He'd died on the side of the hill, three days ago. Now Harper was truly alone. No comfort, no comrades, just him, and still the Corrigal or whatever it was that walked behind him. Blashford's death felt like it had been a very long time ago.

When he had come this way, into this tunnel with Captain Davies, he had thought that it would be easier, in the end, to have fewer people about and not to have to think about anyone else. But this absolute loneliness, just him, and the stalker in the darkness—for he was convinced that there was only one of it—was more than he had bargained for. It was faintly audible if he held his breath and strained his ears—he could just about, just occasionally, hear the step of the other thing behind him.

There was a link between predator and prey, if they remained in those roles long enough. It was not just because of the cold that Harper was shivering—it went deeper than that. His mouth tasted of iron, and he could smell the earth, with an edge of rot, acutely. All he knew was the strange, constant awareness, the monster looming large in his mind and the images of comrades' bodies he had left behind, throats slit, mauled as if by some gigantic, coldly furious beast.

Time moved wrongly; now he was aware of his own movement as it was physically occurring, only for it to dissipate behind him like fog—how long was it even now since he had become aware of being the only survivor? It could have been any length of time; it could have only just occurred to him.

He was holding his pistol, had somewhere along the line taken it out in both hands, and in the pitch blackness that was somehow also a multitude of bright colours he had pushed powder into it, and one of the little pieces of shot. How he had managed to do all of this he couldn't quite be sure—he couldn't even tell if he had loaded the pistol correctly by feel alone, and the striking of the flint would add nothing to his blindness in here that he wasn't already acutely aware of. He held the gun in both hands, still walking forward, his pace still steady.

Behind him it moved, keeping pace in long, slow strides. It must be tall, ten or twelve or fifteen feet tall—and how high was this pathway? Harper had had a candle once, but no longer. He could hear it getting closer, and his heart hammered so hard that he could feel it in his throat. What was it waiting for? When it had been so quick to butcher Ames, Kilburton, Taylor, had been so silent to devour or divert Captain Davies? It was the coward's way out to keep walking, Harper thought. He was not being brave by failing to face it, by letting it force him further and further down, without so much as a by-your-leave. He had never as much as got a glimpse of it at any point, and the bright colours danced and swirled in front of his eyes as if they really could hear his thoughts and were mocking him.

He had come in here to see it. That was what he had wanted to do, and to kill it too, if he could. With more courage than he thought he might ever have had before, than he even thought up until now that he had in him, Samuel Harper stopped walking. The gun was in his hands; he might have been able to pull the trigger but not even that was certain.

Now that he was no longer walking, the footsteps behind him were clearly audible, some twenty or thirty feet away. Bipedal. Step. Step. Step. Step. Nothing.

He turned, very slowly, and in the freezing darkness his cheeks were sticky with tears of terror.

"What are you?" he cried out, and his voice was thin and small in what must have been a cavern bigger than a cathedral.

There was no answer, but something in the depths of the gloom shifted its weight, ready to spring.

Harper held out the pistol, and prepared to fire.

CHAPTER TWENTY-FOUR

Folded In On Itself

HERE WAS THE cave, then, and here was the mouth of the cave, and there was no mistaking it—she knew she must go in. It was still dark, although that was unsurprising; she had been walking for less than an hour after she'd nearly run into the Corrigal. Out of sight of it, when she had been as sure as she could be that it was far away in the other direction, she had got out the little torch. It was one of those with a dynamo that you wound by hand—by getting it out she was tacitly admitting to herself that she was not going to set up camp tonight, not in any meaningful way. Alice was going to walk on, searching, until either she found something that would satisfy her or until she dropped from exhaustion.

And after all, hadn't her instincts proved right all along? Jubilation jostled with a hundred other emotions, but it was still there: she was outside the mouth of the cave, right now. Here was the place she'd been looking for, here was the evidence, as plain as day in the thin light of her dodgy little torch. Maps could be damned, the lot of them. Alice Christopher had found this place through gut instinct and force of character alone. The thought gave her a burning sensation inside, that she had got here, had done this despite all the odds and still there was no one to tell, no person with whom she could share it.

She hoped—it was a momentary stumbling but she hoped—that Nuria had got out of the woods okay. It wasn't the girl's fault that she just didn't have the staying power.

The opening of the cave was maybe five feet tall, and two arm-spans across, a broadly rectangular opening in the sheer side of an outcrop of rock. Grasses drooped to left and right of it, picked out in black and white in the dim beam of the torch. Inside the cave was pitch black. Nothing escaped it. It must go in some way, must not immediately narrow out.

Alice's instinct and her enthusiasm were telling her the same thing, which was to go straight inside and see what she could see. Perhaps there would be cave paintings, evidence of people long since lost, or even still somehow alive in this unnatural place. There was no way of knowing, after all, if the Davies group had actually managed to get this far, but equally there was no reason that they couldn't have.

But going inside was, said a small part of her brain, a bad idea. She wouldn't have advised anyone else to go straight in, at this time of night, however many degrees below zero it was—for it was bitingly cold—where the chances of accidentally destroying evidence of some kind were astronomical. Besides that, there was always the chance she might find the Corrigal again. That gave her more pause, until she remembered what Geoffrey had said—it didn't come this far. That should be terrifying, but it felt almost like respite.

She ought to be so exhausted now that she could barely move. That was what ought to be happening. In truth her mind was racing; she couldn't have slept if she tried.

Something silver flecked the beam of the torch. It looked almost too bright to be simply a light rain. It reminded her of static on an untuned television. Either way, it was the deciding vote, because if there was to be rain or even snow, she could hardly stay outside and sleep in it.

She stepped over the threshold, ducking her head, and her shoulders ached and her pack was still heavy on her back. Now that she was inside, it occurred to her that the cave was like a mouth, a wide cavity that opened up about twenty feet back, with a smaller, narrower tunnel leading off at the far end and sloping downwards. Like a gullet. She had walked willingly into the mouth of this place, which in her mind was worse than the Corrigal and more uncaring. Curiosity and the dregs of her jubilation fought with what she had been calling adrenaline and now recognised as fear. Very definitely, viscerally, fear.

She shone the torch around the walls. They were blank—rough stone, but not hollowed out or decorated by any obvious particular human intervention. There was nothing else visibly suggesting that people had been here before her, although she supposed they must have been, or she'd never have known about the Nest in the first place. Something obvious—a boot mark or a piece of cloth—would have been too easy.

The torch had started to flicker again. She switched it off and stood in the frigid darkness to wind it up. The buzzing of the dynamo echoed around the walls—when she paused, she could hear the light patter of rain or sleet outside, and the more deliberate, echoing drip of water down the walls further into the tunnel, and beyond that something else that might be a slow breathing or groaning or snoring. Whatever it was, it was some way off, but it was also difficult to tell which direction it came from. All the directions, perhaps. She was trespassing somewhere dangerous, where she had not been invited in. She wound the torch dynamo a couple more times, experimentally, and clicked the light back on. It lit up the walls of the little cave, which looked exactly the same as they had done before. Nothing had changed, but now she couldn't rest here either, and she knew it. Onwards, 'til the end, which was coming.

She had to keep going. If there was something to find out, she had to get to it. That was what was moving her forward now, the wish not to remain where she was. Geoffrey Moresby had been right that if she came this way she would not come back—and in her single mindedness she had squandered the opportunity to ask him questions she would now never know the answers to. But her bed was made and now she must lie in it, and forward was really the only way to do that. For a multitude of reasons there was no way she could stay here, in this mouth, at this waypoint on the edge of something enormous.

So it was into the tunnel, or nowhere at all. Alice Christopher started to walk.

For a while, the path went straight ahead, curving gently downward in a way that seemed too regular to be entirely natural. Alice was reminded of the towpaths alongside canals as they went through tunnels. She had walked some of those before, many years ago when she was a student on a low-budget shared holiday somewhere in the West Midlands. The narrow, curving pathways had been disconcerting then. They had seemed to last forever, devoid of light and damping all sound except the gentle lap of water and the hum of the longboat's motor, so that when she finally caught a glimpse of daylight in the distance it had felt strange, unnatural. Those tunnels were a calming and anchoring memory now. She settled into walking again, and as the path remained remarkably similar no matter how far she went, that little edge of doubt that she had been so ready to quash outside crept back in. How far down was she going? What now was she underneath? The shape of the tunnel was remarkably consistent—maybe six or seven feet wide and eight feet tall, and if it was man-made, it hadn't been done recently. Alice kept her torch trained downwards. Not so much as a footprint. She was getting farther and farther away from the world.

This, then, was what it felt like to recede. Strangely enough after the last few hours, her mind was clearer than it had been. It was still bitterly cold, but the stillness of the air meant that she barely seemed to notice it now—the cold went right through her and she was made of nothing, she was lighter than air. Of course there were no footprints on the ground here, even if anyone had come this way before— Alice's own feet probably made no imprint at all if she cared to look behind her, which she didn't. Geoffrey and

Essie Moresby had been real, whereas Alice was a ghost, and this place under the earth, a channel between one thing and another, didn't actually exist at all. And it was not her canvas rucksack that made her shoulders ache this much, but the weight of History itself, folded in and down to the smallest point, then stretched and warped across an entire forest.

Something walked with her, but it was invisible, so she couldn't have seen it even if she had tried to point her torch at it. It was not the Corrigal, who wouldn't have dared come this far. The Corrigal too was a victim of this place, a creature from ancient times when monsters walked the land that would not be called Britain for a long time yet. It was hard to feel sorry for it, exactly, especially having seen it with her own eyes and felt its presence, but Geoffrey had managed to, and he had managed to stay alive out there the longest. Whatever was inside here was older than the Corrigal, and cleverer than it, and although Alice didn't feel like she was its prey exactly she was uncomfortable and knew that she was being watched very closely. A house guest alone in a long hall with a two-way mirror. That was what she felt like. She walked on.

Her thoughts bounced off the walls and ricocheted ahead of her under the beam of the little torch. Several times the light from it began to grow dim and flickering, but each time she rewound it, and the noise the mechanism made was so startlingly loud that every time she was afraid that the tunnel might cave in on her.

Could it be morning yet? Would it be dawn, outside, however many miles above her that might be by now? For the tunnel still sloped downwards, gently, less than it had been doing, but still enough to be noticeable. Sometimes she thought she might be travelling in a spiral, as the tunnel veered left for a time which was long but impossible to accurately assess—but then it would twist back right again and she would be even more disorientated than before. The air at the beginning smelled damp, like earth after a rainstorm, but now after several hours she had grown used to it and smelled nothing at all.

And then, finally, it changed. Ahead, by probably forty yards, the walls of the tunnel seemed to melt away into blackness. Alice shone her torch towards it, and hit nothing—not a far stone wall nor even the ceiling of something sloping further downwards. The small beam was not strong enough to illuminate anything. She gave the torch's dynamo a few experimental twists to try and give it more power, but there was no effect: all ahead was blackness.

As she approached, she could see that the ceiling sloped upwards as sharply as the walls went out. The floor, fortunately, did not bottom out so sharply, although it did look more uneven—as if somewhere in the high eaves, bits of rock had occasionally crumbled down into the cavern below. It was a cavern—a large one, stretching out ahead and above and beyond the beam of the torch.

Alice was lightheaded from tiredness and the cold, too lightheaded to make very much sense of what was around her. Was it some kind of tomb? A natural creation, or formation of the rock? Surely no natural process could result in something so regular, something which to this point had been so decidedly human-sized.

The only sound was the faint drip and trickle of faraway water, somewhere in the darkness. A whistle, too, very occasionally, of air through some small gap. Where was this? How deep under the ground was she?

And then a voice, not close but not precisely far away, said: "Who goes there? I warn you—I—I'll shoot you."

It was a man's voice, with an accent that seemed familiar although she couldn't exactly tell from where.

She said, "I don't mean you any harm," and it was only when she tried to speak that she realised how dry her throat was. The words turned into a cough.

"I mean it," said the voice. "Identify yourself."

"Dr Alice Christopher," said Alice, weakly, and she held the torch up so that it illuminated her face.

A pause. "You're a woman?" Then the clatter of something heavy being thrown to the ground.

"Yes," said Alice. "Can I come towards you?"

"Aye."

So she did, very slowly, in case she had been wrong about him putting the gun down, and she directed the beam of the torch along ahead of her, along the edge of the cavern wall, slowly and carefully until the man came into view.

He was sitting on the ground with his knees up under his chin, and when the light hit his face he scrunched up his eyes. In the half-light it was clearer what he looked like: small in frame, rounded in the shoulders, with wide, dark eyes and a beard that pushed the definition of five o'clock shadow. The gun that lay beside him was an old, long-barrelled pistol, and he wore a dark jerkin that was detailed in ways it was hard to make out. To his left, a metal helmet. Old-fashioned. To Alice, familiar looking.

Her heart was suddenly beating very fast indeed. She towered over him, and he looked back up at her.

"Are you one of the King's men?" He was talking, she realised, about her bright red anorak.

"No," she said. "I'm not a soldier. Are you?"

He squinted into the darkness. "You don't look like a woman. Or sound like anyone I've heard. Where are you from?"

There were several ways to answer that question, but he couldn't possibly know what it was that he was really asking. She said, "Are you Alexander Davies?"

The man looked up at her, and now Alice thought that he didn't look desperate after all, he looked run down. "No," he said. "Davies is gone."

"I came to find him. Do you... Who are you?"

"You still haven't told me where you're from. I'm Harper. Samuel Harper."

"The sergeant?" said Alice. Her heart was beating very fast.

"How do you know that?"

"I just... May I sit down?" It was a stupid thing to say, like she was his guest here. She dropped the backpack laboriously from her shoulders, felt another wave of lightheadedness and swallowed it down. "I've been looking for you," she said. "You went missing." Then, "Everything is different in here. Would you believe me if I said I was born three centuries after you?"

Harper said, "No one will remember us in three centuries. They won't hardly remember us in thirty years." His expression in the torchlight was impossible to read. When Alice sat down, she felt like she could probably never get up again.

"I remembered you," she said. "Some of us did. I spent my

life trying to find out what happened to you. The first time I ever read the deserter's account, I knew I had to find out."

"The what?"

And of course he couldn't know. He couldn't possibly know that some of his comrades had escaped this place. Alice Christopher knew, had always known, more about the fate of the Davies company than this actual living, breathing member of the Davies company. "When was the last time you saw Thomas Edgeworth?"

Harper shook his head. "I thought Edgeworth was dead. The creature came for him, the first night we came into these woods. We thought… We thought some of them ran away, but then we found Roberts near the entrance to the cave. The creature got the others, or that's what we thought. Did Edgeworth really get out?"

"He gave testimony at Tapford, that's how I knew about you. He lived. Edgeworth and—"

"And Moody?" Harper grimaced. "Can make his way out of the smallest holes, I'm surprised it took him so long to leave us for dead." He seemed to notice he was talking to a woman, and regarded her steadily to see if she was shocked. He almost looked disappointed that she wasn't. "Hanging's too good for him."

"He died in debtor's prison."

"That has the ring of truth about it." He shifted slightly, still not taking his eyes off her. Alice got the impression that he was still tensed, still disbelieving, still waiting for her to lash out.

"What happened to Roberts?" she said.

"Mauled. Never saw what did it, and he wasn't for saying. Did you see it?"

Alice said, "It got… one of my colleagues, too. Right in front of us, and we saw nothing."

Harper nodded.

"I think…" said Alice, but then she remembered how the Moresbys had reacted to her suggestion that there were multiple woods. "I don't know what I think. I dreamed about it, even if we couldn't see it in front of us."

"Tall," said Harper. "Like a wolf, but bigger. Much bigger. Stands on two legs like a man."

"That's it. And the eyes…"

"Yes, that's right. It had the measure of us, as soon as we got here. I think Thatch—some of the others saw it too, but the captain thought I was being fanciful."

Alice blurted out, "They wouldn't believe me about the two woods, either. One from your time, one from mine. But then I realised, it's all the same woods, from all the times. That's how the Corrigal could pass unseen. That's how you're here at the same time as me."

He was frowning. He didn't understand what she was saying, and she couldn't explain it in a way that he could possibly understand. To be honest, Alice wasn't sure she understood it herself, and she was beginning to think that it couldn't even be done. With any of the rest, she had worried that they would think her insane, or that she wasn't seeing it clearly at all. But she couldn't see it clearly—no one could. This was as good as it got, here with the only other person with any sense of the magnitude of it.

"What happened to the other men?" she said.

"I hardly know. Even if I saw it, in front of my own eyes, I couldn't be sure I'd got it right."

They lapsed into silence, and her head started to throb.

Truly now she had transcended, she was outside her own body, outside everything at all, and it all hurt, even the bits that couldn't possibly be real. She had reached the end of everything and now she was numbed from it.

And she ought to have been happy. She ought to be thrilled. What historian wouldn't give everything they had to be here, outside everything, with a person from the past—with one of the very people she had dedicated her life to studying? History was frustrating because even when you were studying the people with good records, with copious private letters, hundreds of portraits, an entire library's worth of paper trail, you could still never meet them. The relationship could only ever flow one way no matter how hard you tried or how far you chased; you could spend decades of long afternoons with Queen Victoria or Henry VIII or Isambard Kingdom Brunel, but they couldn't spend time with you. They never looked back at you. They never had opinions about you. You never had to think of something to say to them, or to try and put it in a way they would understand.

Alice Christopher sat next to Captain Alexander Davies's right-hand man, and when the light from her torch died she did not wind it up again. She sat in the darkness and let the tears roll down her face, so he would not see. This ought to have been a triumph. She had spent so long looking for answers.

"How did you become a soldier?" she asked.

There was silence next to her, but he was still there. "It hardly makes a difference now, does it? Feels like a very long time ago, or maybe it happened to someone else and they only told me about it."

"That makes sense."

"It was nice to have that light for a while. A strange light, though. I still have a bit of candle left, if you have a way to light it."

She thought about trying to explain the concept of a dynamo to him, of an electric torch. Of three and a half centuries of enlightenment. But her head hurt. "I like the dark for now," she said. "Have you been here a very long time?"

"A week. Or longer. I'm not hungry, which is strange."

"Nor me," she said.

There was a faint rumbling, like an earthquake or a landslide a mile away, or something vast shifting. Harper said, "It does that sometimes."

"Have you investigated?"

"In the dark? No. I've not really wanted to move, if I'm honest."

"My light, it runs on clockwork. Sort of. I can light it again. We could explore together."

"You want to get closer to whatever made that noise? If it's the Corrigal, I don't want to go near it."

"I don't think the Corrigal comes this far down, anyway. I don't think it has the nerve."

A quiet, wet sniff. Alice wasn't the only one who was crying.

He said, "I can't tell you what you want to know. I can't tell you what happened to him. I'm the only one left!" It echoed off the walls of the cavern.

"There were five of us," said Alice. "We came looking for your company, or what was left of it. I wanted to know what had happened, where you'd gone. I didn't actually think I'd find out. The others turned back."

"You said the Corrigal took one?"

A pause. "I don't know. It's like you say, I was right there beside her, and I don't know what happened to her. Then the others turned back." Saying it now, her anger seemed strangely absent. "I have to try to understand. To make it worth it."

"You'll not find Davies here."

"What was he like?"

Harper said, "Braver than me. A good man. The sort you might say was too soft for a leader, but I saw him shoot a man in the head in these very woods to stop him being the death of the rest of us."

"Who was it?"

He didn't answer but spat onto the ground. "Son of a devil and no better than he ought to be. I'm not one to speak ill of dead comrades, but some of them deserve what they got. And we'll all die in this place. Or maybe we'll sit against this wall forever." A pause again. "I followed him in here, because he's the kind of man you follow into places. Or he was for me. We left three others outside. You didn't see them, did you?"

"It was very dark out there. The middle of the night. But no, I didn't see them. Who did you leave?"

"Byrne. Stiles. Cadwell." He sounded like he was struggling to recall their names. "Stiles was right about this place. We should never have come. Especially... if people came looking for us."

Alice said, "The wood lures us all in somehow. If you're meant to be here, it's where you go. If it's not one reason it's another."

"If it's not a shortcut then you're being shot at."

"Right."

From far off in the distance came the sound again of rumbling.

"Giants," said Harper offhand, although Alice hadn't asked. "Giants from the time of King Arthur, or else it's the end of the world."

"More likely that," said Alice. "I'm so tired."

"I'm not going anywhere," he said. "I'd offer to keep watch but I don't suppose there's much point."

"I suppose not."

"I'm glad it's not just me," he said. "I'm glad I'm not alone." In the darkness, Alice felt him reach out for her. She took his hand, and it was warm, the first warm thing she'd felt in who knew how long.

"So am I," she said, and meant it. The ground was hard, and seemed to be littered with gravel, but she lay down on it anyway, and put her head onto the lumpy pocket of her rucksack. She was so tired, so heavy. She did not turn the torch back on. In front of her eyes, the darkness bloomed into psychedelic, acidic colours. She closed them, and listened instead to the steady breathing of the soldier next to her.

CHAPTER TWENTY-FIVE

Nomansland, Again

THE SUN RISES, in an insipid sort of way, over the place called Moresby Forest. There are other forests around the United Kingdom, many of them of similar size to Moresby, some of them equally old and haunted by as many stories. A few of them even have barbed wire fences around the edges of them, and capital-lettered warnings to would-be ramblers to KEEP OUT—although ordinarily those have more to do with army practice ranges than the signs at Moresby do.

The mist hangs low, so that even from a hundred or so yards away the chain link fence is obscured in thick greyness. Behind it, and further into the trees, the mist seems to grow darker in the thin light of early morning. It gives the place an eerie feel—which, again, is not uncommon for thick forest in the early hours of the day.

There are birds in Moresby, which are audible even if they aren't specifically visible. And at some points—and this probably does set it apart from other fenced-off bits of British woodland—there are gaps under the fence, as if some animal or another had tunnelled its way in, or out.

If you listen very closely, you can hear from the boundary the hum of a far-off motorway. Not so much yet, but in an hour or two it will be rush hour.

In a section of the boundary that faces to the north-east, over a wide, plain stretch of English countryside, there is movement from behind the fence. It looks, to begin with, unnatural: limping awkwardly and slowly, a shade of turquoise blue that is out of place in that green and grey landscape. Then, through the mists that obscured the fence, the shape forms itself into something unmistakably human, and the turquoise becomes recognisable as a plastic anorak, and the woman—for it is a woman—flings herself at the chicken wire of the fence. She bounces off it and falls to the ground, as she must have known she would do, and the metallic clang reverberates in all directions.

Nuria Martins—freezing, sleep deprived, frizzed hair plastered to her face—has found the edge of the woods. She has found—could it possibly be true?—the way out.

But of course there is no immediate way for her to get to it, being on the wrong side of the fence. She has had plenty of time to think since the events of the previous day, and she is more sure than ever that this side is the *wrong* one— she has dragged herself to this point by thinking of this fence, and of being on the other side of it. No more the unfinished thesis, the history department, the stories of men long since dead. If the last eighteen hours have taught

Nuria anything, it is only that she can never look at any of it again. Even if she does manage to find the gate. Her priorities are irrevocably changed. Getting out of here is getting out of all of it.

Having found that the fence is both impassable, and too high for her in her weakened state to climb, she sits on the damp ground and hugs her arms about herself. She is extremely hungry. In one of the pockets of her rucksack is a cereal bar—apparently the last one she has, or at least the last that is accessible without opening and unpacking the whole bag. She finishes it in three bites and feels a little better. It's okay: if she follows the fence round to the south, eventually she will come across the gate, and she can get out that way. It's going to be okay.

In the end, the desperation to get out of that place overcomes her exhaustion and the pain in her blistered feet, and she sets off again, holding out her left hand to the fence like it is her lifeline, and perhaps she is even right that it is the only thing that could prevent her from getting lost inside this place.

She has walked a long way over the last few days, however, and has come a long way from the south side that bordered onto Sibbert Hill, where she and four other women entered the forest, so long ago.

After two hours, the sun is properly up, although it is hidden behind the thick cloud that seems to be the only weather here. She rests for half an hour and then forces herself to get back up again. After another hour, she rests again. One hour on, half an hour off, gritting her teeth, now long past crying. Another hour on, half an hour off. Every time she tries to think beyond the next hour, it is a lead weight in her stomach, making it harder and harder to keep moving. The middle of the day approaches, and the fence finally just about begins to curve around to the south. It feels like the bars of a cage: she is out in the open air, can feel the wind on her face, rolling off the nearby hilltops, but at the same time she is still trapped, and somehow suffocating.

An hour on, half an hour off. She sees stars in front of her eyes. If there had been much more in her stomach, she might have thrown it right back up. But there is Sibbert Hill in the distance now, tantalisingly close.

Then there it is—the gate, and beyond it the Land Rover. Kim's Land Rover. No Kim or Sue—and the thought is suddenly overwhelming again, and Nuria cries dry, unselfconscious sobs.

She is hobbling. It takes several minutes after having seen the gate before she is close enough to get to it. It is the same as it was three days ago, padlocked shut, and with the ladder lying a little way away. That blessed ladder. Nuria ought to rest and get her strength up before attempting to position it against the fence, to climb up with her whole rucksack and—what, jump down the other side? By the looks of things it is the only way—but she isn't inclined to wait. She has to be out of here as quickly as possible. So she gathers up the final dregs of her strength and approaches the ladder.

Her heartbeat is in her throat as she limps towards the Land Rover. It is nearing the middle of the afternoon now. On some level it seems impossible that she should have managed to get out of that place at all; on another level, impossible that she should have while the others have not.

Ahead, to the south, Sibbert Hill rises up. In days gone by, it would have made an excellent spot for an ambush.

On the front passenger seat of the Land Rover, through the window, she can see a washed-out mug, with the words "Dignity at Work" printed on the side.

Nuria Martins fishes in the pockets of her anorak, and her hand closes around the tiny, ancient coin they found at the site of the burnt-out shack. It should not be real. Now she is out of that place, the coin should have melted into thin air. How dare it still be here when Kim, Sue, Helly, even Alice are not?

She tries the handle of the car door, but it won't open. It's locked. Of course it's locked. And Kim had the keys.

Nuria Martins curls up on the ground, with her arms clutched over her head, and weeps.

THE END

ACKNOWLEDGEMENTS

Thank you to the early readers who met this book in various stages of undress, took it seriously, and gave me advice: Kyna, Helena, Emily, Corbin, Sian, Struan, and the folks at NSTB who held my hand through the nerve-wracking bits. Mike gave me the benefit of his re-enacting experience and historical knowledge, much of which I gratefully took on board and some of which I ignored because "it's cooler this way". All remaining errors historical and horticultural are mine alone, which definitely include a few extreme liberties with a firearm – what can I say except that Alice Christopher would probably mark me down for them.

My agent, Anne Perry, saw the potential in this book in about five seconds flat, and has been its greatest advocate ever since. It has been my biggest stroke of luck to have her on my side and I am grateful for her hard work, impeccable judgement, and unstoppable good cheer.

I also owe many thanks to the folks at Rebellion, who have been collectively and individually excellent: my editor, Michael Rowley, very much with me here in the middle of the Venn diagram of interests that is this book; editorial assistant Amy Borsuk, who fielded my nit-pickiest questions with great patience; PR/marketing master Jess Gofton; the copy-editor/typesetter/proof-reader dream team of Paul Simpson, Gemma Sheldrake, and Bridette Ledgerwood; Dominic Forbes who designed that incredible cover(s), and all the rest who pitched in to turn this story from a lot of weird, soggy shouting in my possession to something actually pretty cool (albeit still with the rain and yelling) in yours.

I have a very cavalier attitude to research: I'll do plenty, but only if I can tell myself it's just for fun. Thanks in particular to Martyn Bennett, Charles Carlton, Diane Purkiss, C. V. Wedgewood, and the administrators of the BCW Project for making this so easy to do. Thank you also to Edinburgh University library for allowing me, Not a Student Any More, to take textbooks home to read in my pyjamas, and to Martin for the shedload of tomes which plugged the gap when a pandemic happened and library visits were suddenly off the cards.

My family – Barnetts and Aucklands both – have been supportive of my writing for a very long time, even (some might say *especially*) when I couldn't tell where it was going. Gravy sat on my feet during every round of edits and exuded calm, because he is a cat.

And Ned was there too, all along: patient, encouraging, enthusiastic. Everything I could wish for, really. Thanks, Ned.